SABIKUI BISCO

KARMIC CROWN, FLORESCENT SWORD

4

SHINJI COBKUBO

Illustration by
K AKAGISHI

World Concept Art by
mocha

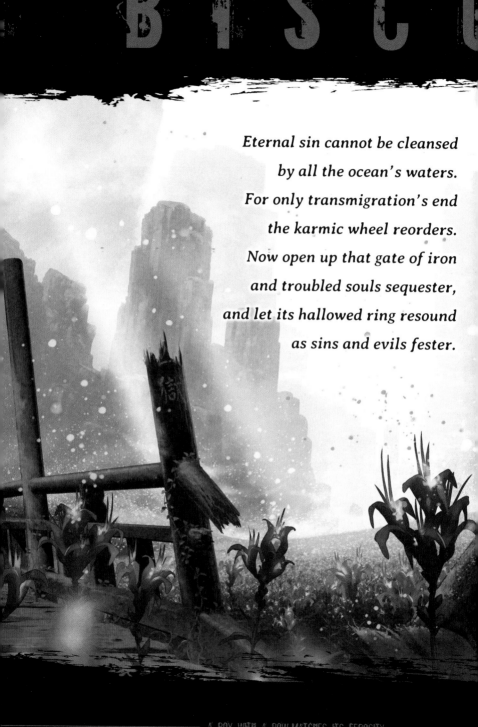

Eternal sin cannot be cleansed
by all the ocean's waters.
For only transmigration's end
the karmic wheel reorders.
Now open up that gate of iron
and troubled souls sequester,
and let its hallowed ring resound
as sins and evils fester.

A BOY WITH A BOW MATCHES ITS FEROCITY

"The king must cast himself aside. Only for the people shall his flowers bloom."

SABIKUI BISCO 4

SHINJI COBKUBO

Illustration by
K AKAGISHI

World Concept Art by
mocha

The Rust Wind eats away at the world.
A boy with a bow matches its ferocity.

4

Karmic Crown, Florescent Sword

SHINJI COBKUBO

Illustration by
K Akagishi

World Concept Art by
mocha (@mocha708)

YEN
ON

NEW YORK

SABIKUI BISCO 4

Shinji Cobkubo

Translation by Jake Humphrey

SABIKUI BISCO Vol.4
©Shinji Cobkubo 2019
Edited by Dengeki Bunko
First published in Japan in 2019 by KADOKAWA CORPORATION, Tokyo.
English translation rights arranged with KADOKAWA CORPORATION, Tokyo through TUTTLE-MORI AGENCY, INC., Tokyo.

Yen On
150 West 30th Street, 19th Floor
New York, NY 10001

Visit us at yenpress.com † facebook.com/yenpress † twitter.com/yenpress
yenpress.tumblr.com † instagram.com/yenpress

First Yen On Edition: January 2023
Edited by Yen On Editorial: Payton Campbell
Designed by Yen Press Design: Wendy Chan

Library of Congress Cataloging-in-Publication Data
Names: Cobkubo, Shinji, author. | Akagishi K, illustrator. | mocha, illustrator. |
    Humphrey, Jake, translator.
Title: Sabikui bisco / Shinji Cobkubo ; illustration by K Akagishi ; world concept art by mocha ;
    translation by Jake Humphrey.
Other titles: Sabikui bisco. English
Description: First Yen On edition. | New York, NY : Yen On, 2021- |
Identifiers: LCCN 2021046139 | ISBN 9781975336813 (v. 1 ; trade paperback) |
    ISBN 9781975336837 (v. 2 ; trade paperback) | ISBN 9781975336851 (v. 3 ; trade paperback) |
    ISBN 9781975336875 (v. 4 ; trade paperback)
Subjects: LCGFT: Science fiction.
Classification: LCC PL868.5.O65 S3413 2021 | DDC 895.63/6—dc23/eng/20211001
LC record available at https://lccn.loc.gov/2021046139

ISBNs: 978-1-9753-3687-5 (paperback)
        978-1-9753-3688-2 (ebook)

10 9 8 7 6 5 4 3 2 1

LSC-C

Printed in the United States of America

The long winter is over.

You are not seeds, to spend your lives trapped underground.

You are flowers, to burst forth and make yourselves known.

Shishi felt steeped in a sticky warmth. The cloying scent of death tingled her senses and knotted her sleeping brow. She parted her lips, and thick water came in, along with a rusty taste that made her splutter.

…

But each time consciousness felt near, the overpowering smell swept her mind clean and dragged her deeper and deeper into death's sweet release. At the very last moment, just as she was about to renounce all hope and surrender herself to its welcoming embrace…

Ssss!

"…Waah!!"

A burning heat on Shishi's toes threw her eyelids open.

"What's this…?!?! It's hot! Aaah, oof, ow!"

Now awake, Shishi realized she was being weighed down by fleshy masses at the very base of some sort of lake, the bed of which was blazing hot. She pushed the oppressive sea aside and clawed her way to the surface.

"Pwah! Haah…haah…… Ah…ah…!"

Her lungs filling with air at last, she surveyed the scene. And then…

"Aaaaahhh!!"

When at last she realized what she saw, a panicked scream escaped her. She had been lying among bodies. Young, old. Women, men. All stewing in the lake of blood that erupted from their severed necks and left the corpses white as snow. It was the sight of tortured sinners, tightly packed, its equal found only in the most grotesque depictions of hell itself.

"Helllp! Oh…ah…oh…"

One gently floating severed head turned over, and upon making contact with its lifeless eyes, Shishi let loose a bloodcurdling scream. Even the girl's own pale skin was so drenched with blood it would make a demon's skin crawl.

I-I'm in the Devil's Cauldron! They've thrown me in while I'm still alive!

Snatching her mind back from the grips of terror, Shishi looked up at the walls of the furnace, now starting to glow bright orange and emit a radiant heat.

I-is this it? I'm going to be burned to ash...and there's nothing I can do...

No! Shishi shook her head resolutely, expelling the last of her fear and exposing a single crimson eye between her long forelocks.

It is just like Father said. A true king seeks victory even where there is none to be found!

The very air seemed hot enough to scorch her lungs, and yet Shishi took a deep breath and swam through the lake, even as the rising heat caused her blood to boil.

There must be an exit chute for ash and debris. I just have to find it...!

She dunked her head beneath the surface, searching the base of the furnace for a drainage hatch of some sort. Sure enough, she spotted it, illuminated by the ever-present orange glow, but as expected, it was locked and didn't seem easy to open.

Oh, Father!

Shishi broke the surface again and filled her lungs with air.

Grant me your power... Grant me your Florescence!

Her eyes flared wide, and in response, the camellia behind her left ear spread its petals, scattering glittering pollen into the air. With this new mysterious power at her side, she swam down once more, pressing both palms against the exit hatch.

As she focused power into her arms, the lake parted her hair, revealing both of her glimmering crimson eyes. Whatever mystical force she commanded, it caused ivy to sprout from her wrists, forcing its way through the stone wall of the furnace in defiance of its blazing heat.

Get to the lock...quickly... I can't hold on much longer...!

Shishi was being cooked alive by the boiling lake of blood, and just as she was about to pass out, she heard the *Clink! Clink!* of rattling chains, and the heavy door suddenly gave way.

…! It worked…!…Waaah!

The rushing liquid pushed her through the hole and dropped her into the cooling pool below. She resurfaced to fill her lungs just in time to see a waterfall of boiling blood crashing down toward her. Shishi cut through the pool, swimming with all her might until, at last, she reached the edge and hauled herself up out of it.

"Haah…! Haah…! *Cough… Cough… Cough!*"

A grim mixture of water and blood spilled from the girl's lips and onto the cool floor.

"I can escape… Now's my chance."

Shishi wiped her mouth and looked back at the scarlet cascade still spilling into the pool. She staggered to her feet, bloodied and burned, but with her crimson eye still gleaming between her bangs.

"I…cannot die. Not while I am still weak. Not until I become the next king…"

Over the din of crashing water, Shishi heard the raised voices of the guards coming from outside. As she looked around, her eyes fell upon a waste disposal chute, and she tossed herself into it. Slick with blood, she slid down the chute before disappearing down a dark tunnel.

SABIKUI BISCO

4

Karmic Crown, Florescent Sword

The Rust Wind eats away at the world. A boy with a bow matches its ferocity.

Illustration by **K Akagishi**

World Concept Art by **mocha** (@mocha708)

Kaso Prefecture was one of Japan's newest municipalities, formed on the southernmost island of Kyushu after the eruption of Mount Aso left behind a flat, ashen region. The people there rebuilt, soon growing the municipality to such prosperity that it rivaled those of their neighbors Oita, Fukuoka, and Kumamoto. Eventually, the area became recognized as a prefecture in its own right.

The Rust Wind had always been strong in Kaso, and of course, the ash deposits left the soil barren and unworkable. Nobody had expected the region to succeed, and outsiders left them well alone, another factor that led to their success.

So just how did this desolate land earn its wealth and autonomy? The answer lay in its so-called Prison City. Kaso possessed a city like none other, called Six Realms Penitentiary, an impregnable mountain fortress well known throughout the country. The ruthless and impartial trials held there by the Iron Judge, the Lord High Overseer Someyoshi Satahabaki, cemented its reputation as a bastion of order in this lawless land.

In a world where it was increasingly difficult to impose strict rule, a prison that accepted even the most heinous of criminals was much welcomed. No prefecture's citizens would turn up their noses at the opportunity to pay a little money and be rid of their captured outlaws forever.

In short, Kaso handled the entire prison–industrial complex. Put up the fee, and Six Realms would take care of the rest. With this system in place, there was no end to the influx of criminals from all across the country, and today was no different.

"You want us to hand over these prisoners?"

The guard peered suspiciously at the two detectives before him, at their Kyoto Police ID cards, and at the mugshots they provided. This man oversaw the temporary holding cells, where captured prisoners awaited sentencing.

The two detectives wore trenchcoats, one white, one black, signifying them as partners, and each was adorned with a badge depicting the Golden Pavilion. Their uniforms were instantly recognizable to anyone even slightly involved with the police.

"Well? Are they here?" one of them asked, "Our Mushroom Keepers?"

"...Hard to say without checking the list. But even if they were..."

Their low-brimmed hats and black face masks were a necessity for secret agents such as these two, but still...

"We couldn't possibly release prisoners who have yet to receive judgment."

That would be an embarrassing loss of face for Kaso, no doubt.

"Of course, we wouldn't be here if we were confident their sentencing would be swift," the one in the white trenchcoat chimed in, "but we have heard that wait times have increased as a result of Lord Satahabaki's absence. We trust the overseer's judgments; that is why we entrusted the prisoners to you in the first place, but if their processing is to be delayed, we would rather see them returned and deal with the matter ourselves."

"Sure, the overseer's away on other business," the warden protested, "but Ladies Gopis and Mepaosha are more than capable of—"

"We only trust the very best on this case," interjected the one in the black coat. "If you've got our Mushroom Keepers in there, then hurry up and hand 'em over. That is, unless you're itchin' for war with Kyoto."

"Urgh..."

The Kyoto police sure turned nasty after their city got destroyed...

Muttering his complaints, the warden tore off the list and disappeared into a back room, from where could be heard the shouts of prisoners. As he left, the two detectives whispered to one another.

"*You really think they're holdin' 'em in a shithole like this?*"

"*If they're anywhere in Six Realms, they have to be here. I checked the court records and couldn't find anything suggesting a Mushroom Keeper went on trial at any point last week. That means they must still be in the holding cells, awaiting sentencing.*"

"*Hmm...*"

The detective in black cracked his neck, apparently bored already, and peered out the window of the reception room. It was a clear spring day and yet all that was visible outside were cold concrete buildings, hardly a pleasing view. Amid all the depressing scenery, only one structure had any style at all: the distant black gate whose iron doors served as the sole way in and out of Six Realms.

"Kaso's very own prison town. What a dreary, godsforsaken piece of—"

Suddenly, as he gazed at the drab view, the detective's eyes widened.

"...What is it?" his partner asked.

"Get down!"

The pair of them hit the deck, milliseconds before the glass shattered and a small white figure, like a doll, came crashing into the room.

...A child?!

The one in the white trenchcoat sprang into the air and caught the figure in the nick of time, rolling across the floor. He felt blood on his fingers and gulped.

"Are you okay?!" he cried. "Can you hear me? Wake up!"

"I...cannot...die..." The figure groaned. "Not here... Not yet..."

The figure's long violet hair parted to reveal a pair of tear-streaked eyes that gripped the detective's heart.

"You have...to help me... Please..."

"You're terribly hurt!" the white-coated detective exclaimed. "Wait right here, I'll—"

But his words were interrupted by another.

"Shishi, you fool. This game of tag is over!"

"How moronic, running right into a dead end. I guess you're just a child after all."

A pair of female voices, one angry and one mocking, came from the room's entrance. Pushing the staff members aside, they stood imposingly in the doorway before walking primly over to the two detectives.

"That's the first time a fool has tried to escape the Devil's Cauldron," roared the first. "I don't know how she did it, but look at the state it's in now, thanks to her! Do you have any idea how this makes me look...?!"

"This could have all been avoided if you just did your job, you know?" the other shot back. "Why didn't you make sure she was dead first?"

"I thought she was!" the first one bellowed. "Her heart had stopped, I swear!"

Meanwhile, the *clack, clack* of their heels rang out across the floor. The one who seemed to speak only in violent outbursts wore a long floor-length red dress that exposed her cleavage, as well as a pauldron made of an ox's skull on her shoulder. Her long blond hair came down in an elegant wave, and from one of her nostrils hung a glittery ring piercing. Her arrogant look made it clear she took great pleasure in humiliating others.

The other also had long hair, but it was indigo-blue and spiky like a pine tree. A pair of spectacles glimmered on the bridge of her nose, and an earring that looked like a horseshoe dangled from one ear. Her dress was similar to the first, only blue instead of red, and over the top she wore a clean white lab coat, so that she appeared, at first glance, to be a scientist of some sort.

"...As of this moment, this matter is under Six Realms jurisdiction!" the blond-haired woman screeched. "What are you fools standing around for? Get out! Unless you want me to throw you all behind bars!"

Everyone working in the reception room immediately scattered, as if not wanting to face the ordeal of objecting. Soon all that remained was a crowd of guards with black executioner hoods that the women had brought with them. Each wore a *wo-dao* sword at her hip, engraved with a cherry blossom design.

The two detectives, finding themselves quickly surrounded, took up stances to protect the mystery child.

"...Oh? I wondered who was stupid enough to stick around," said the blue one. "Looks to me like we've got ourselves a couple of guests." "...Fools from Kyoto's secret police?" added her partner. "Why have you come here?"

Meanwhile, the executioner guardsmen had not expected to find the detectives here and were at a loss as to how to proceed. They remained silent, awaiting their mistresses' orders. After a short while, the blond-haired one cleared her throat and said, "I don't know what a couple of witless detectives want with us, but I don't like your attitude."

Contrary to her cocksure expression, the blond woman gripped her whip tightly, clearly hesitant to lash out against a representative of a foreign prefecture.

"I am Vice-Warden Gopis of Six Realms Penitentiary," she said. "And my gloomy assistant here is Mepaosha."

"Since when am I your assistant, shit-for-brains? I'm a vice-warden, too!"

"Don't interrupt me! Hey you, whitey. That girl belongs to us; she's a highly dangerous prisoner. Hand her over."

"I'd be happy to," replied the detective in the white coat. "Just send proof of her crimes to the Kyoto Prefectural Bureau, along with copies of your ID, and we'll process her release within a month or so."

"Don't fuck with me, fools!"

Vice-Warden Gopis struck the ground with her whip, cracking the linoleum floor.

"Here at Six Realms, we don't just hand over our prisoners to any-body. I don't care if you're foreign agents; you fuck with our business, and I'll slice off your pretty little heads."

"Well, that's a problem," the detective replied. "We don't intend to meddle...but we're on official business, too."

"What...?"

"Explain it to them."

"Hmm?!"

The detective in black gave a start, his partner's sudden gaze catching him off guard, and he hurriedly pulled a notebook out of his pocket. Flipping through it, he landed on a page of text covered in pronunciation aids and began reading aloud.

"Kyoto Prefekshural Police Regulashuns, article two. Protect and give aid to the—" He stopped to read a difficult word. "...Si...ti...zun...ry, wherever and whenever they are in need."

"Nicely done," said his partner.

"Of course we know the police department's motto, fools! But you're not bound by those rules!"

"That's true, we ain't. I got no problem handing one kid over to you... At least, normally I wouldn't."

The detective in black waved his notebook in defiance of Gopis's threats.

"But lookin' at it from a completely neutral viewpoint," he went on, "I realize I can't do that."

"You bastard... You'd declare war on Kaso for one lousy kid?!"

"It's nothin' like that. It's all about politeness. You see..."

From beneath his hat, the detective's eyes glimmered, putting even the executioner guards on edge.

"That's the fourth time you've called us fools, when *you're* the ones who fucked up and lost a prisoner."

The blood vessels on Gopis's forehead looked ready to burst.

"At least the kid had the decency to say *please*!!"

"Die!!"

Gopis lashed her whip, striking the black-clad detective in the face. The attack knocked the notebook out of his hand and tore off his hat and mask, scattering blood. It was such a fierce impact that it would be a miracle if the man's bones were still intact.

"Look what you've done now, imbecile," said Mepaosha. "That's another foreign agent you've killed. You know how much trouble it is to cover this up!"

"Hah. That's your job, ain't it? Sounds like a you problem to me. Besides, that Kyoto snob was askin' for it. While Satahabaki ain't here, *I'm* the law in Kaso!"

"You're mean *we're* the law! When will you get that through your thick skull?!"

Gopis gave a triumphant sneer and coiled up her whip...or tried to, at least, but she found it wouldn't budge. Something held it in place tightly, like a vise.

"...What...?!"

The end of her whip had coiled around the man's face. With his mask flayed off, the whip's tip lay trapped between his teeth...

...and those glimmering fangs bit down like a wolf on its prey.

"Wh-who *is* this guy?!" Gopis shrieked, and the guards all went for their swords. The man's crimson hair, no longer stuffed under his hat, bristled like fire.

"Cut him down! Kill him... Waaah?!"

The man in black suddenly swiveled, like a typhoon. Using only his teeth and neck muscles, he yanked the whip, pulling Gopis clean off her feet. Then he executed a sort of jumping, spinning back kick that met her right in the stomach and blew her backward.

"Ghaaah!!"

Gopis collided into several of her guardsmen and sent them all crashing through the building wall, landing outside.

"All you had to do was ask," the man growled. "If you wanted a fight, I'd have given it to ya!"

"H-how is he so strong?!" asked one guard, hurriedly drawing his sword. "Stay alert! Surround him!" yelled another.

"Heh...heh-heh-heh..."

Mepaosha gave a chuckle, making sure to conceal her astonishment from the men.

"This day just keeps getting worse," she said. "Why did these guys, of all people, have to show up?"

"Lady Mepaosha! You know this man?!" asked one of the guards.

"I'm gonna dock your pay, limp-dick. No prison warden should be able to forget that face."

She pointed at the man's piercing eyes, at the crimson inking that adorned one of them.

"Red hair, and a red tattoo around the right eye. Once public enemy number one and the bearer of a three-million-sol bounty…"

"Y-you don't mean…it's…"

At Mepaosha's words, the guardsmen all turned to face the man, who said…

"You know who I am? Then you know it's me you should be after, and not some kid."

He cracked his neck once and scowled defiantly at his opponents. His jade-green eyes twinkled with such vigor that the guardsmen all took a step back in fear.

"I-it's Akaboshi! The real Akaboshi! The Man-Eating Redcap!"

"He's here! He's here in Kaso! We're doomed!"

As the guardsmen quivered in panic, Gopis wiped the blood from her mouth and bellowed out to them.

"Silence, fools! He's just one Mushroom Keeper! Teach him why the prison guards of Six Realms are feared throughout the land! Surround him! He's only one man!"

"Have you forgotten why we're here, numbskull?" Mepaosha cried. "Kill the white one and take back the child!"

Despite their mistresses' contradictory orders, the guardsmen made to surround detective…or rather, Bisco Akaboshi. His partner in the white coat gave a resigned sigh.

"Why does it always turn out like this? I thought we could talk our way through it for once."

"I put up with that plan for three times longer than I usually do," Bisco replied. "So, what now? We running?"

"As much as I'd like to, I need to treat the girl immediately. Her wounds are grave."

The detective in white tore open his coat, revealing an array of medical tools.

"Keep them away for a bit. I'll just apply first aid, and then we can go."

"Give me something to work with here," Bisco replied. "How far away do you want them kept, and for how long?"

"Hmm."

His partner drew a lizard-claw blade from his hip and held it so it glinted in the light. Then he tossed aside his hat, revealing a head of sky-blue hair. While the guardsmen were enchanted by his beauty, he used the blade to draw a circle in the ground around the young girl and himself.

"Five minutes. Don't let anyone inside this circle."

"Five minutes?"

"And no mushrooms. We can't let the spores contaminate her wounds. Is that okay?" Bisco's partner asked, raising an eyebrow atop his panda-bruised eye.

Bisco clicked his tongue. "Huh. 'Is that okay?' he says..."

"What are you doing, you miserable dogs?!" Mepaosha yelled. "Don't just stand there! Attack! Attack!!!"

"...Just watch. I'll be done in three."

The guardsmen descended on Bisco from all angles, and Bisco flung off his black trenchcoat. As the guards shielded their eyes, he rushed forward and hit them with a spinning kick before grabbing on to a leg and swinging one of them around like a hammer, knocking back the attackers coming from behind.

With the coat gone, Bisco's Mushroom Keeper cloak caught the breeze and fluttered, tangling the arms of one guard who tried to sneak up on him. Twisting the cloak, Bisco sent the would-be assassin flying into a wall before catching the man's sword and knocking down four more attackers with a single swing.

"Lucky these things're only sharp on one side," Bisco chuckled, clearly enjoying the fight. "I don't have to kill ya if I just use the backside."

The fight continued, alternating between the guards' angry bellows and their screams of defeat. But it was almost like there was a bubble in the center of it all where the clamor of combat disappeared.

When Shishi opened her eyes at last, she was astonished by what she saw. The crimson-haired boy was like a god of war, grinning as he tore up the battlefield, while the gentle boy taking care of her seemed to take no heed of the bodies constantly flying overhead.

"Ah, you're awake," he said, pulling aside his mask to give her a peaceful, reassuring smile.

"W-waah! The guards!" she cried. "We need to get out of here!"

"Don't move. You're under anesthetic," the boy replied. "My name's Milo Nekoyanagi, and I'm a doctor. You've been burned terribly and suffered deep lacerations as well. You're in critical condition, but I can make it all better, if you'll trust me."

"B-but...," the girl protested. "We have to...!"

"It's okay. As long as we stay inside this circle, you'll be safe."

True to Milo's word, for all the chaos unfolding around them, it was like magic: Not one hair breached the circle on the ground. And despite the terror, Shishi could not look away; with each passing second, she found herself more and more enamored of the fiery warrior who opposed the guards in combat.

The man's perfectly developed muscles brought to bear the full, terrifying might of his advanced fighting techniques. He slipped between the hostile blades with almost no effort at all, dancing on the edge of death with only a roguish grin and a prayer. His focus, his strength, his almost inhuman courage; it all seemed to flow into Shishi and light the smoldering fires that lay at the pits of her soul.

...That red-haired man... Who is he?! So strong...and so beautiful...!

"..."

Milo smiled, seeing the young girl so fixated with his partner that she quite forgot her own pain. Then, putting his genius talents to work, he set about patching her up with astonishing speed.

"Bisco, I'm done! You can stop— Whoa!"

Just as Milo turned around, he saw one of the guards' hoods, knocked loose in the fight, flying directly toward him. But just as he put his arms up to stop it...

Fwippp!

Like a bolt of lightning, an arrow swept across his vision, catching the hood and pinning it to the far wall.

"Hey, did that touch you?" came Bisco's gruff voice after he'd cleared away the surrounding guards.

"Huh? D-did what?"

"Did that hood touch you?! Did it get inside the circle?!"

Milo chuckled at Bisco's characteristic seriousness and drew the emerald bow on his own back.

"No, it's fine!" He smiled. "You did it, Bisco! Mission complete!"

"Hrm? Really? ...All right, if you say so."

Despite not really understanding his partner's mirth, Bisco looked satisfied. All around him, the guards lay in a defeated pile, each of them groaning in pain.

"Look at all this, Bisco. I don't suppose I could ask you to bring it down a notch?"

"Hey, they're still alive, ain't they? If you wanted to do this peacefully, you shoulda just given them the kid."

"You know, you're awfully stubborn for someone who can't read."

"What's that got to do with anything?!"

As she watched the pair quibble, Mepaosha grinned a nervous smile.

"Heh...heh-heh-heh... You took out my pawns like it was nothing. You're even stronger than I expected, Akaboshi, and yet you're still so young. How?"

"Quit eyein' him up, fool! Who knows what Satahabaki will do to us if we don't bring back the child?!"

"This is all *your* fault! *I've* called for reinforcements. Even Akaboshi can't hope to hold out against a force five times that size!"

Sure enough, the reception building was soon surrounded by a veritable horde of the hooded guards.

"Don't worry about taking them alive. Kill them! Kill them both!"

At Mepaosha's command, the guards all raised their swords and rushed inward.

"Looks like they're serious this time," Milo said.

"No worries, I can take 'em. Hey, let's do the circle thing again. That last one was too easy."

"What are you talking about?! We need to run!"

Milo's sky-blue hair seemed to twinkle in the light as he scooped his white trenchcoat off the ground and kicked it up. Swiftly pulling back his drawstring, he fired an arrow directly into its center.

Gaboom! Gaboom!

A cluster of dull yellow mushrooms exploded out of it, releasing a pungent ochre cloud that engulfed the guards.

"Arrgh, it's so itchy! What's with all this dust?!"

The guards fell to the floor, quickly succumbing to the fearsome effects of the tickleshroom spores.

"We have to get this girl somewhere safe," said Milo, watching the guards writhe. "Let's go, Bisco!"

"Didn't you just say no mushrooms a moment ago?"

"It's okay if I use them. *I* know how to hold back."

Milo fired an arrow directly overhead, and a cluster of clamshell mushrooms blew the roof off with a *Gaboom!* Dazzling sunlight flooded into the room, and Milo swept up the girl in his arms before the two of them sprang to freedom as nimbly as a pair of acrobats.

"Come back, fools! After them, after them!"

"Hah! It doesn't matter how many you are, you'll never catch a Mushroom Keeper!" Bisco laughed, their cloaks flapping in the wind. Then he turned and said, "Well, this sucks. We came to free the Fukuoka Mushroom Keepers, and now we got a kid to deal with as well."

"She's hurt! What did you want me to do, leave her? She's not in the clear yet, either; I need to begin proper treatment as soon as possible!"

By now the anesthetic had fully taken effect, and the girl was asleep once more. Milo could feel her soft breathing through his back.

"That warden lady packed a real punch with her whip," Bisco said. "Tore up my nose and ear bad. If that's what the kid had to deal with..."

"Yeah, I can't believe it," said Milo. "Those are the vice-wardens of Six Realms? This prefecture's just as rotten as all the others...!"

"Huh? Oh, yeah, I guess so."

"What, were you going to say something else?"

"Oh, I was just thinking...the kid must have had some real guts."

The two Mushroom Keepers flitted from rooftop to rooftop, quickly escaping the sea of black-hooded guards who attempted to pursue them.

Let's take a moment to rewind and learn just how our boys found themselves engaged in this intrepid infiltration.

It all began with the Akaboshi Mark I, a humanoid robot created during the incident with Tokyo, based on the genetic code running within Bisco's blood. Deriving his personality from Bisco's, the robot turned out to be exceedingly violent and went on a rampage that made national news. A rampage that wouldn't have been too out of character for the old Bisco, back when he earned himself the title of Man-Eating Redcap.

Bisco, meanwhile, thought of the robot as his own brother. Even though they weren't both human, the two *were* related by blood in a sense. And so, feeling responsible for the whole mess, Bisco had come all the way to Kyushu to put a stop to him.

However, things were not as they seemed, and soon after landing in Fukuoka, the two boys started to get a sense of the strange goings-on that troubled Japan's southernmost isle.

"Phah! Just smell that air, Pawoo!"

"Indeed. And I daresay the view is not bad, either. The northern parts of Kyushu are famous for their lack of ferocious beasts and make a popular sightseeing destination as a result. I have heard the food is more substantial around here, too... The buffalo stew is to die for, supposedly."

Pawoo, sitting in Actagawa's saddle, and Milo, poking his head out from the luggage, were enjoying the warm spring breeze, engaged in pleasant conversation. Now far from Imihama, Pawoo had discarded her stuffy suit and changed into something more comfortable. And since this was Pawoo, we weren't talking about yoga pants and a sweatshirt. She sported an expensive white dress, elegant in its simplicity, a wide-brimmed hat with a few ornamentations, and long white iguana-skin gloves, looking for all the world like a prize-winning actress at the Academy Awards ceremony.

"Did you hear that, Bisco? Buffalo stew! Let's see if we can have that today!"

"You two sure are havin' fun, ain't ya? You think this is a freakin' cruise?!"

Bisco's loud voice and bloodshot eyes made it clear he was not finding the voyage anywhere near as relaxing as the Nekoyanagi siblings were.

"You can think about eatin' and sightseein' after we catch the Mark I!" he bellowed. "Ain't that what we came here for?!"

The reason for Bisco's frenzied urgency was that the Akaboshi Mark I had already destroyed a shrine dedicated to the Mushroom Keeper god Yatanaten. The extraordinarily devout Bisco was so afraid of divine punishment that he had been having nightmares night after night, and all he could think about now was capturing his accursed brother and begging the gods for forgiveness.

"Once we pass this mountain, there's a village hidden up ahead," Milo reassured him. "We'll stop there to stock up on arrows and poisons."

"Sounds good," Pawoo replied. "These clothes have gotten a little dirty, and I shall need to change into new ones."

"Just how many changes of clothes did you bring?!" yelled Bisco. "And not one of 'em's good for crabriding, either! What was wrong with your biker suit?"

"Hmph. Don't be absurd. How could I go on a trip with my husband without sparing a thought for my appearance?!"

Pawoo's counterargument was so fierce it caused her hair to flutter, and Bisco's eye twitched in defeat...until the distant mountain peak came into view and a host of brilliant pink flowering trees caught his eye.

"...Huh? What's with that...?"

"Wow, it's so pretty!" Milo marveled. "What kind of trees are they, Bisco?"

"Trees? I didn't even know trees grew here."

Bisco lashed the reins and urged Actagawa forward, heading down from the peak toward the trail that led to the village Milo had mentioned. On the way they passed more of the same trees, and when they finally arrived at the village, they found it blanketed in them.

"It's so beautiful...," said Pawoo. "It's a shame a village so pretty has to be hidden."

"...That's strange," muttered Bisco. "Mushroom Keepers would never let their home get so overgrown."

Milo got down from Actagawa, leaving the other two to stare in wonder at the village, and ran over to one of the nearby trees, catching one of the falling petals and eyeing it closely.

"There's no doubt about it, Bisco. These are cherry blossoms."

"Cherry blossoms? Do they grow in the wild? I ain't never seen one before."

"No, they don't. They only exist in a conservation center in Kyoto. All plants were destroyed by the Rust Wind. So how did they end up here...?"

"I heard that after Tokyo, the Rust Wind weakened across all areas of Japan," offered Pawoo, climbing down after Bisco and walking over to her brother. "Perhaps that is what has allowed these species to reemerge?"

"But it doesn't make any sense," replied Milo, furrowing his brow and biting his thumb. "The soil is far too weak to support this rampant growth. Just where are they getting their nutrients from...?"

Milo turned, flapping his cloak, and set off toward the center of the blossom-covered village. Bisco shared a glance with Pawoo before shouting, "Actagawa, wait right there!" to his trusty crab, and the two of them chased after him.

"What the hell happened here...?!"

After he'd laid eyes on the center of the village, Bisco no longer looked confused but angry. Each and every one of the Mushroom Keepers' homes lay wrecked, holes torn in the walls by the cherry blossom trees. The expired husks of giant crabs littered the settlement, their corpses the seedbeds for more of the trees that grew through the cracks in their shells.

"The town's been destroyed by cherry blossoms!" replied Milo.

"There must have been some kind of attack!"

"I can see that, dumbass! But how…?!"

The homes here were all made out of giant, hollowed-out mushrooms called houshrooms. The magnificent beauty of these fungi all standing in a line was famed even among Mushroom Keepers, but now the cherry trees had sucked all the nutrients out of them, so that they looked more like a row of mushroom mummies.

"…! Bisco, watch out!"

An arrow came flying toward Bisco from some unseen corner. Pawoo quickly leaped into its path, deflecting it back with a kick from her stiletto heels. When the arrow hit the ground, it exploded into a cluster of clamshell mushrooms. Pawoo landed, snatched her hat out of the air, and placed it back atop her head.

"Who's there?! Show yourself!" she yelled.

"Back for more, huh? Take this!" came a voice.

"…Huh?!"

"I'll show you fiends what an old woman can do! Give me back my son and grandson!"

A truly ancient yet unbelievably sprightly Mushroom Keeper sprang from the shadows. Unfazed by Pawoo's fearsome display of agility, she began firing off more arrows with a *Twang! Twang!* of her bow.

"You've got it all wrong!" Milo pleaded. "We just got here!"

"Taste my vengeance, demons!"

At Milo's voice, the old woman swiveled and pointed her bow at him, but Bisco nimbly leaped off a wall and tackled her in midair, bringing her to the ground.

"Aaaargh! You scoundrels…m-make it quick!"

"Chill out, lady! We're not gonna kill you; we're on your side! We're Mushroom Keepers!"

"Huh…huuuh?"

The old woman made a bewildered noise and began running her hands all over Bisco's face, squinting. At long last, after confirming his story, she let out a deep sigh.

"Why, you're not demons at all! You're human! Don't give an old lady a scare like that..."

"You're the one scarin' people, you blind old bat! Don't shoot what you can't even see!"

"Do you know what happened here, old woman?" asked Pawoo. "We haven't met anybody else besides you. And going by what we've seen..."

"...Aaagh... Waaaahh!"

The old woman, her fighting spirit all but gone, now began sobbing loudly in Bisco's arms.

"It was the Blue Devil! The Blue Devil was here!"

"Blue...Devil...?"

"An enormous brute! He marched into town...and not even all the village's crabs could stand against him. He took the younguns away! All of them!"

Bisco looked at Pawoo, who frowned, before turning back to the old woman and shaking her roughly by the shoulders.

"But how the hell'd he beat a whole village of you? Kyushu Mushroom Keepers are s'posed to be tough as nails!"

"We shot him with our mushroom arrows...but he only devoured."

"Devoured...? Devoured what? The crabs? The Mushroom Keepers?"

"It was the Blue Devil's flowers... The flowers devoured everything. Even the younglings...were powerless against them. He took them all away..."

It was painful to even listen to the old woman's voice as she attempted to recount the tale.

"Hmm," Pawoo grunted. "There's not a lot to go on. I don't blame her, though. It sounds like it was quite the panic."

"Yeah," replied Bisco. "But if they were taken, then that means they're still alive, right? Hey, Granny, take a deep breath. Hold it, one, two, that's right. Try to remember for me. Where'd the big guy take 'em? Do you remember?"

The old woman followed Bisco's directions, and at long last, after gathering herself, she began to speak.

"T-to Six Realms. That is what he said," she went on, occasionally flinching at some terrifying recollection. "He said they would pay for their crimes in the Six Realms of Rebirth."

"Hey! Doesn't that just mean he killed 'em?!"

"Bisco," Pawoo interrupted. "I might have an idea. Perhaps this *demon* of ours was referring to Six Realms Penitentiary. It is a massive prison complex in Kaso Prefecture, a little south of here."

"A prison?"

"Yes. I can't see anywhere else one might take a bunch of criminals. Perhaps some local police force has developed a new weapon that could do all this and is cracking down on Mushroom Keepers in the area."

"...Hmm, I see."

Bisco thought for a moment before nodding in comprehension and lifting the old woman up onto his back.

"If that's the case, they might have other villages on their radar, too. I'll go send Actagawa on a run. He can take this old woman to Shikoku and warn the others there while he's at it."

"While we'll continue on to Kaso, correct? What about the Mark I?"

"My tribe comes first. Come on, Milo, we're going!"

Milo was still standing a short distance away from the others, staring at the petals on the trees. But at his partner's voice, he whirled around.

"I'm coming!" he yelled. But just as he turned to leave, he spotted something. The cherry blossom petals suddenly swarmed together, blanketing the clamshell mushrooms the old woman had fired previously. In just a few seconds, a trunk began growing from the mushrooms, and before long, the only thing standing there was a miniature cherry tree.

"..."

Milo felt a faint chill run down his spine.

"They devoured the mushrooms...!"

The old woman's tearful lament replayed in his head. Milo wished there was some kind of clue he could take from it all, but with a sigh, he gave up and ran back over to where his partner and sister were waiting.

Back in the present, in the western commercial district of Kaso, Bisco and Milo had succeeded in outrunning their pursuers and had taken refuge in a run-down inn town, girl in tow.

Many of the business owners here were criminals on suspended sentences, and so while they projected a facade just like that of ordinary citizens, who knew what they got up to in secret? It was not a very pleasant place for upstanding folk like Milo and Pawoo to be.

Bisco, on the other hand, knew there was honor to be had among thieves, and the Man-Eating Redcap's name was known far and wide. A sympathetic Mushroom Keeper would have no reason to turn them in, so long as they paid a fair price for his services.

And so it was that the three of them found their current digs, a room in a questionable inn run by one tattoo-covered old man.

"Okay, I don't think they're after us anymore," said Milo, looking over his shoulder. "We must have lost them by now."

"Heh. Obviously. Just who do you think I am?" said Bisco.

Pawoo butted in. "Someone who lost the Kyoto police uniform I went to great pains to arrange."

In preparation for battle, she had changed into her bodysuit (a souvenir from Tokyo!) and sat down next to Bisco, who was cleaning his bow.

"I thought it might come in handy," she went on, "and it wasn't easy to procure in secret. If word gets out it was me, I could lose my job."

"Well, what're you gonna do? What's gone is gone."

Bisco was unsympathetic, as if to say it had been a necessary price to pay. Not many people could rival his brazen tongue, except perhaps his master, Jabi.

"Our little game of spies didn't turn up nothin' good, either," he continued. "You sure our Mushroom Keepers are here, Pawoo? I'm startin' to think even your gorilla instincts are off the mark this time."

"Wh-wha...?! How dare you talk to me like that, fool!!"

Pawoo hit her husband across the head in anger. Though she had meant it as a light slap, with her strength, it was like a mighty punch, which knocked Bisco face-first into the ground.

"A-aaargh! What the hell was that for?!"

"After all I've done for you... And another thing! You've got some nerve, talking to me like that after bringing me out here on false pretenses! What happened to our honeymoon? What happened to visiting the temples? I'm such an idiot for thinking you were serious about any of that!"

"I didn't have a choice! I needed someone strong to come with us... Wait! Put that staff down, please. It's dangerous!!"

"Don't worry, my love. Even death shall not separate us."

"Oh, damn, you're serious, aren't you...? You're really gonna kill us both for this?! S-stop!"

"BE QUIIIET!" yelled Milo. "I'm trying to work!! You can fight when we get back!!"

Pawoo's anger shrank back inside her, and she gave a small, embarrassed cough.

Milo turned back to the patient stretched out on the table before him: the young girl they had just rescued. Normally, Milo would be done by now, but her treatment had proved more difficult than expected.

...This girl's not human. My usual medical techniques won't help me here.

When Milo had gone to extract the girl's bullets, a strange ivy-like plant tried to block off his scalpel.

It's like it's protecting her, even while she's unconscious.

The ivy ran like a tattoo across the girl's white skin, lending her innocent physique an odd beauty. Another strange feature was the flower bud that rested just behind her left ear. So enigmatic was this patient that even the talented Dr. Panda had to throw up his hands and admit her condition was like nothing he had seen in his years of practice.

It doesn't seem to be malignant, but what could it mean...? No, I have to treat her, not study her.

Milo persisted and eventually succeeded in extracting the bullets. He gave her a transfusion, using some artificial blood that was unlikely to be rejected, before sighing and wiping his brow.

"Never known a patient to give you that much trouble," said Bisco.

"Yeah. The lurkershroom medicine didn't work the way I expected," Milo replied. "These plants just suck up the mushroom spores. Looks like I have to do things the old-fashioned way. Next up is treating the burns..."

"The lurkershrooms didn't work? You're shittin' me. They work on anything..."

Bisco came over to see the patient with his own eyes. "Hey, stop!" Milo protested, but his partner brushed him aside. When he spotted her lying there, naked from the waist up, Milo left a huge slap across his cheek.

"Gyaagh?! Not you as well! Why am I gettin' beaten up today?!"

"You mustn't look!" scolded Milo, staring his partner down. "Haven't I told you about modesty? Remember, you're a married man now!"

"W-wait, that kid's a girl? I coulda sworn she was a boy..."

"Oh, shush! I'm not done yet anyway!"

Milo shooed away his partner and turned back to bandage up his patient...when he spotted a pair of gleaming eyes staring back at him from between the girl's violet bangs.

Milo froze. For several seconds, he didn't even breathe.

Sh-she's awa—

"Waaaaghhh!!"

The pale girl let out a terrified shriek and attempted to crawl out the window. Milo grabbed her and tried to hold her back, but she was surprisingly strong.

"Wait, please! We're not with the government; we're trying to treat your wounds!"

"Let go of meee! How long will you violate me before you're satisfied?! Get your hands off me!"

The girl put her burned legs to use, repeatedly kicking Milo in the face, causing him to see stars. Each time he opened his mouth to say something, he took a foot to the teeth, unable to get a single word in.

Just then…

"Hey, get off him!"

At Bisco's yell, the young girl froze.

"That ain't no way to treat the guy who saved your life," Bisco said. "If you got problems, we're happy to hear them, right after you show us some manners."

Obliviously blind to his own faults, Bisco strode over the girl and grabbed her by the hair, staring deep into her crimson eyes.

"…Rhhh. Ah…!"

As soon as the girl saw Bisco's jade-green eyes once more, she suddenly remembered the sight of him on the battlefield. The flower behind her ear instantly exploded into bloom, and her face lit up in delight.

"Brother!!"

""""Whaaat?!"""""

Her words shocked every person in the room. Even Pawoo, leaning against the wall some distance away, joined in the bewildered chorus. Every last trace of the distrust the girl had been showing up until that point was gone, replaced with a bright, adoring smile. She slipped free of Milo's grasp and threw her slender arms around Bisco, leaping on top of him.

"Brother!!"

"Gaaagh?! What's gotten into you?!"

"You are like a god of war! I've been searching for someone like you for so very long! A true warrior, someone who can lead me along the path of kings…! I will never leave your side, not for a moment!"

"W-wait! P-put on some clothes!"

Milo and Pawoo rushed to wrap some bandages around Shishi's upper body, red-faced and flustered, but Shishi herself never took her eyes off Bisco for a second.

"You were like the great Enbiten himself, fighting against over-whelming odds! Even the god of death would flee from your visage. You are the Man I've been dreaming of all my life! From now on, I shall be your younger brother. Ask anything you wish of me!"

"What are you talking about? We ain't related!"

"My name's Shishi!"

Ignoring Bisco's bewildered tone, Shishi somersaulted off the table in defiance of her injuries and landed with a *plop* before Bisco.

The violet hair she allowed to fall messily over her eyes was nonetheless smooth and pretty, and the skin of her slim, gentle arms was white as snow. When combined with the ivy's pattern, she looked just like a tiny orca.

The clear beauty she'd once possessed made the scars and burns all that more painful to look at, yet the scarlet camellia flower behind her ear bloomed brilliantly, as though a reflection of the girl's very life force itself. Bisco was unable to take his eyes off it.

"If it is my birth that worries you, then lay your fears to rest! I am the biological child of King Housen...a true prince by blood, as young and foolish as I may be."

"King...Housen? Who the hell is that?"

"My father taught me that if I am to become a true successor, I must leave the king's path and find a master. A man who lights a fire in the depths of my heart. And when I do...I am to make him my Brother and learn all I can from him. Now, Brother, order me as you wish! Allow me to become your arms and legs!"

"Just sit down and let Milo treat you! You're covered in burns!"

Bisco somehow managed to retain enough of his dignity to put the young girl in her place, but as soon as he did...

Grrrr...

...his stomach rang out loudly. Now that he thought about it, he hadn't eaten since their infiltration began.

"...It seems you are hungry, Brother!"

"Uh...no, that was just... Hey! Where do you think you're going?!"

"Wait there, Brother! I'll go get the guards to give us some rations!"

"Ahh, wait, stop!" Milo cried, but Shishi evaded his grasp as effortlessly as if she were completely unharmed. She threw open the door to their room and started heading down the nearby staircase, when…

Clunk! Thunk! Ker-dunk! Thunk!

…her foot slipped and she went tumbling all the way to the bottom like a stone.

"Ouch…," said Milo, screwing up his face in secondhand pain. Pawoo quickly dashed down the stairs and brought Shishi back. She had passed out once more.

"Well, she's energetic, I'll give her that," she said. "Just needed a little more time for the anesthetic to wear off."

"She shouldn't have been able to wake up in the first place," said Milo. "I'd better apply the burn ointment while I still can."

Pawooo leaned over and whispered, *"Milo. Just a suggestion, but you might want some of that ointment on your right eye, and don't look at Bisco just yet. I'll lend you some makeup later."*

"…Pawoo? What do you mean?" asked Milo, turning in confusion. But as soon as Bisco laid eyes on him, he burst into laughter.

"Gaaah-ha-ha-ha-ha!!"

"Too late."

Pawoo sighed and offered Milo a mirror, whereupon he realized that Shishi's kick earlier had left a large bruise around his good eye, matching the other eye perfectly.

"It's a panda! A real freakin' panda!" Bisco howled. "What's the matter, little fella, need help gettin' back to the zoo?"

"You son of a…!"

The boys grappled. Pawoo sighed and cast her eyes down at the girl lying on the table. She found her eyes drawn to the girl's wounds, and they told her just how much hardship she had been subjected to.

"I am sorry, Milo," said Shishi when she awoke sometime later. "Did I do that? When you were trying so hard to make me better, too…"

"Don't worry about it! Everyone suffers some haziness in recollection right after the anesthetic wears off. It just means you're a tough and determined young kid!"

"But, Doctor, you have two black eyes now because of me…"

"Oh, ha-ha-ha… Well, the thing is…"

"S'fine. One of 'em's all-natural. Thanks to you, he's got a matching pair."

"You stay quiet, Bisco!!"

"…But I am thankful," Shishi said. "If you two hadn't saved me, I'd be…"

The three shared a glance as Shishi gently held her own trembling body. With the treatment complete, the girl's nerves had settled to the point that she could hold an honest conversation, but what had not changed was her sudden, mysterious, and unwavering dedication to Bisco.

Now the girl thought back on her close encounter with death and of the undoubtedly fierce struggles she'd gone through to get here.

"That just goes to show that fate has great things in store for you," said Pawoo. "We are travelers, with no duty to this land. Whenever you feel comfortable talking, we are happy to lend an ear to what troubles you."

"Thank you, Pawoo…!"

Shishi was currently dressed in one of Milo's spare tunics—the closest fit for the girl's small size—in an attempt to shield her strikingly pale skin from suspicion. What the three found a lot harder to conceal was Shishi's distinctive violet hair and the alluring smell of flowers that surrounded her at all times.

"'Ere you go, lads and lasses, sorry fer the wait."

"'Bout time," grumbled Bisco. "How hard is it to cook four bowls of soup?"

Since all of them, Shishi included, had not eaten in some time, the four had ventured out into the villain-riddled streets to find a restaurant where they could secure a quick meal. Bisco gulped down his miso soup with vigor, which Shishi eagerly watched before sidling up to him.

"You are hungry, Brother. Here, have mine as well!"

"Don't give it to him, Shishi!" cried Milo. "You need to eat first!"

"He's right," Bisco agreed. "We ordered that for you."

"You ordered this…for me?"

Shishi's face lit up in delight, and the flower behind her ear, which had retracted back into a bud, burst into full bloom once more.

"I am so happy, Brother! ...But I insist. I cannot possibly eat when... Ah, I know! You are still worn out from your battle, are you not? Here, I shall feed you!"

"Is your head full of flowers, too?!"

"Say *aaah!*"

"Cut it out! Get off me!"

...What on earth is she up to?

Milo's eye twitched as he watched Shishi cling to his partner, sometimes getting very touchy-feely indeed. Even Pawoo, the man's own wife, didn't seem to have anything to say, only eyeing the girl's actions with more confusion than anything else.

"Shishi," Pawoo said at last. "If Bisco is indeed the true man you seek, then he doesn't need you to feed him. Eating properly is a part of Milo's treatment, so you had better get on with it."

"I am okay! These are mere scratches..."

"Listen, kid. It ain't me who saved your life, it's Milo. Show him the proper respect," said Bisco flatly. "And eat that food we got for you. Understand?"

"Y-yes. I am sorry, Brother..."

Shishi shrank after Bisco's stern warning and turned to Milo before giving him a small, apologetic dip of the head.

"I apologize, Milo. That was no way for me to act after all you've done for me."

"O-oh, no! Not at all! I'm just glad to see you up and about. It's nothing you have to apologize for..."

Milo quickly hid his displeasure with a smile, but he noticed that contrary to the girl's pleasant and polite demeanor, the camellia flower in her hair had curled up into a bud once more.

"I will drink this soup as you command, Milo. Will that make things better?"

"Oh...um...I guess...?"

"Brother! Milo forgave me! That makes it okay!"

Before Milo could even finish speaking, Shishi turned back to Bisco, her camellia flower exploding into bloom, and with wide eyes and a beaming smile, she snuggled up to Bisco again.

"Listen, kid. The problem wasn't about whether he forgave you or not..."

"Let's try this again. Say *aaah*! ...Come on, Brother. You have to open your mouth!"

"You don't understand a thing that just happened, do you?! You're supposed to eat that yourself!"

Milo's eye began twitching again, but Pawoo only gave a half-amused, half-resigned laugh and clapped her brother on the shoulder.

"*Do you see that flower, Milo?*" she whispered. "*Quite fascinating, I must say. It seems to be reacting to the girl's emotional state. It's like a built-in lie detector.*"

"*Pawoo, don't you have anything to say?! That's your husband she's feeling up...!*"

"*Ha-ha! Milo, you think I'm so jealous, don't you? Give me some credit.*"

Pawoo stroked back her long, silky black hair and proudly puffed out her chest, crossing her arms.

"*She's just a kid. There are certain areas where we simply can't compete.*"

In Kaso, the food was mostly prepared by the inmates, so it tended not to be particularly refined. The region's specialty was a kind of *mochi* made from rice flour and helmet potato, called a "Kaso cake." It wasn't bad as such, but compared to the sumptuous feasts the boys had enjoyed back in Shimane, these dry and tasteless rice buns filled with crushed beans left something to be desired.

"...? Ow."

"What's wrong, Bisco?"

"What the...? Urgh, there's a tooth in my bun."

"Ha-ha-ha! Looks like you got unlucky, brother! Here, you can have mine instead..."

"Shut up and eat! Still, a tooth? Freaks me out to think about how it got there..."

"I suppose two of the cooks must have gotten into a squabble on the kitchen floor. One of their teeth probably fell in then."

"And they just served it up like that?! I'm gonna file a complaint!"

"I'll come with you, Brother!"

Shishi immediately clung to Bisco's side as he rose from his seat. Capitalizing on this distraction, Pawoo leaned over and whispered into Milo's ear.

"*Milo. I've been observing for some time, and it doesn't seem like Shishi's human.*"

"*I think you're right,*" Milo replied as he bit open his Kaso cake and checked for any offensive material within. Then he ate the whole thing and washed it down with tea. "*Shishi appears to be one of the Benibishi. I saw one at the clinic once, and Shishi reminds me very much of them.*"

Back when Japan was still rebuilding, before achieving what could tentatively be called its current stability, a corporation called Benibishi Bionics sought to augment the workforce using a race of artificial life-forms. They were created to serve humanity, biologically engineered to feel a sense of obligation toward their masters, and genetically spliced with plant DNA to allow them to subsist off light instead of needing to be fed. From there they were sent all across Japan, where they were employed as slaves.

But as reconstruction went on and humanity regained the use of heavy equipment, the demand for strong, unthinking laborers decreased. Benibishi Bionics changed direction and focused on creating more lovable, attractive servants for the purposes of companionship.

"Each generation of model was more attractive than the last. They became musicians, dancers, entertainers, and eventually sex workers..."

"Milo. Shishi's coming back."

"Ah, s-sorry..."

"Milo! Pawoo! Look at this!" Shishi squealed with delight. The Nekoyanagi siblings put aside their discussion to listen to her. "They gave us this big meat on the bone as an apology! All Brother had to do was give the shopkeeper one look, and—!"

"Terrorizing the locals again?" asked Milo. "I told you not to do that, Bisco!"

"All I said was there's a tooth in my bun," replied Bisco without a shred of guilt before swiping one of the meat shanks out of Shishi's hand and taking a bite from it. "Then he started makin' excuses, so I just glared at him. He's the one who struck the first blow."

"It's your glare that should count as the first blow—," began Milo, but Shishi cut him off.

"Isn't my brother amazing?" she sighed with delight, and the sweet scent of her camellia wafted through the air. "*A true king moves minds without resorting to words*; that is what my father used to say. It is only through mutual understanding that we can avoid unnecessary bloodshed."

"Sounds like your old man knew what he was talkin' about. Perhaps you oughtta take a page outta his book."

You're the one who needs to learn to avoid unnecessary bloodshed, Bisco!

Milo caught the hunk of mutton he was tossed and glared back at Bisco's self-satisfied smile, grinding his teeth in frustration.

"So where are you off to next, Shishi?" asked Pawoo. "Do you have a plan of what to do after this?"

"A plan...?"

"Such as a family, or someone who can look after you. We'll take you there...if you have any, that is."

"...My father... He is the only family I have left."

"I see," Pawoo replied with a look of surprise. "Then that is good. I had thought perhaps he was also gone. So where does this father of yours live?"

"...Over there."

Shishi pointed out the window...toward the Devil's Gate, the black structure towering over the drab concrete townscape.

"Over there...? Shishi, you don't mean...!"

"Six Realms Penitentiary. That is where they are holding him."

Shishi made short work of the tough lamb shank and began chewing a second one, staring out the window.

"I cannot live free while he is still imprisoned. Once my wounds are healed, I will march back in there to retrieve him...before he is subjected to the same things I had to go through."

"You want to sneak into Six Realms? But that's—!"

Pawoo cut Milo off. "Shishi. I've been meaning to ask you something. Your father, could it be that he is a man of some renown?"

"There are none among the Benibishi who do not know my father," Shishi replied with pride before her face fell a little and she continued. "He is King Housen of the Benibishi, a great hero who led us to overthrow our oppressors. We all believe...that he will one day deliver us from internment."

The petals of her flower fluttered a little as she continued, "He is my father, our king, and leader of our people..."

"Shishi's father is king of the Benibishi...?!"

"I suspected as much. Shishi's determination seems much stronger than that of the other Benibishi. However..." Before Pawoo even said anything more, she saw Shishi's face fall. "...I was under the impression that King Housen was moved to death row only a few days ago. He lost his mind, killed several of the prison guards, and is now tied to a post, awaiting his execution."

"That's not true! Gopis made it all up!" Shishi growled in anger before grunting in pain at her wounded chest. As Milo rushed over to support her, she continued, "That cruel woman. She seeks only to disgrace my father, since he would not kneel to her. She thinks that by killing him she can crush the spirits of the Benibishi...!"

Shishi's voice quivered with anger, and both Milo and Pawoo found themselves unable to respond.

"...I came to her on my knees, begging her to revoke my father's execution. Then she whipped me over and over again until I lost consciousness..."

"...But you managed to escape the incinerator and make your way to freedom, and the rest is history."

Pawoo finished off the story that Shishi was struggling to complete, and she nodded, deep in thought.

"Pawoo, do you have an idea?"

"Hmm. It would not be wise to use my influence to demand King Housen's release. It may only succeed in making them more wary. However..." Pawoo smiled to set Shishi's heart at ease. "Vice-Warden Gopis is only in temporary command of Six Realms. The true ruler is Lord Satahabaki, a man of steel-like resolve and unwavering judgment. If we inform him about the corruption Gopis has been up to in his absence, I am sure he will agree to cancel your father's execution."

Pawoo looked down into Shishi's eyes and gently took her hand. It seemed to calm her down a little.

"Lord Satahabaki is a man in great demand, and his travels take him all over the country, but fortunately I have heard that he will soon be returning to Kyushu. We must get in touch with the man and speak to him directly."

"You mean you will help me rescue my father?!"

"Hey, ain't anyone going to run this by me first?!" roared Bisco after he'd downed his sixth lamb shank. "We ain't got time to be respondin' to every little sob story that comes our way. We can help other people with their problems once we've taken care of our own! We got plenty enough on our plate as it is, remember? First we gotta save the Fukuoka Mushroom Keepers, then we're goin' after the Mark I!"

Shishi cast her eyes sadly downward.

"But, Bisco," protested Milo. "If we go to meet Lord Satahabaki first, then..."

"If that's what you're gonna do, then leave me out of it," Bisco shot back. "I'll go out on my own if I have to."

"Oh, come on! At least let me finish!"

Just as Milo tried to come up with a way to change his partner's mind, something appeared on the nearby television that piqued his curiosity.

"...Bisco. Bisco! Look at that!"

"What, who cares about sumo wrestling? We all know Ikaruba's gonna take the belt anyway."

"No, it changed to the news! Just look!"

Bisco begrudgingly turned to see the screen…

"We interrupt tonight's tournament to bring you a special news report. We've received word that Lord High Overseer Someyoshi Satahabaki has just reentered Kaso after concluding his business trip across Japan! Our correspondent Yamano is on the scene!"

The reporter gave his announcement with a sense of agitation, while the ticker tape along the bottom read, *Lord High Overseer Returns to Six Realms after Six-Month Absence.* The image then changed to reveal a giant of a man, possibly three meters tall, clad in thick navy armor and a helmet that covered his eyes and nose. Only his mouth could be seen, a splendid, bare-toothed grin that inspired fear even through the TV screen. The very earth shook as he plodded along the highway, making his way toward the city.

"It's Satahabaki! Brother, that is Lord Satahabaki!"

"That guy's a judge? He looks more like the executioner!"

Just as he said that, though, Bisco noticed the figure that Satahabaki dragged along the ground behind him. It struggled to break free of its bindings, expelling bursts of smoke as it did so. Bisco's jaw dropped.

"Hello! I'm here at the north gate! As you can see, it seems that Lord Satahabaki has succeeded in capturing the crimson giant who has been terrorizing the northerly regions! Even the other prefectures struggled to contain this criminal, who—"

"*"It's the Mark I!!"*" Bisco and Milo shouted at the screen before Shishi and Pawoo clasped their hands across the boys' mouths.

"Welcome back, Lord High Overseer! Your loyal subjects have long been awaiting your return!"

"…"

"I see you have apprehended yet another dangerous criminal! Is there anything you would like to share on the matter?"

"…"

"Erm… My Lord…?"

Satahabaki kept on walking, without sparing so much as a glance toward the rookie news anchor by his feet. Of course, so incredibly tall was the man that the microphone would not have reached him anyway.

It was almost impossible to tell, given the spectacular shaking of the screen that occurred with each step, but besides the Mark I, there appeared to be something else wrapped up in a cloth on Satahabaki's back. Like him, this luggage was so large that it couldn't all fit on camera at once.

"I...I see you've brought quite a lot back with you, My Lord. Just what might this...umm, could you please— Wah!"

The news anchor tried their best to keep pace with Satahabaki, running alongside him, but tripped on a stone and fell, grabbing the cloth wrapping for support and pulling it away. It drifted gently to the ground, revealing...a pile of iron cages, all filled with people.

"Erk."

"Erk."

Bisco's and the reporter's reactions to the sight were exactly the same. The camera panned upward to show that the mountain of cages was easily ten meters high. Satahabaki had fastened them all to his back with stout iron chains.

Inside each and every one was an exhausted warrior, who was thrown into the air each time the Iron Judge took another step.

"Mushroom Keepers...! They're all Mushroom Keepers, Bisco!"

"I can see that!"

"...This group of bandits concealed themselves in the mountains of Fukuoka and threatened the townsfolk there."

At long last, Satahabaki spoke in a loud, booming voice.

"They are criminals and not for your amusement. Switch off the cameras."

"Oh...er...well, I... Waaah!"

Satahabaki lowered a single gauntlet-clad finger and flicked the camera away. Only the cameraman's scream could be heard as the image cut to static. Then the news show cut back to the studio.

"...Er... Well, thank you, Yamano, for that update. Things should be back to usual in Six Realms by tomorrow. Anyone wishing to attend the trials should..."

After a short while, Bisco muttered to himself.

"…Hmm. So that's the Blue Devil," he said, casting his mind back to the navy-colored helmet he had seen during the broadcast. "An' here I thought that crazy old lady was just talkin' shit. If that guy took out a whole village of Mushroom Keepers, not to mention the Mark I, then it ain't just a case of the camera addin' a few pounds."

"But I thought the misunderstanding surrounding the Mushroom Keepers was dispelled when we all banded together to fight against Tokyo," said Pawoo. "Why is Lord Satahabaki still opposed to them at this stage…?"

"Who knows? We'll find out if we ask him, I bet."

"Hear that, Shishi?" said Milo. "It seems that Bisco needs to speak with Lord Satahabaki as well. We can all go see him together!"

"Brother!" Shishi threw her arms around Bisco, almost ready to cry. "That's such good news! I am sorry about what happened to your friends, but this must be fate! Heaven has freed me from that prison and led me to you! Brother, you must lend me your power…!"

"Put a sock in it. We just happen to be headin' in the same direction, that's all."

Bisco's flippancy could not fool Milo, and it was clear to him that Bisco really wanted an excuse to help the girl. The problem was that these days, the two could practically read each other's minds, and Milo had to be careful whenever there was something he didn't want his partner to know.

"Gopiiis! Gopis! Where are you?!"

"Silence, fool! Your voice is making my bones hurt!"

Six Realms Penitentiary, entry yard.

Mepaosha's screeching voice resounded in Gopis's shattered ribs. Mepaosha snatched her by the collar and pulled her in.

"Wh-whoa, let go, fool! You're pulling on my dress…!"

"Since when do you care if your tits are hangin' out, skank?!" The normally smug Mepaosha was now coated in so much sweat that her glasses had steamed up. "Listen to me! He's back! He's returned!!"

"I don't give a shit if your ex is back in town," said Gopis, breaking free of Mepaosha's grip and turning to leave. "Don't you dare bother me again when I'm busy humiliating the slaves!"

"Nooooo! It's Satahabaki! Lord Satahabaki is on his way here right now!"

"…Whaaaat?!"

Upon hearing that ten-letter name, she whirled around in shock.

"Th-that can't be right. I thought that foolish warden was headed to Kagoshima next…"

"He was, but he came across a den of bandits and… *Cough! Cough!*" Mepaosha suddenly began coughing violently. "…He wanted to personally make sure they came here. M-m-m-maybe he already knows that we let Akaboshi get away…"

"Why didn't you tell me any of this earlier, you fool?! We can't let him find out about Shishi, or there'll be hell to—"

"The Lord High Overseer has retuuurned!"

"Open the great dooooors!"

""Waaaaarghhh!""

The two turned to look in horror as the huge black gate slowly opened.

"..."

Tilting his navy helmet, the man in the enormous suit of armor stared at the doors slowly creaking open.

"Warden! Welcome back from your long—"

Several guards hurried out the gate to greet their Lord High Overseer at his sudden arrival, but their mouths fell agape at the sight of the tremendous mountain of cages chained to his back. From within could be heard cries of *"Let me out!"* and *"Release me, you brute!"*

"These prisoners," began Warden Satahabaki in a booming voice that rattled the cages and silenced the captives, "are a band of Mushroom Keepers I arrested in North Fukuoka. "They are villains, but they are powerful villains. They have the potential to become strong guards. Keep them locked up until the Sakura Storm sets in."

"A-as you wish, My Lord. But...," replied a guard, looking timidly up at Satahabaki's enormous frame. "We have not the room to house such a large number of criminals. We are already overcrowded, as you can see..."

Sure enough, at either side of the gate were more piles of iron cages, stretching as far as the eye could see. These were the criminals that Satahabaki had already sent back from his trip across Japan. The prison had long since exceeded capacity, and so these cages were left out here.

"Hmm."

Satahabaki curled one massive finger around his chin and pondered.

"Very well. Then pile these up with the others."

"As you wish, My— *Waah!*"

The earth shook as Satahabaki dropped the mountain of cages to the ground, causing the Mushroom Keepers trapped within to pass out. A huge swarm of guards came pouring out the front gate and split themselves into groups to help carry the cages inside, which were so heavy it took ten men to lift a single one. It was impossible to imagine what strength the warden of Six Realms possessed that allowed him to carry them all by himself.

"...Warden, that villain you carry with you is another of them, is he not? Please entrust him into our care."

At the guard's words, Satahabaki looked down at the criminal tucked under his arm (who was also fairly large himself), then slowly shook his head.

"No. This one is too strong for you to contain."

"But, Warden..."

"The gate is no swifter than usual to open, I see."

The rumbling doors of the great gate were weighty indeed. Not only to prevent an escape but also to showcase the magnificence of the penitentiary itself.

"I apologize, My Lord. We currently have one hundred men working the mechanism. We are opening it as fast as possible..."

"No need. I shall do it myself."

"Huh...?"

As the guard looked on, puzzled, Satahabaki pushed past him and, without word or warning, placed his hand to the black iron gate and began pushing it open. The rumbling intensified, and the doors swung back faster than ever before.

"W-witness the might of Lord Satahabaki, Keeper of Justice!"

"He is returned! Lord Someyoshi Satahabaki is returned!"

The prison guards extolled their words of praise as Lord High Overseer Someyoshi Satahabaki, the Iron Judge of Six Realms, forced open its gate and returned to his mountain fortress.

The overseer's respect for the ways of Old Japan was well known, and his navy and sky-blue armor was heavily based upon the samurai of the Edo shogunate. Of course, all who laid eyes on him were first struck into submission by his enormous size, and not out of any appreciation for ancient history.

Looking up at him now with those exact feelings were two figures.

"*H-he's huge... Is he even human?*"

"*Look at those teeth... Think he ever flosses?*"

The two prison guards whispered to each other as they kneeled in worship. Of course, those two guards were, in fact...

"*Bisco. Remember we're only here to scout things out. Don't get excited and try to fight him.*"

"*Whaddaya think I am, a dog?! You don't have to keep me on such a tight leash!*"

They were none other than Bisco and Milo, who had knocked out two guards and stolen their uniforms.

Thud! Thud! The ground echoed with each step, and as Satahabaki passed in front of them, the two held their breath. In one hand he held an enormous flat *shaku* scepter, so large that any ordinary person would be squashed beneath its weight, while in the other he held the struggling form of the Akaboshi Mark I.

How did he capture him?!

The robot was based on the Mokujin design. Even a seasoned warrior could not stand against it, much less defeat it. That Satahabaki had managed to capture the rogue alone was testament to the warden's monstrous might.

"You certainly are a boisterous one."

"*Vrrr.*"

The Mark I only whirred in response.

"Do you understand your sentence?"

"*Vwoo.*"

"Then I shall explain anew."

Satahabaki tossed the Mark I to the ground. Before any of the guards could react, the robot sprang to its feet with surprising agility for its size and launched a rocket-enhanced punch at the Iron Judge.

"*Vrrrr!*"

"Before the law..."

The Mark I's fist connected solidly with Satahabaki's torso, but not one crack appeared in the warden's mighty armor.

"...Your sin is POWERLESS!!"

Ker-rangg!!

Satahabaki swung his enormous fist down on the robot's skull, smashing him into the ground like a nail. Sparks and even a couple screws flew all over the place.

"Still, you fail to comprehend?"

"*V-vrrr…*"

"GUILTYYY!!"

Kerrang! Ker-ranggg!

Satahabaki grabbed the Mark I by the arms and slammed him left and right into the cherry trees that lined the yard. Each time, the blossoms scattered and filled the air.

"*That bastard…!*"

"*Bisco, wait!*"

Milo hastily grabbed on to Bisco before he could leap in to help. Luckily, the other guards were so awed by what they were seeing that none of them seemed to have grown suspicious of the pair. Once all the surrounding cherry trees were completely bare, Satahabaki stopped at last.

"Now do you understand?"

"…"

"…You cannot answer. Then, guards, take him to the Devil's—"

"*V-vr…*"

"…Hmm."

Satahabaki watched the half-broken Mark I, whirring and throwing off sparks, and gave a nod of satisfaction.

"Your spirit speaks to your admirable will. Splendid! Six-Tenths Bloom!"

Satahabaki swung his arm, tossing the helpless Mark I high into the air.

"Deliver him to the Preta Realm!!"

A shrill cry answered Satahabaki's booming voice, and a trained eagle appeared out of nowhere and snatched up the Mark I in its talons before transporting it away to a distant part of the prison. Bisco instinctively went to draw his bow, but Milo stopped him.

This all went unnoticed by the grand Satahabaki, who barked an order to the other guards.

"Once the brainwashing is complete, he shall become a fine guard of steel. Have a programmer brought here at once. He appears to be a robot of some kind."

"B-but, My Lord, his trial has not yet—"

"I have already passed judgment. Here are the charges. Keep them safe."

Satahabaki tossed down a scroll that enumerated the Mark I's crimes in carefully penned letters. The brushstrokes, while impressive, were difficult to make out, given their creativity, but the guard only bowed and took his leave.

"It has been a while since I last returned. I believe I shall first make the rounds."

Satahabaki stood and surveyed the row of guards all kneeling before him.

"I detect the scent of sin among you."

…!

"Two of you, to be precise."

The two boys gulped at Satahabaki's oppressive voice. They stayed as still as possible, trying their best to blend in.

"Those of you who flinched at these words…"

Satahabaki crossed his arms, peering down at the line of guards.

"…You are innocent. A true scoundrel would hide their thoughts."

"…He tricked us…!"

"Bisco, don't move!"

"Enough. Stand and face your punishment!"

As Bisco and Milo kneeled there, drenched in sweat, Satahabaki lifted his enormous hand…and snatched a pair of robed figures sitting directly behind them, fishing them out of the crowd and depositing them in the center of the yard.

""Kyaaaagh!!""

Their robes came undone, revealing the flashy dresses of the two vice-wardens, Gopis and Mepaosha.

"Why are my two best lieutenants sneaking around like gutter rats?"

"Uh…uhhh…"

The two women prostrated themselves once more, and Milo breathed a sigh of relief.

"*Thank goodness. I thought we were done for.*"

"*That's those two vice-wardens from before. Looks like they're in trouble.*"

"I hear you have been neglectful in my absence, Gopis, Mepaosha," said Satahabaki, not even glancing at the two women as he ascended the staircase that led to the splendid black seat reserved for the Six Realms judge. Gopis was sweating so hard that her bandages were sopping wet.

"We shall begin with you. Kneel, Vice-Warden Gopis."

"O-overseer. I can explain! Y-you see—"

"I said KNEEL!!"

"Y-y-y-yes! R-right away, My Lord!" Gopis shrieked and tumbled to the floor before Satahabaki's seat.

"Your wounds degrade you. Is this a prisoner's doing? You must not show weakness before them."

"Y-y-y-yes..."

"Minus two points. Next, in the course of giving orders, you foolishly injured a subordinate. Minus another two points."

"...? R-right..."

"You object?"

"A-absolutely not!"

Nose still to the ground, Gopis felt the color return to her face.

That's strange. These are all minor infractions. Could it be...he hasn't heard about Shishi yet?!

"I find it hard to forgive your reckless behavior...but considering you have kept the place well, I shall not charge you with a crime. However, you are forbidden from leaving the premises until you prove yourself mindful of your duty under the law."

"Y-yes!" Gopis screamed, pressing her head into the dirt. While she was drenched in sweat, a faint smile appeared on her face.

Satahabaki, meanwhile, struck the *shaku* scepter against his knee and nodded.

"Court dismissed. Next..."

"Please wait a moment, Lord High Overseer."

Just as Gopis breathed a sigh of relief, Mepaosha's shrill voice echoed over the court.

"Gopis concealed her greatest wrongdoing from you. Her true crime far outweighs those...heh-heh-heh...petty misdemeanors."

"...Mepaosha, how dare you!!"

The bespectacled woman named Mepaosha recoiled in mock fright while a cluster of guards held Gopis back. "Hee-hee. How scary," she taunted.

"I'll kill you, you foolish woman!" yelled Gopis. "Don't think I won't! I'll tear you limb from limb and feed the bits to the prisoners!!"

"Just try it, you cow. This is what you get for making me do all the hard work. Now's *my* chance to claim the vice-warden's seat."

Her mocking eyes met Gopis's bloodthirsty gaze, and Mepaosha continued.

"While the warden was away, Gopis became more selfish than ever. She especially took delight in picking out the most beautiful of the Benibishi and ensuring they got the whip...indulging in her own selfish desires within these hallowed halls of justice!"

"Do you speak the truth?" Satahabaki inquired.

"Hee-hee-hee... The overseer's eyes are not so easy to fool. What do you see, My Lord?"

"Hmm."

Satahabaki clenched and unclenched his massive teeth.

"It...it wasn't just me! She took part in it, too! She made the Benibishi serve her...!"

"The problem is what came after, My Lord."

Gopis's face suddenly turned pale. Mepaosha went on.

"Just a few days ago, one of her favorite Benibishi, Shishi, managed to escape the Devil's Cauldron and break free of Six Realms."

"Stop...don't tell him anything else!"

"You mean to say...," came the warden's thunderous voice, shaking the very air and preventing both women from speaking any further, "...that Vice-Warden Gopis has been cavorting with the prisoners and brought the security of this impregnable fortress into question? This 'Shishi' managed to deceive her, and as a result..."

The air continued to shake until eventually there was a *Bwoom! Bwoom!* as a pair of cherry blossom trees grew through the chinks in Satahabaki's armor, scattering their *somei-yoshino* petals.

"...a prisoner has succeeded in ESCAPING from Six Realms Penitentiary? Am I understanding correctly?!"

"W-Warden!" Gopis wriggled along the ground, clasping her arms around the overseer's leg. "Th-that little fool has not yet left Kaso! Any Benibishi would be stopped at the checkpoint! We will get her back, trust us! I'll mobilize the entire prison if I have to!"

"For allowing a prisoner to escape, minus one thousand points."

"Ah..."

"Repent, you wretched simpleton!!"

Satahabaki's condemnation seemed to split the sky above, and he snatched up the trembling Gopis by her bare legs before smashing her into the ground, much the same way he had to the Mark I.

"L-Lord Satahabakiiiii!"

"Please have mercy! Lady Gopis will surely die!"

A group of guards came running up to Satahabaki and begged him to stop before he passed judgment a second time. He let out an indescribable roar of either rage or frustration before tossing the passed-out Gopis to the ground. Then, like jets of steam from his ears, a bunch of cherry blossom trees burst into being beneath his armor, causing his large frame to quake. The subsequent petals that fell like snow were pretty to look at, but nobody had any time to appreciate the aesthetic.

"I have failed," he boomed, concealing the fury in his voice. "I was blind not to see that my own officer harbored such depravity. See that she lives; I still have use for her. She shall receive her punishment at a later date."

"Hee-hee-hee. Warden, surely you're not thinking about retrieving Shishi yourself?" Mepaosha sidled over to Satahabaki, pushing up her glasses.

"My officer's sin is my own. I must deal with this personally."

"Y-your dedication is admirable, My Lord, but there is no need for the overseer to trouble himself over a single Benibishi child. Forget about Gopis…and allow me to go in your stead. Give me but a couple of days, and I'll see to it that—"

Before Mepaosha could finish wagging her tongue, Satahabaki wrapped his thick gauntlet around her body. Her bones creaked, and she tried to scream.

"G-gaaaagh! …W-war…den…"

"Why is it you knew of Gopis's treachery but did nothing?"

"Eeeep! P-please forgive me… I'm too pretty to die…!"

"The reason I employ two of you is that each is too weak by yourself. You must each cover for the other's faults. Next time you allow Gopis to fail, Mepaosha, consider your life forfeit."

The Iron Judge dropped Mepaosha on the ground and stared down at her as she writhed in pain.

"Do you understand what I am saying??!" roared Satahabaki in a voice that could level mountains.

"Y-yes!" squealed Mepaosha. It almost seemed like the warden's grip had made her a few sizes smaller. Satahabaki took one look around at the busy prison grounds before gnashing his exposed teeth.

"I invited this corruption into our midst. The scales shall be righted by *my* hand," he said. Then he took a deep breath, and…

"Come to me, Winter Cherry!"

…he gave a sky-rending shout, and an enormous stallion, its coat deep red, as if it were stained in blood, appeared at the gate. Satahabaki hopped atop it, but the mighty horse did not even drop an inch beneath his weight.

"Follow the scent of fugitives, Winter Cherry. Do not let them escape!"

Satahabaki's steed gave a magnificent whinny before galloping out of the front gate and dashing through the streets of Kaso like a bolt of flame.

The two Mushroom Keepers, still wearing their disguises, stood in the gateway of the busy courtyard and watched the rapidly receding figure disappear into the distance.

"He's even crazier in person than on TV," muttered Bisco in disbelief. "How're you even supposed to negotiate with a guy like that? ...You think he likes sushi?"

"That's exactly what we're here to find out. The place has just been thrown into chaos; if we want to get to work, now's our chance!"

"Get to work? Weren't we here to speak to that big guy?"

"I knew you'd forget! Just follow me!"

At this rate, it seemed quite likely that Satahabaki would kill the young girl if he ever got his hands on her. Nevertheless, the two Mushroom Keepers blended into the crowded uproar left in the warden's wake, disappearing into the confusion like mist.

"Lord High Overseer Satahabaki Simultaneously Executes 100 Prisoners in World First!"

"Six Realms Incarceration Rate up 850 percent on Previous Year!"

"Refusal to Offer Seat Earns Death Penalty! The Crazy Laws of Kaso Prefecture!"

Pawoo flicked through the Kyoto newspapers, eyeing their disturbing headlines as she walked along the Kaso streets, her white coat and long black hair fluttering behind her. Her striking beauty turned even the heads of the downtrodden and melancholic townsfolk, though Pawoo herself wore a troubled frown.

I always knew Satahabaki to be a strict and judgmental man, but according to these newspapers, he's only gotten worse ever since the war with Tokyo ended. What could have caused such a rapid and dramatic change?

So engrossed was Pawoo in the paper that she failed to notice a utility pole ahead of her and walked straight into it with a *thud.* Hastily looking around to make sure nobody saw that, she cleared her throat with a cough.

"I won't get anywhere just thinking about it. I must go and meet with him in person."

Muttering to herself, Pawoo turned a corner and was met with the flashy shopfront of a confectionery store.

Hmm. Far from the worst place I've seen around here.

Pawoo nodded at the shop's clean curtain and entered, looking around at the neatly arranged rows of sweets.

"Welcome," said the shopkeeper, an elderly woman sitting behind the counter.

"This is a cute little place you have here," replied Pawoo. "A welcome sight after the dreary streets outside."

"You are very kind to say so, madam. Many times I have thought it was a foolish idea to run a confectionery store in a city like this, but your gracious words make it all worthwhile."

The old lady stood, using her cane for support, and dipped her head in appreciation. Pawoo laughed and gestured her down before pointing to the row of sweets.

"I'll take some of those ant-honey-coated ones, please."

"Certainly, we have fire strawberries, tomatoes, and wart-potatoes."

"Then I'll take one of each... Anything else you recommend?"

"These were just made today."

The shopkeeper lady retreated into the back and brought out some lattice-shaped wafer cakes with red-bean filling.

"What a curious design," said Pawoo.

"They're a famous delicacy around these parts. They're called Exoneration Cakes."

"Exoneration Cakes?"

"The wafer symbolizes prison, while inside the filling there's a human shape made out of mochi."

"Ugh..."

"A famous Kaso belief claims that if you can eat the whole thing at once, it will keep you out of prison for an entire year."

Pawoo had been lulled into a false sense of security by the old woman's charm, and the grotesque nature of the treat startled her. The sweetly smiling old lady seemed genuine enough, however.

"Th-then...I'll take one..."

"Just one?"

"Y-yes. Here, keep the change. Th-thank you very much!"

"Do come again."

Pawoo nearly ran from the shop, sweating, before taking the Exoneration Cake out of its wrapping and examining it.

"The molding is very lifelike...*too* lifelike. It looks just like a prison. I was hoping to get something that would cheer Shishi up, but this..."

As she walked, Pawoo took a bite.

"...Mmm. Doesn't taste half bad."

She stuffed the rest of it into her mouth, subconsciously heeding the old woman's tale, and swiftly made her way back to the cheap hotel where the group was staying.

"Shishi! I'm back! I thought you might be bored stuck in here, so I bought..."

Pawoo peeked her head around the doorframe, but what she saw there stunned her into silence. Shishi was dancing with a fan in her hand, and the tiny beads of sweat on her pale skin glistened in the sunlight that flooded into the room.

She leaped and turned, following the motions of her fan, displaying a balance of passion and elegance that was unlike any style Pawoo knew. And astonishingly, for all the girl's skips and prances, her feet were completely silent against the ground. It was a level of control known only to the greatest masters of martial arts.

It's...beautiful...

When it was over, Shishi expelled a deep breath and snapped the fan shut before landing, feet wide, in a stunning finishing pose. When she opened her eyes, the first thing she saw was Pawoo staring right back at her. Stunned, Pawoo dropped the bag of sweets to the floor and began applauding.

"Ah...ahhh!" Shishi's gallant face suddenly went bright red with embarrassment. "P-Pawoo! How long have you been there?!"

"That dance was wonderful, Shishi! I didn't know you could do things like that!"

"Ohmigosh, you saw the whole thing?!"

Shishi rolled onto the floor, covering her face with her fan, and nestled herself in a corner of the room, presumably waiting for a large crack in the ground to swallow her up.

"It's nothing to be embarrassed about," said Pawoo, walking over and placing a hand on Shishi's shoulder. "You're a very talented dancer, young lady."

"Y-you really think?" Shishi peeked out from behind the fan and looked up at her. "D-did you think I looked...strong? Was it scary enough to make you freeze in terror?"

"S-scary??" Pawoo looked quite taken aback by Shishi's question but answered honestly, "I wouldn't say that, but it was graceful and sweet... Even a Philistine like me was impressed by the artistic quality."

"...Graceful...and sweet?"

Shishi sighed a despondent sigh and curled herself up again.

"Hmm. It appears I said something I shouldn't have," said Pawoo.

"I am still not ready. The dance of a king should not be seen as sweet. It must be a powerful dance, a dance of men, or else I shall never succeed my father."

Pawoo gave the crestfallen girl a gentle stroke and offered her the honey-glazed fire strawberry.

"It will be okay. Here, have something sweet to chew on... I thought your dance was very moving, and all of us know you're a very strong girl."

"..."

Shishi took the candy in her mouth and sucked on it for a while... and soon large tears came to her eyes, and she had to wipe them away with her hands.

"...It tastes so good."

"Then I'm glad I went out to get them. If you're happy, I'm happy."

"Thank you, Pawoo... I don't know how you managed to find a confectioner in Kaso."

"Hah. A simple task compared to dealing with my husband and my brother... I thought you deserved something after all you've been through. It must have been tough on such a young..."

Just as Pawoo was about to say the word "girl," she stopped herself. The more she got to know Shishi, the more cognizant she became of the boy she was at heart. When Shishi spoke of strong *men* or true *kings*, those choices of words were not accidental; they spoke to the way she chose to identify. She needed the body of a man if she stood any chance of becoming just like her beloved father.

Or at least that was what Shishi seemed to think. Pawoo's feelings on the matter were something along the lines of, *It doesn't matter. There are no genders in war anymore. All you need these days is the will to see it through.*

Still, Shishi was at a delicate age for young boys. That was no doubt compounding her worries.

To live with the body of a girl... She must feel so estranged from the sort of man she seeks to become.

Shishi lay cradled in Pawoo's arms, drying her eyes and weeping her laments to Pawoo's sympathetic ear.

"...My father always used to tell me that since I was born a girl, I should forget the crown's burdens and seek my own happiness. But I don't want to. I've lived my whole life looking up to him, seeking the strength I need to rule in his place..."

"..."

"But it's just not possible, all because of the way I was born..."

"Shishi. This strength you speak of, is it simply a male body you seek?"

"Huh?"

Shishi raised her eyes to see Pawoo's smiling face. She stood up, took the staff lying against the wall, and gave it a thunderous swing. The blast of air blew back Shishi's violet bangs and exposed the shock in her crimson eyes.

"I think it's my turn to show you a dance of my own."

Pawoo twisted her iron rod as lightly as if it were made of wood, causing the air in the room to grow so turbulent that the beams of the hotel walls creaked with age. With each roar of her staff, Shishi's hair was blown back by the gale-like winds. Pawoo's own black hair fluttered as she brought her demonstration to a close and, without a single drop of sweat anywhere to be seen, tossed her staff to Shishi with a smile.

"Wawawa! Waah!"

Shishi staggered under the staff's weight and fell backward, but her face lit up and she sprang back up, grabbing Pawoo's arm and looking up at her. The camellia behind her ear was in full bloom.

"Did that seem *weak* to you?" Pawoo asked.

Shishi enthusiastically shook her head. Pawoo's effortless display of staff wielding had so encouraged the young girl that she found it impossible to put her thoughts into words.

"That was amazing, Pawoo! To think a woman could be so agile yet so strong!"

"You're young," Pawoo replied. "That's the only reason you're still weak. Anyone can be a warrior, regardless of gender. Keep up your training, and you'll be every bit the hero your father is."

"Ah...!" A glimmer of hope appeared in Shishi's eyes as she watched Pawoo swish back her hair with confidence. "I see. I may be young now, but so long as I keep the heart of a man like you do, my strength will come!"

"Yes, see? You understa— Hmm? Hold on a second, I didn't say I have the heart of a man..."

"...? Pawoo, I hear someone coming! Perhaps my Brother is back at last!"

"Wait, Shishi! You've got it all wrong! I'm—!"

Crash!

Suddenly, the entire wall was blown out, along with half the room itself. Shishi was launched back by the explosion, and Pawoo caught her before leaping backward.

Who's there?!

It was as if a bolt of lightning had come down, blasting off the roof of the building and letting in the midday sun. Pawoo took her staff and peered down the stairs to see the innkeeper shaking in fright and...

...the giant in blue armor, who had stood over him and used his back to shield the landlord from the falling roof, now brushing himself clean of debris.

"I misjudged my strength," he said.

"Eeep..."

"Please accept my apologies. Use this to rebuild your inn."

The giant took a wad of sols from his armor and scattered them before the innkeeper's eyes.

"And please. Do not tell a soul about what happened here today."

"O-o-okay..."

"Answer me CLEARLY!"

"Yes, sirrr!!"

It baffled the innkeeper that a man so eager to keep the whole thing under wraps would immediately produce such an earth-shattering yell, but the giant seemed to find the outcome satisfactory. It was then that he looked up and locked eyes with Pawoo.

That's...Someyoshi Satahabaki!

Pawoo held her breath. For a second, she felt a strange sense of anxiety. Satahabaki did not allow that second to go unnoticed. He jumped up into the air and landed with a *Crash!* before the guarded Pawoo.

"You. Woman. Why is it you feel nervous? Do you have something to confess? Then speak. A repentant mind may result in a lighter sentence."

"If I had committed any wrongs, I would admit them freely, Your Honor."

There was no fear in Pawoo's voice. Satahabaki's imposing figure was enough to terrify even the bravest soldier, but Pawoo was made of sterner stuff by far.

"My soul is clean. Or is Kaso so struggling with its finances that it would trump up charges to arrest an innocent woman?"

"You have a sharp tongue. But you are without sin, I see."

Satahabaki folded his arms and nodded, but just as Pawoo found time to relax, he barked once more.

"Then what of the Benibishi girl hiding behind the cupboard over there?"

Pawoo tensed up again at his question.

"It is admirable to give shelter to a wounded child, but you should know that she is a miserable fiend who has committed the sin of jailbreak. You must hand her over—"

Before Satahabaki could finish speaking, Pawoo sliced with her staff, executing some kind of technique that split the cupboard into four pieces without hurting Shishi at all. Then she scooped her up and fled through the window.

"Such finesse! Splendid! That earns a Seven-Tenths Bloom."

Satahabaki's teeth rattled as he watched the pair go. It was almost as though he was attempting to laugh.

"It seems the game is truly afoot! Look kindly upon me, Tadasuke Ooka!"

Satahabaki set off after the fugitives, aiming to leap out the open window as elegantly as Pawoo had, but seemingly ignorant of his own monstrous size, he only did so by taking the entire wall with him.

Pawoo fled from the destruction without looking back. "He's even more ridiculous than I'd heard! Shishi, don't let go!"

"But, Pawoo! Didn't you want to talk to him?"

"Not yet! Milo and Bisco are still inside Six Realms, looking for evidence! We can't do anything until they get back with…"

At this point, Pawoo glanced behind her, only to see that Satahabaki had somehow caught up already, his massive arm raised high overhead.

How is he so fast?!

"GUILTYYY!"

Kerrang!

There was a deafening boom as Satahabaki swung his scepter, striking Pawoo in the side. Pawoo just barely managed to catch it on her staff, but the force sent her flying off like a baseball, where she remained airborne for all of four seconds before landing in a sandpit in a nearby park.

"*Cough! Cough!* Pawoo, are you all right?!"

"I-I'm fine… But how is he so strong? He's like a monster!"

The two were not badly hurt, thanks to Pawoo's quick reflexes and their fortunate landing place. However, never before had Pawoo been struck with such force. Bisco's superhuman strength was erratic at best and came only in short bursts. Meanwhile, there was so much mass behind Satahabaki's blows that it felt more like fighting a train.

"A true master of their craft! Surely, I must know you…," said Satahabaki, landing nearby in a cloud of dust and flattening a sign that said KASO PUBLIC PARK—NO BALL GAMES. "…However, my memory fails me. Please remind me of your name."

"Imihama Governor, Pawoo Nekoyanagi." Swiveling her staff, Pawoo introduced herself. "Lord Satahabaki, I heard tales of your deeds during the Tokyo War. You defended the island of Kyushu from enemy forces. We are both of us this nation's protectors. What reason have we to fight?"

"Ah." Satahabaki's teeth chattered. Shishi came out of hiding to face him, but Pawoo stood over him defensively. "Pawoo, the Whirling Steel. I knew you were a reputable fighter. …However, I cannot comprehend why you have come here, to Kyushu, and why you stand up for a Benibishi you do not know."

"Wouldn't anyone stand up for a child who is under attack?"

"Splendid! Your virtuous creed earns a Seven-Tenths Bloom!" Satahabaki swung his scepter with a *Bang!*

"Lady Pawoo. Your reasons for protecting the child are noble, and as such I shall not press charges. However, I am the Iron Judge of Kaso, tasked with upholding this land's laws. My scepter shall not show mercy upon one who gives safe haven to an escapee of my prison!"

"If you oppose me, I'll make sure you regret it, Satahabaki!"

"The only one tasting regret shall be you. I cannot be harmed."

Satahabaki raised his scepter aloft once more and smashed it into the ground. The powerful impact shattered the earth, sending the slender Shishi flying.

"Waaagh! Pawoooo!"

"Oh no! Shishi!"

"The sentence…is DEATH!"

Pawoo leaped to her feet and jumped after Shishi, but Satahabaki's scepter got there first. Just as the Iron Judge was about to cleave the girl in two…

Gaboom!

"…?! Nrrrghh?!"

…a pair of arrows stuck into the ground between Shishi and Satahabaki, exploding in an instant into a great big King Trumpet mushroom. The warden's massive iron frame was tossed up into the cloudless sky like a rubber ball.

Shishi was thrown back by the blast and caught by Bisco, cloak billowing, who landed heroically near the mushroom's base.

"Hit that one outta the park!" he said.

"Brother!!"

Shishi wrapped his arms around Bisco, and Milo landed next to him.

"We made it!" the boy doctor said. "Shishi, are you okay? You're not hurt, are you?"

"Milo!" Shishi replied. "Satahabaki is even more fearsome than the legends said. Can we really hope to talk peacefully with such a man?!"

"Eh. I'd say the chick who protected you is the more fearsome of the two," quipped Bisco.

"I heard that! If you're trying to talk behind my back, lower your voice!"

"I'm just sayin'. You held that freak off with only your staff, while lookin' after the kid, too."

Bisco heaved a deep sigh and helped Pawoo to her feet, meeting her gaze with his dazzling jade-green eyes.

"Ain't nobody else who could do somethin' like that. Your strength and will are second to none."

"…Y-you mean that was meant to be a compliment? You can't fool me. I bet you're just—"

"It's just 'cause I'm weak? Just say so if that's how you feel." Bisco adjusted the skullcap that had fallen ever so slightly out of place in Pawoo's long black hair. "When we got married, I said I'd do anything to protect my family, and that includes you. If I ain't strong enough to do that, the gods are gonna burn me to a crisp."

"Th-that is not true. Y-you are everything a husband should be, Bisco…"

When she looked into his brilliantly gleaming eyes, Pawoo found that all the complaints she had accumulated over the past few days seemed to dissolve into nothing. Her face turned bright red, and she couldn't meet his gaze.

"Milo, are Pawoo and Brother having a fight?"

"No, this is supposed to be them flirting. They're just not very good at it."

Milo watched the married couple with an indescribable look of *what-are-they-doing* on his face before his battle instincts came to the fore once more and he called out to his partner.

"Bisco! He's coming back!"

"Figures. I'd be disappointed if the King Trumpet was all it took."

"Brother, I shall fight by your side!"

"Like hell! You'll just get in the way! Pawoo, take this kid somewhere safe!"

Bisco and Milo readied their bows and aimed them upward.

"Nnnrrruuugghh!!"

Satahabaki had landed atop the sloping caps of the King Trumpet and tucked himself into a ball. Now the metal sphere was rolling at top speed toward them.

"What is this, a bowling alley?!"

"Bisco, fire!"

But even the pair's armor-piercing arrows merely ricocheted off Satahabaki's thick plate. As he reached the base of the mushroom, he popped open like an armadillo, flying through the air and swinging his scepter into the ground.

"Milo, jump!"

The earth shook again with the force of Satahabaki's blow. Bisco and Milo barely managed to escape the fractured earth but were unable to stop themselves from tumbling into the weeds.

"Nrghhh! Rrraaaghh!"

The two Mushroom Keepers heard something slowly tearing apart. They sprang to their feet to see Satahabaki in the process of uprooting the King Trumpet with both hands.

"Y-you're joking…"

"Hraaaahhh!"

Satahabaki finally succeeded in wrenching the giant mushroom free of the earth, and with a spin, he tossed it far into the distance. It twinkled in the clear blue sky before dropping in a cloud of dust on some far-off part of the city.

"…Article 115. Menacing a public space of relaxation." Without any heed for the damage he had just wreaked, Satahabaki jabbed his finger and barked at the Mushroom Keeper duo. "If you continue to obstruct justice, then be prepared to face the law!"

"What about all the people *you* just menaced?!" Bisco yelled, but Milo put his hand up to stop him.

"Please wait, Your Honor!" he said, stepping forward. "We apologize for resorting to violence, but we absolutely must speak to you about something. It's about how Shishi escaped from prison…and the cruelty that Vice-Warden Gopis has been engaged in."

"Mmm?"

Upon hearing Gopis's name, Satahabaki froze. Now that he was aware of the tyranny he allowed to pass in his absence, this was one of the few chinks in his otherwise impenetrable armor.

"…The penalty for jailbreak is death. No exceptions. Gopis's conduct has nothing to do with the child's case."

"It has everything to do with it, Your Honor!"

"You dare object to the ruling of the Lord High Overseer?! Hand over the child without complaint, or else—"

But just as Milo was about to respond, Shishi stepped in his way.

"I will not run or hide from you, Satahabaki!"

"Shishi!"

She was trembling with fright, drenched in a cold sweat, but somehow, she found the nerve to walk up to Satahabaki and stare up into his eyes.

"You stand before me of your own accord. Do you not value your life?"

"I do not!" Shishi's eyes flickered beneath her bangs, and the camellia behind her ear flared in response to her indomitable will. "I do not value my life in the slightest. You can have my head on a spike if need be, but only after you hear what I have to say! It is for that reason that I slipped my bonds, and for that reason I stand before you now!"

"Do not think you can save your life with trickery, child."

"Then slice off my head before I can speak! Or is the Warden of Six Realms too cowardly to hear the last words of a dying *man*?!"

Sh-she's insane!

…

Milo and Bisco watched carefully. Shishi was sweating hard from the raw power that emanated from Satahabaki's very being. Her shoulders rose and fell with every breath, but the single camellia flower behind her ear, red as blood, seemed to shine with the girl's will. The sight of this small child and the miraculous courage she displayed shook even the Iron Judge Satahabaki to his core.

"Hmm…!"

Satahabaki thought for a moment and then stood up straight, arms crossed, as if inviting the child to speak. Milo looked over at Shishi and urged her on.

"…My father, King Housen of the Benibishi, has been charged with killing the guards and sentenced to death," she began.

"I am aware. Murder of a prison guard is one of the gravest sins imaginable. Housen has been well-behaved during his incarceration, but I cannot allow such an act to go unpunished."

"…I am disappointed, Lord Satahabaki. I had thought you wiser than to be fooled by your subordinate's deceit."

"What…?"

"King Housen's crime was a complete fabrication!"

Shishi's bellowing voice rattled Satahabaki's armor.

Shishi's losin' her cool. If she angers Satahabaki, he's just gonna step on her! Wait! I—I think it's all right…!

Bisco and Milo watched, hands on their weapons, ready to immediately leap to Shishi's rescue should Satahabaki make a move. Strangely, however, the warden seemed to give the matter careful thought, pondering the issue calmly without sacrificing his posture.

"All of it was Vice-Warden Gopis's doing. She schemed to have good

King Housen executed, all because he would not submit to her cruel whims. All she cares about is crushing the hopes of the Benibishi and forcing them to obey!"

"I still have my doubts. Gopis is prone to...extreme behavior, but she is a fine keeper of the law. Is it not merely your hatred of justice that drives you to view her that way?"

"In that case, look at this!"

Shishi tore open the coat she was borrowing from Pawoo, revealing her pure white skin.

"Behold! And then tell me if you still think so, Lord Satahabaki...!"

The young prince bit her lip in humiliation as she forced herself to display the signs of her submission, the marks of the slave-beating whip. Milo and Pawoo couldn't bring themselves to look at the tragic scars upon scars that marred the girl's beautifully soft skin.

"You claim that Gopis inflicted all these?!"

"It was not just me," Shishi said, close to tears. "She whipped all the young girls of the Benibishi. She enjoyed watching their minds break. I watched as she killed any that disobeyed her...mere children, every one of them..."

"Mrrh?!"

By now, Shishi could no longer hold back the tears, and Satahabaki gave a troubled grunt. Any misdeeds of Gopis's were his burden to bear, and as such, Shishi's claims were hard to accept.

"Never would I have imagined this. Your testimony will be required at Gopis's trial."

"Th-then...!"

"However! That has no bearing on King Housen's crimes! Proof of her villainy is not proof of his innocence!"

"Your Honor! I believe these hold the answer you seek!"

Milo, seeing that Satahabaki was open to reasoned judgment, suddenly cut in. Up above his head, he held out five photographs, each depicting the dead body of a prison guard.

"What's this? The Six Realms morgue?"

"These are photographs of the five guards that Housen supposedly murdered."

"How did you obtain these, scoundrel?!"

"I'll explain that later. For now, allow me to show you something."

Milo pointed on the photos to the wounds the corpses had suffered.

"King Housen is supposed to have killed the guards using a stolen sword. However, these wounds were caused by something moving in a far larger arc. For example…"

"…A whip." Satahabaki's rumbling voice shook the earth as he compared Shishi's wounds to those in the photos. "There is only one in all of Six Realms skilled enough with the whip to take a human's life: Gopis. Grrr… Could it be she went to such lengths to frame the Benibishi king?"

"Warden, you must call off King Housen's execution!" Forgetting all honor and fear, Shishi fell to the ground and groveled at Satahabaki's feet. "You can do whatever you want with me, but spare him! Spare my father, I beg of you!"

"Do not touch the JUUUDGE!!"

Satahabaki's mighty bellow caused a gust of wind that blew Shishi and Milo away.

"Grrr! Decided to fight after all, eh?!"

"Court is now in session! ALL RIIISE!!"

At Satahabaki's roar, the ground quaked and split, and dozens of trees sprouted out of the ground with tremendous force. After forming a large circle around everyone, the trees all burst into bloom simultaneously.

"Wh-what the hell? More cherry blossoms…"

"I shall now hand down my verdict!"

Bisco and the others could only stare, dumbstruck, as Satahabaki yelled. Nothing they had ever come across before could make trees blossom instantly.

"My prolonged absence does not excuse my ignorance as to the corruption taking place behind my back. As this prison's highest authority,

I am equally guilty of Gopis's crimes. Furthermore, my blindness to her plotting has thrown the good name of Six Realms into disrepute!"

Bang! Satahabaki struck the ground with his scepter.

"I hereby sentence the defendant, Someyoshi Satahabaki, to one hundred years of hard labor!!"

The air rippled, catching the cherry blossom petals and scattering them on the wind. Bisco and Milo stood frozen, their mouths hanging open in shock and amazement.

"Wait...*who* is he sentencing?" asked Bisco in confusion.

"Himself!" said Milo. "He just sentenced himself, the judge, to one hundred years! Just how devoted to upholding the law *is* he?!"

"You call that devotion? I say he's lost his goddamn mind!"

"Shh! There's still more!"

"In addition! I shall issue an amendment to the sentencing of the Benibishi, Housen!"

"Wardennn!" Shishi ran joyfully over, but—

"SIT DOOOWN!" The judge's roar sent her flying back. "...I hereby acquit Housen of the crime of murdering a prison guard. Accordingly, he shall be spared an execution and moved back to the Human Realm."

Shishi's eyes filled with tears, and she flopped down to the ground, all her strength drained. It was like all the feelings she had been bottling up until that moment suddenly vanished, taking her soul with them.

"That's wonderful! That's wonderful news, Shishi! Your father's going to be okay!"

"Milo...!"

Teary-eyed, Shishi went to accept Milo's hand, when...

"Fools! Do not think my judgments to be over so swiftly!"

Baring his enormous teeth, Satahabaki expelled a hot breath of air, like steam.

"King Housen's case was but a trifle. There is an even larger matter that requires the attention of this court. Benibishi Shishi, you and your kind shall face the traditional punishment for your jailbreak."

Shishi fell to the floor, and Bisco and Milo stood over her protectively.

"Surely you can overlook somethin' like that, big guy! This girl just risked her life to help her father!" Bisco's hair bristled with rage. "And the only reason she broke outta prison in the first place was because your head guard dog was gonna roast her alive! What's wrong with that?!"

"It is not a question of right and wrong." Satahabaki's booming voice made Bisco's seem like a whisper. Its sheer force blew the hair out of the boys' eyes. "The Benibishi were created to serve humanity unconditionally. The fact that one acted to protect its own life means that it has managed to overcome its genetic code. This ivy that wraps around the child's body is proof. Proof that the Benibishi have evolved to throw off their shackles of servitude."

Satahabaki pointed his scepter at Shishi, and the oppressive blast of wind that followed gave her the chills.

"The fires of evolution have been lit. Shishi shall not be the last Benibishi to be born emancipated. There will be more. It is too dangerous to leave them unchecked. Therefore, I declare!"

Satahabaki slapped his enormous scepter against the ground.

"One week from now! All the Benibishi imprisoned in Six Realms shall be put to death!"

A billowing shock wave burst forth from his body, scattering cherry blossom petals on the wind.

"All the Benibishi...will be killed?!" repeated Shishi, deathly pale and shivering. "All because of me...? Th-that can't be... This can't be happening!"

"That's ridiculous!" Milo yelled. "Evolution is a natural part of life! Is it a crime to live?! Is it illegal to adapt and survive?!"

"For the Benibishi, yes. They are a dangerous race. Enslaved, they pose no threat, but if all of them were to be freed, Japan itself could be in danger. The problem must be rooted out."

"But killing them all?! Even you must think that's far too cruel a solution!"

"What I think is of no consequence. The law is the law."

"It's no use, Milo! He's not gonna listen to anything unless it's written down in his precious rules."

Bisco took on a combative air, and his jade-green eyes glimmered. He drew the bow from his back, and Milo followed suit.

"We're gonna have to teach him a lesson. Let's see if you'll listen to *this*, big guy!"

"Khaaah!!"

Riled up by the fighting spirit of the two boys, Satahabaki began shaking as trees exploded all over his armor.

"Drawing your bows against me only hastens my verdict. Let us move on to the final trial of the day."

"Trial this, justice that!! Man up and draw your weapon already!"

"The law is my weapon. The world has trusted me to rid it of vermin like you. Do not think I fail to see you for what you truly are."

"Grrr... Does that mean he knows we're—?"

"Vile Mushroom Keeper Akaboshi, the Man-Eating Redcap! Long have I awaited the day you appear in this court! Feel the weight of the law!"

Crash!

Satahabaki's scepter leveled the earth and created a circular crater in the ground around him. The two boys leaped over to the other side of him and turned, bows drawn.

"B-but wait, Your Honor! Our bounties have been rescinded!"

"This is bullshit! I wanna speak to a lawyer!"

"For ruining Gunma's tourism industry by covering Mount Akagi with mushrooms! Forty years of hard labor!"

Satahabaki swung his scepter, and the cherry blossom petals all flew toward the pair as though they had a mind of their own.

"Whoa! What the hell?!"

"Bountiful Art: Crimson Petals!"

Almost as if the petals were tiny razor blades, the cloud engulfed the two boys and tore their signature cloaks to shreds. Without them, a Mushroom Keeper's mobility was much curtailed.

"What's does he mean, 'the law is his weapon'? It's these flowers! That musta been how he attacked the village, too!"

"For riding your giant crab, Actagawa, across the land, terrorizing the people and disturbing the peace! Twenty years of hard labor!"

"Say what?! I'll have you know Mushroom Keepers consider crabridin' to be an elegant and noble sport!"

"Don't get sucked into his game, Bisco!" whispered Milo, rolling over to him. *"Our mushroom arrows won't work on his armor! We need to break through it somehow to get a clear shot!"*

"How're we supposed to get through his armor with nothin' but our daggers?!"

"We need to crack it open. If only we had some sort of round, blunt weapon..."

"Blunt weapon, huh...?"

"And other crimes too numerous to mention!"

The scepter came down just as Bisco was about to leap, and he rolled sideways out of the way. Then he rummaged around in his front quiver for an arrow that would do the trick and nocked it to his bow, taking careful aim. The fire in his eyes was so intense it seemed that his glare, and not the arrow, would burn a hole in the target first.

"...Mrh! There it is! Those glowering features of yours are the arrow that threatens law and order! The world will not truly be safe so long as your foul face exists! Another twenty years of hard labor!"

"Take a look in the mirror, Jaws! If ugly's a crime, they should lock *you* up for life!"

Bisco's hair and tattered cloak fluttered in the wind of Satahabaki's yell, and he pulled his drawstring tighter. The Iron Judge ran toward him, unable to focus on anything else, the ground quaking with each step.

"No arrows can harm me, Akaboshi!"

"We'll just see about that...!"

Bisco drew a deep breath. His crimson hair flared in defiance, and his jade-green eyes twinkled.

"Mrrrgh?!"

In the face of the overwhelming sense of threat, Satahabaki instinctively raised his scepter to protect his face. That left him open to...

Bang! Bang! Without even a breath between them, Bisco's two arrows stuck into Satahabaki's knees, tearing the armor apart and leaving two large cracks. But the arrows came to rest just centimeters away from his skin.

"...You did well, to create an opening using fear alone. However, you have failed to land a scratch on—"

Gaboom!

"...Urghhh?!"

"From now on, you have to say, *Only Bisco's arrows can harm me!*"

Gaboom! Gaboom!

From Satahabaki's knees swelled clusters of anchorshrooms, their bulbous caps glistening gray. Their terrifying weight brought the inhuman Satahabaki to one knee, where he let out a roar of pain before falling to the other knee as well.

"To think there was a technique that could immobilize me. Only Akaboshi could be capable of such a thing!!"

"Pawoo!"

"Bisco! Use this!"

In perfect sync, Pawoo tossed her staff into the air, while Bisco took aim. His anchorshroom arrow hit the staff's tip and grew into a sturdy iron ball, creating a sort of sledgehammer that then stuck into the ground at Bisco's feet.

"You think this can stop me...?"

Even with mushrooms growing out of his legs, Satahabaki attempted to stand back up, but as he did so, Bisco pointed the anchorshroom hammer at his chest.

"It might be *your* job to beat people down, but I don't like watchin' you trample all over the little guy!"

"My job is not to beat people down! It is to uphold the law!"

"Really? You coulda fooled me!"

While Bisco yelled, he kept swinging the hammer around in a circle, gradually building up speed.

"Maybe someone needs to teach you to recognize what gettin' beat down is like!"

Smash!

Bisco released the hammer, which went flying straight into Satahabaki's breastplate. The incredible force of the impact shattered not only his armor but the weapon's anchorshroom tip as well.

"Rrrrgh! What?! My armor!"

"Milo, now!"

Bisco leaped into the air alongside his partner, and both of them drew their bows tight.

"Oyster mushrooms, on three!"

"Got it! One, two…!"

Pchew!

Satahabaki raised his scepter to defend himself, but the two arrows broke right through it and stuck into the warden's exposed chest muscles.

Gaboom! Gaboom!

Two oyster mushroom clusters burst forth, one red and one blue, blowing off the back and shoulders of Satahabaki's armor.

"Ngh! Grrrooooaaahhh!"

The mushrooms' explosive growth sent him flying backward, skidding against the ground a couple times. Each time he did, he gouged up great clods of earth before finally coming to rest after carving out a trench twenty meters long.

Shishi coughed on the clouds of dust kicked up by the battle but stared on, wide-eyed in wonder.

"W-wow! Brother brought him down! The warden of Six Realms!"

"Of course he did! That's my husband and my little brother, working together! However…hmm. I fear killing the Lord High Overseer invites its own problems…"

"He didn't give us much choice," said Bisco, he and Milo landing nearby just as the other two ran over. "It was us or him." He put away his bow and popped his shoulder back into place, after its dislocation from swinging the anchorshroom hammer. "Why don't we just say you did it? Then you can take over his lands or whatever."

"What exactly do you think being a governor is all about?" asked Pawoo in disbelief.

"Wait a minute! Something's not right…"

Milo silenced the pair before things got out of hand and directed their line of sight over to the dust where Satahabaki had fallen. There was a huge shadow, silhouetted in the cloud. With one swing of the warden's scepter, the dust cloud was dispelled, revealing the magnificent body of Satahabaki himself, standing once more on his own two feet.

"Krhhh…!"

"Waah! Bisco! He's still alive!"

"I have taken on a hundred Mushroom Keepers at once and won," declared Satahabaki. "I had expected this battle would be trifling compared to that."

Satahabaki lowered his mighty fists and tugged on the anchorshroom caps embedded in his knees. Their lead-like weight yielded to his monstrous strength and tore off almost immediately.

"Your techniques are like none I have ever seen. Splendid, Akaboshi! Nine-Tenths Bloom!"

"What the hell?! Is this guy even human?!"

There could be no mistaking the cluster of mushrooms that grew from Satahabaki's chest, scattering their spores even now, yet he refused to go down. The two Mushroom Keepers stared in shock. There had been giant organisms that shrugged off a direct hit from their mushroom arrows, but never once had a human done the same.

"I…am not human. I am Benibishi. One who wields the cherry blossom in defense of the law."

"B-Benibishi?! The Lord High Overseer is a Benibishi?!"

"Behold! Witness the Sakura Storm that graces Six Realms!"

Satahabaki summoned all his energy, and miraculously, cherry blossoms grew forth from his mushroom-riddled chest, twisting around the stalks. They then began to feed off the fungi, channeling that life force into Satahabaki himself, until magnificent *somei-yoshino* trees sprouted from his shoulders with a *Bwoom! Bwoom!* in a stunning display of vitality.

"That bastard… He's eatin' the mushrooms!"

"Bountiful Art! Rechaaarge!"

Satahabaki began trembling with the fearsome new life force he had absorbed from the oyster mushrooms.

"Your techniques are impressive," he said, his huge white teeth chattering. "However, so long as your strength stems from mushrooms, you shall never defeat me!"

"Uh-oh! Bisco! Get out of the way!"

"Bountiful Art: Nature's Coffin!"

Satahabaki thrust out his chest and howled, and out flew enough cherry blossom petals to blot out the sky.

"Shishi! Let's run! This way… Waagh!"

Pawoo tried to lead Shishi away, but the petals swooped down on them like a swarm of locusts and enveloped them, leaving only a pair of flowery cocoons that fell to the ground.

"Pawoo! You bastard…!"

"Bisco! What if we burn him with an infernoshroom?!"

"I thought I told you…!"

The two swiftly nocked and fired their arrows, which landed with a thud in Satahabaki's chest. They exploded into being with a *Boom! Boom!* but…

"…Mushrooms will never work on meee!!"

Once again, the cherry blossom trees wrapped around the fungi and hindered their growth.

"They ain't growin'. Our aim was perfect, too!"

"Bountiful Art: Revelation! Hidden Art: Weeping Dance!"

"Bisco, watch out!"

The willowesque branches that drooped from the weeping cherry trees on Satahabaki's chest lashed out like whips, striking Milo hard as he jumped in the way to protect Bisco from harm. He cried out in pain as the attack launched him back.

"Milo!"

"I will have ORDER in my court!" roared Satahabaki, tugging his whip back and wrapping it around Bisco's leg just as he readied an arrow in retaliation. Bisco suddenly toppled onto his back as if the floor had been pulled out from under him and was dragged flying toward the overseer.

"Woooaaah?! Damn!"

"Foolish Akaboshi! Without your mushroom techniques, there is nothing you can do!"

"…Nothin', eh? How about *this*?!"

While Satahabaki reeled him in, Bisco drew his lizard-claw blade with lightning speed and kicked off the ground, aiming a swing squarely toward the helmet atop the warden's head. However, just before the exceptionally keen blade could slice the metal open...

"Khaaah!"

Satahabaki exhaled a deep breath, and the dagger was immediately cloaked in cherry blossom petals, whereupon it quickly fell apart like falling leaves.

"Your might. Your will. Your ambition! Splendid, Akaboshi! It will be a shame to watch you die."

"Shut the fuck up!"

"Mmrh!"

His enthusiasm uncurbed, Bisco seemed, if anything, wilder than ever before as he continued flying toward Satahabaki, swinging only his bare fists. The Iron Judge swiped him out of the air, holding him by the scruff between his enormous fingers, and brought him up to eye level.

"I have decided. You shall be my Iron Deputy."

"Grrr...ghh! You bastard... What are you—?!"

"Bountiful Art: Revelation! Full Bloom: Magistrate's Mark!"

"Grrrrhhhhh!"

As Bisco hung there in his viselike grip, a cherry blossom tattoo spread from Satahabaki's palm to Bisco's skin.

"Ha-ha-ha...! As I thought, the blossoms take quickly to Mushroom Keeper blood."

Bisco struggled as he felt a searing pain, like a branding iron pressed to his flesh, but he could not struggle much in the warden's grasp. The tattoo wrapped its way around Bisco's neck, up his shoulder, and onto his left cheek.

"The Sakura Storm," explained Satahabaki, throwing Bisco to the ground. "I bestowed it upon all the other Mushroom Keepers I captured, too. It ensures strict adherence to the law, inflicting an immobilizing pain when its standards are not met... In the end, it even dominates the mind, transforming the bearer from a villainous scoundrel into a faithful servant of justice."

"You asshole... What's your problem?! Why do you hate Mushroom Keepers so much?!"

"So long as criminal behavior continues to spread its vile roots, I will always be in need of stronger prison guards to contain it. By eliminating the formidable and crafty Mushroom Keepers and making them my servants, I can address both problems at once. I shall ensure they become my most loyal and hardworking agents of the law."

"The only law that Mushroom Keepers follow...is the god that lives within!" Bisco roared in defiance of the paralyzing pain and shot a piercing glare at his captor. "Don't think I'm gonna let you trample all over our beliefs! I'm gonna kill you and free the others, just you wait!!"

"A star burns ever so brightly on the verge of its demise. You are like nothing else on Earth, Akaboshi! You will make a fine candidate to uphold the law after I am gone!"

"What the fuck are you talking about...?!"

"I am a Benibishi. And even the judge abides the gallows. In one week, I shall be put to death alongside all the others."

Satahabaki tapped an impressive finger to the side of his helmet.

"By that time, the Sakura will have spread to your brain, making you every bit as loyal a servant of the law as I. From then on, it shall be you who welcomes sinners and judges them in my place, in the new Six Realms, free of our kind."

"Holy shit..."

"But until then, you must observe the law. Break it wantonly, and the Sakura Storm shall break you in turn."

"Grh... Aaagh!"

"Stop hurting him! Bisco!!" cried Milo.

"Fear not. You shall be joining him in short order."

Coughing up blood and crawling along the ground to help Bisco, Milo was soon engulfed in a similar breath of cherry blossom petals. The two boys were wrapped up in cocoons of petals, like a pair of bagworms, before falling to the ground, wriggling impotently.

"D-dammit...! Let us out...!"

Satahabaki took a look around at the four cocoons that lay shaking in the park. Giving a thoughtful nod, he raised his scepter high...

"I hereby DECLAAARE! Court ADJOURNED!"

With the shower of petals that fell about his striking stance, Sataha-baki made for a spectacular sight indeed, but unfortunately, there was nobody left to see it. Satahabaki only mimicked the graceful strum of a *shamisen* to finish things off and relaxed his posture.

Then he quickly strode over, collecting first the cocoon containing Pawoo.

"*Cough! Cough!* This ruling satisfies naught but your own ego, Over-seer!" she protested from within her flowery prison. This is a mistrial! If you are to execute yourself, then do it right now!"

"I have not found you guilty of any crime. I shall therefore see that you return to Imihama."

Then Satahabaki heaved Pawoo's body into the air, where a large eagle appeared out of nowhere, taking the cocoon and flying off toward the east. Pawoo's cries quickly disappeared as she receded into the distance, while Satahabaki took the remaining three cocoons. "Winter Cherry!" he yelled, and an enormous horse with bloodred fur galloped up to its master.

"You gonna throw us into prison like this?! You'll regret not killin' us while you had the chance!"

"As I already said, you are to be my replacement. I have no intention of killing you at all. I have also heard that your partner, Milo Nekoy-anagi, is an illustrious doctor who uses his talents to cure the people's ills. He shall await his judgment in Six Realms!"

As Satahabaki leaped atop his moving horse and grasped the reins, there was a strangely energetic quality in his voice.

"And while this may be unbecoming to admit, as an officer of the peace..."

"Wh-what is it?"

"Nekoyanagi, Akaboshi, I must thank you. It has been far too long since last I enjoyed a hunt so!"

What a strange man...!

This guy's fucking nuts...

Now powerless before the might of the law, or at least the might of Satahabaki's strange flower power, Milo and Bisco, along with Shishi, were ferried on horseback all the way back to Six Realms Penitentiary.

Charge Sheet

1. First-Class Criminal, Bisco Akaboshi

The accused is feared across the land as the Man-Eating Redcap.

Charge 1: Destruction of city buildings and checkpoints through the use of mushrooms.

Charge 2: Terrorizing humanity with his evil countenance and diabolical features.

While his crimes are deserving of capital punishment, he has been judged to have a supernatural strength of will that makes him fit to be the next Lord High Overseer. Accordingly, he shall be sentenced to imprisonment in the Preta Realm.

2. Second-Class Criminal, Milo Nekoyanagi

The accused is feared across the land as the Man-Eating Panda.

Charge 1: The creation and distribution of hazardous drugs and chemical concoctions.

Charge 2: Destruction of the pharmaceutical industry through the development of new medicines.

To his merit, he treated the people of this land with no obligation or expectation of payment or recompense. Accordingly, he shall be sentenced to forty years of imprisonment in the Human Realm.

3. The Benibishi, Shishi

The accused, while being of Benibishi origin, has engineered an escape from Six Realms Penitentiary.

The Benibishi are condemned to capital punishment, and the accused will receive no special treatment on that front.
She is hereby imprisoned in the Preta Realm until her execution.

Lord High Overseer
Someyoshi Satahabaki

Warden of Six Realms Penitentiary

Six Realms Penitentiary Blueprint

Asura Realm

Devil's Pot

Body Dumping Ground

COMMERCIAL DISTRICT

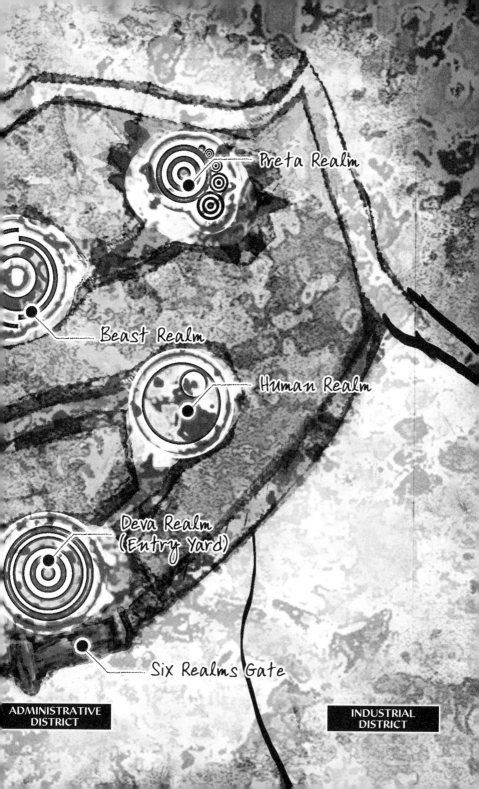

Preta Realm

Beast Realm

Human Realm

Deva Realm
(Entry Yard)

Six Realms Gate

ADMINISTRATIVE
DISTRICT

INDUSTRIAL
DISTRICT

Six Realms Penitentiary covered a large area and exploited the natural mountains and valleys of the region. It was quite different from an ordinary prison, where all the inmates might be locked up in a single building. Everything was arranged in a long, winding path surrounded by cliffs that led all the way from the main entrance to the deepest chamber, and it was divided into sections such as the Human Realm and Asura Realm, where different kinds of punishments were meted out.

Beyond all the other realms lay the Preta Realm, where imprisonment was effectively a life sentence. And it was to this deepest part of the prison that Bisco and Shishi were headed.

"Dammit, that bastard. He sure did a number on us. How is he so damn strong?!"

Within the cherrywood bars of his cage, Bisco cracked his neck, which Satahabaki had knocked out of alignment in their fight. The cage was in the claws of one of Satahabaki's giant eagle riders, the trademark jailers of Six Realms, on his way to the so-called Preta Realm at the heart of the prison. Bisco's bow, dagger, and mushroom poisons had all been confiscated, of course, but they even went so far as to take away his cloak. On the other hand, Satahabaki seemed to consider Bisco's goggles to be part of his face, and so he had managed to keep hold of those. Bisco sat completely disrobed from the waist up, and his muscles, firm as a whip, shivered in the cold air, while upon his body was still tattooed the strange mark Satahabaki had given him, the blizzard of falling cherry blossoms he had called the Sakura Storm.

"Fuck, it's cold! Hey! Can't you fly a little lower? There's too much wind up here!"

Bisco called out to the rider who sat atop the eagle, but the jailer was wearing a pair of headphones with the volume turned up, and so he simply hummed to himself, not hearing Bisco at all.

"B-Brother...you should not taunt the guards..."

"Listen to me, dumbass! Take us lower or I'll roast that overgrown turkey of yours and eat it for dinner!"

"Brother!"

Shishi, who was in the same cage but had only been watching Bisco nervously until now, suddenly jumped onto him and clasped her hands over Bisco's mouth.

"Mmrgh!"

"Brother! The Sakura Storm is not to be taken lightly!" cried Shishi, straddled atop Bisco. "It has stolen the minds of many a prisoner before now! Any who turn against the guards risk invoking the effects of the curse! I understand that you are angry, but you must bear with it for now!"

"Mrrrgh!"

Bisco made a disgruntled sound, but Shishi was right. Bisco had felt a burning pain across his collar just as he had begun to speak ill of the guardsman. He gave a reluctant nod.

"...Dammit. This freakin' flower tattoo. He thinks he can use it to make me do whatever he wants, that fuckin' ward—"

"Shh! You must not say the f-word, Bisco! Or the s-word or the c-word, either!"

"...Uhh, okay... In that case... That...flippin' blue bubblegum Popsicle..."

It seemed like insults were a core part of Bisco's personality, and not being allowed to use them put him under a large amount of stress. He ground his teeth in frustration and attempted to sit back up...only he couldn't, because Shishi was still sitting there.

"...You can get off me now, kid. I get it already."

Shishi's concern seemed to have shifted from Bisco's behavior to his body, and there was a biting envy in the girl's deep eyes.

"Brother... Your wounds... There's so many!"

Shishi ran her eyes along the many marks that scarred the flesh of Bisco's torso. Surely there was not a person in all the land who had taken so much punishment as he. Kurokawa's bullets, Kelshinha's spears, Apollo's black bow—all had left deep scars that remained visible even now, an ever-present reminder of his past struggles.

"Proof of a man's battles," said Shishi. "Just what have you been through, I wonder?"

"...Hey, get off. Get off, I said! Whoa, hands off! Don't touch me!"

Shishi's eyes twinkled behind her forelocks as she slowly looked over Bisco's scars and caressed them with her slender fingers.

"Was this...a beast's fang? And this, a spear...? Wow, there's even more on your back! There's more!"

"I said cut it out! That tickles!"

Shishi ducked and weaved, checking each and every one of Bisco's marks while avoiding his grasping arm, giving almost excited sighs as she did so. Bisco tumbled around within the cage, eventually pulling the young girl off him and setting her down in the center of it.

Shishi was breathing hard, her face flushed, and the flower behind her ear was in bloom once more.

"Listen, you! You can't just go runnin' your hands all over people! Didn't your parents ever teach you some manners?!"

"Ah, um, well... I am sorry, Brother, I just...got excited. Your body was so manly I just...had to inspect it."

With Bisco shouting at her, Shishi soon returned to her senses and turned red with embarrassment at her prior behavior.

"Phew... What's the matter, anyway? You never seen scars before? You've been whipped plenty yourself."

"They are not like yours, Brother. I was whipped to be tortured, not killed. I could never even survive such deep scars as yours."

"Hell, I *didn't* survive a couple of 'em..."

"...???"

"...Huh?! Get down, Shishi! We're falling!"

The pair could continue their conversation no longer, because the eagle suddenly released the cage from its talons, which fell to earth as Shishi screamed. The cage struck the valley walls and tumbled down into the gorge below.

"Ow...! Brother, are you all right?!"

"I get it. So this is like a natural prison, huh?"

The cage had now fallen on its side. Bisco gave it a kick from within, reverting it to its original orientation. He then peered through the bars at his surroundings.

The Preta Realm was like a huge cylindrical region carved out of the mountains themselves, such that the inmates were surrounded on all sides by vertical cliffs. Looking closer, Bisco could see that there were holes all throughout the cliffs, through which he was able to spot inmates coming and going. It appeared this hard labor he had been assigned to involved mining work of some kind.

"Yes," said Shishi. "Six Realms Penitentiary is a prison that makes use of nature's bounty. The Deva Realm essentially means release, while the Hell Realm equates to execution. In between those two extremes lie four facilities that represent the Human Realm, Asura Realm, Beast Realm, and Preta Realm."

Shishi gave her explanation while patting tiny clouds of dust from Bisco's body. "The graver the crime, the deeper they are incarcerated. And in the deepest, darkest part of the prison..."

"...You'll find this place, the Preta Realm, fresh meat."

The one who finished Shishi's sentence had a thick dark voice, like tar. Bisco wheeled around to see a crowd of hooded prison guards walking over toward their cage.

"Well, well, well, would ya look at this? Ain't he one o' the Kyoto dogs from the other day?"

One guard, evidently the leader of the bunch, peered into the cage with a look of mock surprise, and a chorus of cackles erupted from behind him. He looked down his nose at Bisco and sneered.

"Been a hot minute, Man-Eater. Been itchin' to see you again."

"And who are you supposed to be?"

"Well, you wouldn'ta recognized me, what with the masks an' all. You did a real number on me, though. Look, one swing of your sword and you messed up my perfect face, see?"

The guard pointed to the large scar that went from his cheek to his eyebrow, and he chuckled with glee. He and the other guards seemed to have been part of the group that tried to stop Bisco from rescuing Shishi, for they all wore the same look of vengeful delight.

"You're lucky you're still alive, then. If I'd used the blade, you'd all be dead."

"Oh yes. We're very happy you left us alive. From today on, you're gonna see just how grateful we are..."

"Let me just open his cage, captain."

"Watch out. He's like a wild tiger, this one."

With their captain's approval, one of the guards roughly undid the lock on the cage, and several of the men dragged Bisco and Shishi over to the edge of the prison yard, near the cliff face.

"Welcome to the Preta Realm, Akaboshi. I gotta say, I reeeally love making guys like you cry. Try to hold out as long as you can; it's boring if you crack too early."

...Assholes...

Under normal circumstances, Bisco wasn't one to let small fry like this get under his skin, but right now he wasn't in the best of moods. His jade-green eyes flashed wide, and he glared at the leader of the guardsmen.

"Urgh... Wh-what're you givin' me that look for? You're on *my* turf now, and you'll show some damn respect!"

The captain quailed in fright, just as the tattoo around Bisco's neck activated, growing scorchingly hot.

"Brother!"

"Grr... All I did was scowl a little!"

Through gritted teeth, Bisco acquiesced to Shishi's hushed admonition. The Sakura Storm was even less forgiving than he expected. Move even a single muscle in defiance of the guards, and he was punished.

"Did you just scowl at me? You did, didn't you? Listen to me when I'm talkin' to you, Akaboshi."

"Not really. I was just thinkin' about how pretty that scar makes you look."

"I'll teach you to run your fuckin' mouth!"

The guard, furious, snatched up his baton and began pummeling Bisco repeatedly. One of those blows hit Bisco on the head, scattering blood across his face.

"Brother!!! Please, stop this senseless violence, you cowards!"

"Hurgh? Stay outta this, kid, an' just... C-captain! Check this out, the Benibishi's a *girl!*"

Just as Shishi attempted to intervene, one fat guard grabbed her by the hair and leered.

"It's my lucky day! I'll be takin' this one! Heya, girlie! Say hi to your new master!"

"U-unhand me! Let me go!!"

Flailing wildly, Shishi scratched the guard on the cheek, drawing blood. The guard immediately turned nasty, drawing his baton.

"You little shit! Listen to your master!"

Shishi squeezed her eyes shut and braced herself for the moment the baton struck, but...

Bisco dashed over at the very last moment, delivering a kick into the neck of the fat guard and sending him flying off into the hard stone wall. As all the other guards looked on in disbelief, Bisco spoke up.

"Oh, sorry 'bout that. Thought I saw a mosquito."

Even as the burning pain in his neck caused him to sweat, he managed to crack a devilish grin.

B-Brother!

Shishi watched as the Sakura Storm tattoo spread farther across Bisco's body. Bisco fell to one knee in pain and coughed blood onto the floor.

"...H-hold him down. They won't recognize him when we're done!"

Bisco was too weak to fight back now. As they attacked, Shishi screamed, but then an arm wrapped around her neck and held it until she passed out.

* * *

"Prisoners, LINE UUUP!"

At seven AM sharp in the sunlit courtyard of the Preta Realm, Satahabaki bellowed with his big white teeth through a megaphone.

"Six Realms exercise routine step ONE! Alternate punches! Stretch out those AAARMS!"

Down in the courtyard itself, the prisoners of the Preta Realm lined up and followed the warden's instructions, as they did every morning. This time, however, they were joined by one prisoner whose technique stood head and shoulders above the rest.

Swoosh! Swoosh!

Bisco's punches audibly sliced through the air as Shishi watched in shock.

"B-Brother...a-are you feeling better already?!"

"I'm fine, obviously. My soul's like a clean river."

Shishi couldn't help but feel that Bisco's answer was a little off the mark as they moved on to step four of Satahabaki's boxercise plan, consecutive front somersaults.

"I've always been a pretty chill dude, you know. So this freaky flower tattoo's no big deal. Whenever I feel a little bit angry, I just recite a *haiku.*"

"Oh? You know *haiku*, Brother?"

"Yep. My master used to tell them all the time... *'The still mountain air/Hides amidst the silent crags/Hippopotamus.'"*

"Isn't it *'The cicada's cry'*?"

"Maybe. Do you have to be such a buzzkill?"

"Brother, I meant physically, are you okay?"

Watching Bisco take part so energetically in the workout routine, it was hard to believe he had taken such a beating only the night before.

His wounds have completely healed already! What is Brother made of?!

It wasn't as if Bisco had received medical treatment following his decidedly unmedical treatment at the hands of the prison guards, but one night was all it took for Bisco to be in perfect fighting shape again. Shishi was right to suspect that his vigor was far from normal.

"Warm-up's over! Get to work!" shouted a prison guard from a platform, and the prisoners flooded to the walls in droves, clambering up their ladders and into the holes.

The Preta were the hungry ghosts of Six Realms, and given this, the job of the prisoners here was the procurement of their own food. The mountain was home to a breed of tuber called the Preta potato, and any prisoners who failed to unearth any with their pickaxes simply starved—a severe punishment befitting the deepest section of the prison, where the most heinous of criminals resided.

In the caverns, dimly lit by hanging lanterns, the hungry inmates swung their pickaxes as best they could, given their constant weariness. All of them except for one, that is, who beat at the earth so tirelessly the other prisoners could only stare in wonder. Without a hint of fatigue, Bisco bored his way through the rock like a drill, his cat-eye goggles fixed over his eyes.

"Shishi! Pick up some of this crap and chuck it outside for me!"

"O-okay, Brother!"

Shishi assisted Bisco with his noble task for some time before timidly asking a question.

"Brother, you have dug plenty already. Would you not like to rest awhile?"

"Rest? I can't rest yet, I ain't even found any."

"Yes, you have! You've found all these potatoes!"

"Wait... There's one!"

Shishi came over and looked, puzzled at Bisco's latest find. It was something pitch-black, like coal... A mushroom, illuminated by the lantern light.

"What a beaut. This one should be all we need."

"Brother, what kind of mushroom is that?"

"It's... Hold up, someone's coming."

Bisco quickly hid the mushroom in his back pocket just as a bunch of nasty-looking prisoners came strolling over.

"Well, would you look at that? 'Eard we got a fresh face about these parts, but I didn't expect to see a celebrity down 'ere."

The leader of the men strode over to Bisco and whistled. He had a muscular build, with a buzzcut and a tattoo around his eye that Bisco recognized immediately.

"Looks like the mighty mushroom god has gone and found 'imself in another right pickle, wouldn't you say, Akaboshi?"

"Could say the same about you guys," Bisco responded. "Goin' by your tattoos, I'd say you're Kumamoto Mushroom Keepers. You sound like you've been here awhile; surely you ain't findin' it *that* comfy."

"You got that right, but we're stuck here, same as you. This blasted tattoo stops us from doin' a bloody thing about it."

The one with the buzzcut pointed to the tattoo on Bisco's shoulder and revealed his own that stretched across his back. All the other Mushroom Keepers in his chain gang seemed to have ones of their own as well.

...So it wasn't just Fukuoka. He's got Mushroom Keepers from all the surrounding regions in here.

"That bast—erm... I mean, the warden was too strong, even when the whole lot of us teamed up on him. Well, no matter. Us Kumamoto folk are always ready to act as the situation demands, and down here in the Preta Realm, Mushroom Keepers are top of the food chain."

"Suit yourselves, but I ain't about to give up so easily. And I don't team up with anyone 'cept my partner, and he ain't here."

Bisco turned to leave, but the other prisoners blocked his path.

"Whoa, there, Akaboshi. Perhaps they treated you like a god in Shikoku, but here in Kyushu, we're a little more skeptical, you know? We can't let some young lad do whatever he pleases. It'll reflect badly on us! Listen up. First rule of the Preta Realm is—"

"You after my potatoes? Here, have as many as you want. Take 'em."

"Huh?"

The buzzcut man looked surprised and even a little disappointed that he hadn't gotten to deploy his trademark threats. Shishi walked up beside him and dumped an armful of Preta potatoes onto the ground.

"Wh-whoa! What the hell?!" shrieked one of his underlings. "You dug up all of these in one—?!"

Thwack! The boss man slapped some sense into his loose-lipped lackey and attempted to keep a calm expression.

"H-huh. Well, I guess Akaboshi lives up to the legend after all. Nothin' *too* special, though..."

But while the man was talking, Shishi went back into the tunnel and came out with another armful of tubers, which she dropped by the buzzcut guy's feet. And another, and another...

"Wait, wait, wait, wait! Hold up, how many did you get?! We can't eat all these! They'll rot before we even get close!"

"Then go share them with everyone else. There's plenty more back there in that hole."

Bisco gave a tired yawn and tossed the pickax aside before beckoning Shishi over.

"And share with *everybody*! Don't just let the Mushroom Keepers hog them all! C'mon, Shishi, let's go."

"Yes, Brother!"

Shishi turned back to the buzzcut man and gave him a proud smile before following Bisco back to the pair's cell.

"...What a lad that Akaboshi is. He's every bit as bonkers as the rumors said..."

The brawny Mushroom Keepers of Kumamoto shared a bewildered glance and just watched Bisco and Shishi leave, with looks of pure astonishment.

"All right, Preta! It's time for the one joy in your miserable lives! Mealtime!"

The sound of a gong reverberated through the hollowed-out yard, drawing everyone to the dining hall that was carved from one of the walls. Here, the prisoners used the potatoes they'd excavated to prepare their own meals. The only problem was that the Preta potatoes grew through the solid rock of the mountain, and so they were almost as tough as stones themselves. Even after being cooked, they were far from what might be called a flavorsome meal, and the usual atmosphere around the dining table was a chorus of sighs that really did make the place sound like a congregation of ghosts.

However, today things were a little different than usual...

"Hee-hee-hee. Now it's time for us guards to have *our* meal."

"Captain. Looks like today's menu is bleakfish and seal fat. Not much to get the appetite up..."

"Don't be so picky. You should count yourself lucky Lady Gopis saw fit to make us guards instead of leaving us to rot with the other prisoners. Besides..."

The guard captain sipped his pungent seal soup as he looked down over the dining hall floor.

"Don't watchin' those chumps down there just make the food taste that much better? Mopin' around eatin' their dirty potatoes day after miserable—"

Suddenly, he paused.

"Captain? What's the matt...er...?"

Another of the guards followed his gaze, and when he saw what the captain had seen, his eyes went wide.

Down on the floor, the mood was completely different from anything they had ever seen before. The prisoners were all cheerfully lining up to be fed, and the place was bustling with activity.

"So soft and delicious! Is this really a Preta potato?"

"They said you can come back as many times as you want!"

"I want seconds! Move over! Get outta my way!"

At the center of the hubbub was what appeared to be a young girl, stirring a large pot.

"Don't push, everybody! There's plenty to go around! You won't get any more unless you're all fine ladies and gentlemen!"

"Shishi, this stuff's freakin' delicious! I could eat it all day!"

"That's great! Have as much as you like, Brother. Here, have some more!"

"You sure? Shouldn't I get in line?"

"You don't need to line up, Brother. You're the reason we have so many in the first place!"

Shishi had placed herself in charge of cooking and distribution and had turned the humble Preta potato into a mouthwatering delicacy the likes of which the denizens of the Preta Realm had never tasted in their lives. Not only that, but there was so much of it that the hungry prisoners could come back as many times as they liked. It was almost too good to be true.

"I didn't know you could cook," said Bisco. "How'd you make somethin' this tasty outta that stuff? Those potatoes taste like sand."

"'A man who shies from the kitchen is no man at all.' That is what my father used to say."

Shishi gave an embarrassed smile at Bisco's praise, and the flower behind her ear burst open.

"These Preta potatoes grow in the mountains, where nutrition is scarce, but because of that, they only need a little encouragement to become drastically more delicious. So I boiled them and added some festerleeks—with the poison removed, of course. That created a delicious soup stock to which I merely added some crushed lily-of-the-mountain seeds in place of chili pepper for a little spice."

"Huh. You can get the poison outta veggies with your flower power? That's pretty handy."

"It is too weak to be called a 'power.' Compared to my father, I am nothing. Cooking is all I can use it for... I am an embarrassment to him."

"That ain't true. Look, everyone loves you...or your food, at least."

Bisco pointed with his chin to the line of prisoners waiting for seconds, their eyes sparkling. Even with full bellies, they kept coming back for more of Shishi's delicious creation, some even going so far as to beg, hands pressed together in supplication.

"Ain't it a king's job to keep the people happy? I'd say you're doin' a pretty good job so far, so don't stop now."

"...Yes, you're right!"

At Bisco's encouraging words, Shishi's flower bloomed bright red, and she returned to nobly handing out food to the starving prisoners.

Bisco stretched, having already eaten his fill, and was just about to return to his cell when he spotted a group of prisoners in one corner of the dining hall, beckoning him over. As he approached, he recognized them as the Kumamoto Mushroom Keepers from earlier in the day. Bisco strode over and sat himself down opposite their leader, the buzz-cut gentleman.

"Akaboshi. I wanted to thank you for filling our bellies. We can speak freely here; this table's out of sight of the guards."

"Thought I told you before," Bisco growled back. "I ain't got no interest in joining you or your gang."

"That ain't it," the leader replied. "Akaboshi, we're talkin' about you. I know you're not plannin' to stay down here for the rest of your miserable life, are you? You're thinkin' about getting outta here and riddin' yourself of that tattoo as fast as possible."

"..."

"Well, so are we. We're not content to sit around till the warden's curse turns our brains to mush. So how about it? With us helpin' you..."

But Bisco shook his head. "No thanks. You'd only get in my way. Besides, I already got a plan," he said, standing up. "But don't worry. I'm gonna free all of you from this tattoo. That's the whole reason I came here in the first place... Anyway, I'm leavin' before they realize somethin's up."

"Wait! Wait, Akaboshi. I get it, we won't get in your way. Just...take a look at this before you go."

The buzzcut leader took a rocklike mushroom from his pocket and crushed it in his hand, forming a powdery sand that he scattered onto the desk. The rust-colored powder moved as if by magic, slowly forming into what looked like a handwritten diagram.

"Huh, a magnetshroom. So? What's this supposed to be?"

"It's a map of this part of the prison. Or at least, as much of it as we could find out. We made it out of iron sand on this table." The buzzcut man looked carefully around, then pointed to a part of the map. "Look 'ere. This is the dining hall, here's the cells, and this 'ere's the guards' quarters. A little ways from there is a bone coal storeroom."

Bisco stared at the surprisingly detailed map and gave an impressed nod before burning the information into his memory.

"Well? Think it'll 'elp?"

"Yeah. I was gonna take a look around myself, but this'll save me some time. What's this underground bit?"

"That's solitary confinement. But everyone taken there is blind-folded; we don't know much about—"

"Boss, the guards!"

At his buddy's warning, the leader wiped the table clean, and Bisco punched himself hard in the face, giving himself a nosebleed.

"You lot! What are you whisperin' about?!"

The same guard captain from earlier with the scarred face came over and slammed his fist on the table. The map that had been sitting atop it mere seconds prior was nowhere to be seen.

"All right, honcho?" said the buzzcut Mushroom Keeper. "We was just teachin' the new guy how things work around here. Knocked a couple of his teeth loose, but he's still gotta learn a bit of respect."

Bisco was resting his head on his fist, with blood dripping down his face. The captain crossed his arms and grumbled for a moment before shouting to the other guards, "Hey! Round 'em all up and take 'em to be reeducated!"

"Whoa, whoa," said the buzzcut Mushroom Keeper. "We was 'elping you out! What gives?"

"You should be thankin' us! Not takin' us to be punished!"

"Oh, put a sock in it! You caught me in a real bad mood today. Teach 'em all a lesson they won't soon forget!"

As the guards dragged the Kumamoto Mushroom Keepers away, their leader gave a knowing wink to Bisco. Bisco nodded before the guard captain gave him a tug, too.

"Stand up, Akaboshi. You been causin' trouble ever since you got here. I'm gonna wipe that smirk off your face, and I'm gonna enjoy every last second of it!"

"That'll teach you to keep your nose outta trouble, Akaboshi!"

"Ain't it weird that I get beaten for doin' my job properly?"

"Can it. Get inside your cell, prisoner!"

The guard thrust Bisco inside and slammed the bars shut, waking up Shishi.

"...Brother...you're back...? Ah, you're hurt!"

"Hmm?"

It was way past lights-out by the time Bisco returned to his cavernous cell, and Shishi had been worrying about his sudden disappearance for quite some time. She was given plenty more to worry about, however, when she saw the terrible whip marks that covered Bisco's skin.

"What did they do to you?! Those cowards! To think they would wear their vengeance so openly! I shall take care of you, Brother, so please lie down."

"Don't bother. These are just scratches."

"Scratches...?!"

"Listen. Every day, my wife beats the shit outta me with a metal staff as thick as your arm. Those weedy little police batons ain't got nothin' on her. And at least it ain't as painful as the tattoo."

Sure enough, Bisco didn't seem the least bit put off by his injuries. He wiped away his nosebleed and pulled from his pocket the black mushroom he had unearthed during the day.

"This is what I was concerned about. I was worried they might find it, but luckily they were too obsessed with kickin' the shit outta me."

"...Brother. I knew it. Is that...?" Shishi lowered her voice and sidled right up to Bisco. "Is that something that will help you break out of here?"

"You wanna escape, too, right?"

"Of course!"

Bisco raised his finger to suppress Shishi's enthusiastic reply. The girl lowered her voice again before continuing.

"Satahabaki was furious at my last escape. If we do nothing, all the Benibishi will be put to death. We have to tell Father, so he can lead my people to revolt!"

"What I don't get is... Your father's a wise man, right? Surely he don't need you to tell him what to do. How come he ain't started a revolt already? He's had plenty of time to do it. Is it 'cause he's too scared of the big fella? Knows he can't beat him no matter what he does?"

"That…that's not true!!"

Shishi cried out once more, in a louder voice than she ever seemed capable of. It was enough to give even Bisco a fright.

"Shh! Keep it down, dumbass!"

"My father is a mighty king. He would never allow his people to live in suffering! He must surely be locked up and unable to fight back! We must free him before they see fit to torture him any further!"

"All right, all right! I get it already! Calm down! You'll never get anywhere if you keep losin' your shit like this!"

Bisco flicked Shishi's forehead, causing the young girl to yelp in pain. Rubbing her sore forehead, Shishi took a deep breath and nodded.

"I…I apologize. Still, I worry for my father. We must leave this place at once—"

"We're gonna. We just need some friends first. If I go up against the guards myself, I'm gonna get shocked, and I can't exactly leave the fightin' to you."

"Friends? But Brother, the other Mushroom Keepers bear the same tattoo as you, and all the Benibishi here are emaciated and weak. I do not think there is anyone here who could help us."

"There is one person. Hmm? Is 'person' the right word? Well, whatever."

Bisco reached into his other pocket and took out a long thin stick before putting the mushroom into his mouth. Then he blew, and a thick black mist flew from his lips and onto the tip of the stick.

"*Cough! Cough!* Brother, what is this?!"

"This is a special kinda mushroom called a pseudocoal. It can't grow well in this rocky habitat, but it can turn into different kinds, dependin' on what it touches."

"Different kinds?"

"This here's an antenna I broke off one of the guards' radios while we were fightin'."

Bisco went on, but Shishi found it hard to take in what he was saying alongside the astonishing sight unfolding before her eyes. As she watched closely, a small yellow mushroom sprouted from the side of the antenna.

"Wow, that's so cute!"

"The radioshroom's a mushroom that's receptive to radio waves. It's usually pretty useless, since it just picks up everything, but here in the prison there's no interference to worry about, just the guards' radios."

"Th-that's amazing, Brother! We can eavesdrop on the guards' communications!"

"Shh. I'm pickin' something up... Come stand a little closer."

The radioshroom flickered on and off and swelled and contracted like a speaker as a faint noise began to issue forth. Shishi huddled up to Bisco, and the two pressed their ears to the device.

"This is the basement level, solitary confinement. Nothing to report."

"Very good. You may come back up."

"But, captain, what are we gonna do about the big guy in cell eight? The other day, I watched him tear off his chains with his bare hands. He gives me the creeps."

"Well, he's a robot, so the Sakura Storm ain't gonna work on him. There should be a programmer arrivin' in the next couple days, he'll take care of it. Don't be such a 'fraidy cat, he'll be on our side soon enough."

"He will? It don't bear thinkin' about."

"Well, if he don't play nice, we can send him to the scrap heap. Anyway, over and out. I'm headin' to bed."

The pair heard the click of the guard's transmitter, and the conversation on the airwaves returned to idle banter. Having heard enough, Bisco gave a satisfied nod and crushed the antenna in his fist.

"Cell eight in the underground disciplinary chamber, he said."

"That's where they're holding your friend? But getting down there without being seen will require a lot of preparation. Do we have the time for that?"

"We don't need to do all that. There's a much quicker way."

"There is?"

"We just need to get ourselves thrown in there. Startin' a fight oughtta do it."

Bisco leaned forward, a roguish smirk on his lips that revealed his glimmering canines.

"Hey, don't gimme that look. We're in the same boat here. I'll go easy on ya…"

He hit me!

Shishi sat crossed-legged on the bed, rubbing her bruised cheek, surrounded on all sides by the cold, hard stone of the solitary confinement chamber.

During the morning's exercises, Bisco and Shishi put their plan into motion. A simple conflict of words quickly escalated into violence, and as a result, Shishi figured, the guards must have brought them down here. The reason for Shishi's uncertainty was that Bisco's first punch laid her out stone-cold, and she woke up here without any memory of what exactly had happened.

She remembered saying, *"Brother, I am a prince! You do not need to hold back,"* and so in a sense, Shishi supposed she had been asking for it. But did Bisco really need to knock the girl off her feet? It was far beyond Bisco's capabilities, Shishi suspected, to produce anything between the lightest of taps and a punch like a human bulldozer.

…But he hit me. He hit me without holding back at all…

In addition to her displeasure, Shishi felt an admiration for Bisco unlike any she had felt before. All her life, Shishi had failed to live up to the ideal image of manliness she idolized. Whether it be martial arts or dance, the only image she seemed capable of projecting was that of a helpless princess who needed sheltering and protecting. So as strange as it seemed, Shishi wasn't at all put off by Bisco's unrestrained punch. In fact, it made her feel a little happy.

It is almost as if Brother sees me not as a girl, but as a—

Gaboom!

Shishi's thoughts were put on hold as an explosion rocked the cell, and the dust cleared to reveal a hole in one of the walls. Bisco poked his head through and said, "Damn, coulda done with makin' it a bit bigger."

"Brother!"

"Well, I'll just have to squeeze," he said. "C'mon, Shishi, gimme a hand here."

Bisco reached through the hole, and Shishi helped pull him through. She heard the cracks as Bisco dislocated his own joints to make it through the tiny hole before popping them back into place once he was on the other side and flashing Shishi a cheery smile.

"And because I didn't go against any guards, the curse doesn't mind that I blew up a wall. Everything's going according to plan so far. Well, 'cept you passin' out, that is."

"I know I said to hold nothing back, but I did not expect that! Even a tiger or a hippo would be felled by your punch!"

"Well, that *was* me holdin' back. Maybe it was just 'cause your punches were quite strong, so I fought back outta habit…"

"Y-you think my punches are strong?"

"You left a bruise here, see? So let's call us even stephen, yeah?"

Bisco pointed to the mark on his cheek and smiled. Then he pressed an ear to the wall of Shishi's cell, tapping as he went along, checking the thickness.

Even stephen…

Shishi rubbed her bruise and watched Bisco get to work, half-dazed. The flower on her head softly unfolded.

"…Hello? Shishi, snap out of it! Stay with me, we're breakin' outta prison here!"

"Ah. S-sorry, Brother!"

"This is where the wall is thickest," he said. "Cell eight should be on the other side. I'll have to try a larger blastshroom to get through."

"I am amazed," said Shishi. "To think you are capable of all this, even when your possessions have been stripped away!"

"You can never keep a Mushroom Keeper locked up," Bisco replied. "The big guy's gonna learn that lesson soon enough."

He took a pseudocoal mushroom from his pocket, broke it up in his hands, and placed it in his mouth. After chewing noisily for a few moments, he took it out again to reveal that it had turned soft and pliable, like gum. He smeared the substance on the chamber wall, then collected some nuts and bolts that had fallen from the earlier explosion and stuck them into it.

"I will help, Brother!"

"Stay back. You're not trained in the mushrooms. Keep down and cover your eyes and ears."

"O-okay!"

"...Okay, ready."

Bisco nodded at the result of his work, then he nimbly spun around and delivered a lightning-fast kick to it. The impact caused the mushroom gum to tremble, and soon, bright-red mushrooms began swelling up like bubbling magma, growing out of the implanted metal parts.

"...Hmm? That's not good. Maybe I did it too hard."

"What?!"

"Stay down, Shishi!"

Bisco leaped aside, covering the girl's body with his own, when suddenly...

Gaboom!

...the wall exploded, and thick black smoke filled the room. Shishi kept her head down and tried not to inhale any until it cleared.

"Brother! *Cough!* Brother, are you okay?!"

"This way, Shishi. We ain't done yet!"

Shishi breathed a sigh of relief once she heard Bisco calling out but gulped when she saw the hole the explosion had torn in the metal wall. Bisco's arts were fearsome indeed, to be able to do all this only using mushroom spores and no specialized equipment.

"Seems he's still napping," Bisco said. "I dunno how he slept through that explosion just now."

"...Oh, my! That's...!"

After passing through the opening into cell eight, Shishi felt her eyes fall upon the body of a giant nearly twice Shishi's height and clad in crimson plate. At first, she thought it to be armor, but upon closer examination, it appeared to be the metal body of the being itself. It was a giant robot, held down by multiple lengths of iron chains.

"...A robot! Brother, is this the friend you were talking about?!"

"He's got a name, by the way. Akaboshi Mark I. And watch out, 'cause he doesn't like bein' called a robot... For cryin' out—why'd they have to tie him up like this?"

Bisco expressed his displeasure at the sheer quantity of chains that had been used to restrain the Mark I and the time it would take to deal with them. It just went to show the lengths to which the guards were willing to go to suppress the monstrous strength of the Mokujin robot.

"The guards are out cold, thanks to the sleepshroom concoction I burned, but they'll change shifts at mealtime, so we gotta do somethin' about the chains before then."

"Understood. Then let's get started, Brother!"

"It ain't that easy, kid; I'm not a wizard. I'm gonna need somethin' if I wanna break through these."

Shishi went up to the Mark I and squinted at the chains. Specifically, at the dozens of keyholes on the locks that held them in place.

"We shall need nothing of the sort," she told Bisco, giving a confident snort. "Just leave this to me."

"I dunno where you get that confidence from," Bisco replied, "but we ain't got time to waste."

"It shall take me ten seconds at most," said Shishi. "Just watch. I shall prove to you that I will not be a burden!"

Before Bisco could say anything in response, Shishi took a deep breath and placed both hands on the cold disciplinary chamber floor. As Bisco watched in shock, ivy plants grew from Shishi's wrists and into the padlocks.

"...Shishi, what the hell?!"

"...The mechanism is even simpler than I anticipated. I might stand a chance...!"

Shishi clenched her teeth and yelled, and her hair flared into the air around her so that her crimson eyes, normally hidden behind her bangs, now shone brighter than ever before. The flower behind her ear blossomed in full glory, and then...

"Flourish!"

Crack! Crack! Crackkk!

…with Shishi's cry, the ivy twisted, splitting apart the many locks from the inside all at once.

"Whoa," said Bisco, honestly impressed.

"…I…I did it!"

Shishi collapsed to the floor, panting for breath.

"Shishi! That was wild! You shoulda told me all along you could do somethin' like—"

Bisco turned to Shishi but stopped when he saw the paleness of the girl's face and the blood seeping from her wrists.

"That hurt you, didn't it? Before you push yourself, you should at least tell me."

"Have I…redeemed myself in your eyes, Brother?"

"I wouldn't say *redeemed*. I always—I mean, yeah. Well done, Shishi."

"I'm just glad I was able to be of use…"

"Don't be such a drama queen. Check yourself out and stop the bleeding first."

Bisco tore off a part of his trouser leg and wrapped it around Shishi's wounds. Suddenly, from behind him came a *Vwm!* noise, and a pair of jade-green flashlights illuminated the two of them.

"Wah!"

As Bisco and Shishi stood there, startled, the flashlights moved between the two as if examining them before turning on the robot, now completely unrestrained.

"*Vwoo!*"

The robot gave a deep cry, and sparks flew from its body like fireworks. A jade-green light coursed through the robot's wires like blood through veins, stirring its arms, first the left, then the right. Clenching its fists, it pulled itself free from the huge spike pinning it to the wall.

"W-waaah!"

Shishi could barely sit still in the face of such overwhelming strength, but Bisco stood before her protectively and stared up at the robot, which wrenched the chains Shishi had unlocked off its body and stood up, filling the chamber, striking an imposing stance as though actively showing off its size.

"Vwoooo!"

"You're finally awake, Mark I!" Bisco cried out, as if answering the robot's call. "You've been chained up and sleepin' this whole time! That can't have been good for your back!"

The rebellious and independent Mokujin, the Akaboshi Mark I, scrutinized Bisco, while the cables coming out of the back of its head fluttered like hair.

"Figured you might be gettin' bored of prison life," Bisco continued. "We came to see what's up. How're you doin'?"

"Brother? Why are you attempting to make small talk? He's a robot."

"Shush," Bisco whispered back. *"This guy's no ordinary robot; don't forget that. Nothin' pisses him off more than takin' orders. And when he gets pissed off, he'll kill you."*

"N-never have I heard of a robot like that!"

"Just stay calm and it'll be fine. Once ol' Bisco here turns on the charm, he'll be putty in our— Wh-whoa?!"

"Vwooo. Vwoo!"

The Mark I approached while Shishi and Bisco were whispering and swung its huge log-like arms. Bisco just managed to bundle Shishi under his arm and spring aside before the ground was crushed beneath the weight of the killer robot's fist.

"Hey, what the hell is wrong with you, you scrap-iron knucklehead?! We came here to save you! Is that any way to repay us?!"

"Brother, I thought you just said not to make him angry!!"

"Oh, whatever. *I'm* the one you don't wanna piss off!"

The Mark I's follow-up, a mighty left hook, was met and deflected by Bisco's whirlwind kick. Then Bisco leaped into the air and punched the robot right in the face plate, while also being simultaneously struck by the Mark I's right fist. The two were then blasted apart into the opposite walls of the cell.

"B-Brother!"

"Cough! Cough! I'll teach you some manners…," grumbled Bisco,

crawling to his feet and wiping the blood away from his nose. "What the hell have you got against me anyway?!"

"Brother, please calm down!" Shishi yelled. Then she turned to the robot. "Mark I, listen to me! Whatever happened between you and Brother, we must put it behind us! We need to escape from this prison right now!"

"..."

"With Brother's mushrooms and your mechanical strength, we cannot fail! Please, you must help us! You can save your fighting for after we all escape this place together!"

The Mark I, upon hearing Shishi's heartfelt words, stared at the two for a while, unmoving. It emitted a series of beeps, apparently performing some sort of calculation in its head, but of course, it was impossible for Bisco and Shishi to detect precisely what it was thinking.

"It's useless, Shishi! He doesn't understand what we're sayin'! We just gotta knock some sense into—! Waargh!"

Bisco's eyes fell upon the Mark I, and he screamed out in fright. The robot's arm was now folding away, transforming from a fist into the shape of a massive rocket launcher.

"Waah! What is that?!"

"Shishi, get down!"

Bang! The robot's superheated projectile singed Bisco's hair as he dived to protect Shishi, and it burned a big round hole straight through the thick iron door of the cell as though it were merely made of ice cream.

"...Grrr... What the hell?!"

"*Vwoo.*"

With hulking steps, the Mark I strode over to the door, stuck both his hands through the hole he had made, and began prying the thing open. With the rear thrusters engaged, it didn't take long for him to tear the huge iron door apart like a pizza box before throwing the parts aside.

"W-wow! Look at how powerful the Mark I is, Brother!"

"*Vwoo.*"

The Mark I looked down at the awestruck Shishi and motioned with what must have been his chin, urging the young girl through, before disappearing through the hole himself.

"Heh. Guess we finally got through to him. Took him long enough."

"*Vwooo.*"

"Hurry, he says. Guess we'd better go, Shishi."

"You understand what the Mark I is saying, Brother?"

"Nah, not really, but, like…we're brothers, so I sort of get him, you know?"

Shishi couldn't claim to understand what Bisco was saying herself, but she opted to let it go. Bisco leaped through the hole and started running after the Mark I, and Shishi just watched him go in mute amazement for a while before shaking herself back to her senses and hurrying off to join them.

"It's supposed to be spring, but down here in the Preta Realm, the chill's as bad as ever."

"That's 'cause we're surrounded by all this rock. They should pay us more for this, but instead, the wages at Six Realms are the same as at any other prison. I can't handle it."

"Heh-heh. Well, at least these robes are thick enough— Aha, *ron.*"

"Damn. Your round again, captain."

"Three color fires, all simples, *dora* three."

"That's *baiman*! Geez, my score… There goes all the bribes I took from the prisoners…"

"Ha-ha-ha! Looks like you're on chore duty again this week!"

In a room carved out of the cliff face, the prison guards shirked their duties, noisily enjoying a game of Divine *mahjong*. Here in the Preta Realm, very few prisoners had any fight left in them, and so there was generally little for the guards to do. Mostly they just killed time playing games like this one.

"But damn, what a letdown. We beefed up security at the gate for the great Man-Eating Redcap, and he ain't even *tried* to break free. What was the point?"

"It's 'cause of that tattoo the warden gave him. Now, I don't know how it works, but Akaboshi can't do shit against it. He's only mortal, after all, unlike the big guy... Hold up, ain't it about time to come off break?"

"Huh, so it is. Are the other two still down in the disciplinary chamber? They shoulda been up to change shifts by now."

"Hee-hee-hee. Well, they got ol' Akaboshi down there now. Bet they're havin' the time of their lives messing with him. Seriously... Welp, guess that means we got time for one more game. This time, let's wager next week's patrol duty."

All of a sudden, there was a worrying *Clunk!* from the bone coal stove in the corner of the room. The guard turned to see that the flames had died down.

"Damn, we're outta coal."

"No wonder it's so cold in here. Well, get on with it, handyman. Go get some more."

"What a joke. First I lose my money, now I gotta lose my dignity..."

The downtrodden guard grumbled to himself and left the room for the nearby bone coal warehouse.

"...Waaagh!!"

After a few moments, there came a scream.

"Come on, it can't be *that* cold out there, you big baby."

"N-no, it's not that! It's gone! It's completely gone!"

"Yeah, I know your money's all gone; it's in my pockets now. Stop dawdling and get on with it!"

"No, the coal's all gone! There's no sign of it, or the warehouse, either!"

At this, the guard captain came with his underling, and together the pair walked back down the long tunnel, but when they reached the end, the captain let out the same scream.

"Waaagh! It *is* gone! Not a damn sight of it!"

"But how? We just finished squeezin' all we could off the prisoners, too!"

"Wait...come look at this!"

Following a burning smell, the guard captain came across a huge hole in the ground that stretched downward far out of sight. All the bone coal, as well as the warehouse itself, must have disappeared down it.

"Where the hell did this hole come from?!"

"Look how deep it is. It must go all the way to the basement. When did they make this?"

"The basement…? Wait, the basement!"

When he realized the implications, the color drained from the captain's face. He spun around and bellowed at his subordinate.

"You know what's right below here, don't you? It's solitary! This has gotta be that Akaboshi punk; he's up to somethin'! Get down there and see what's goin' on! And take the whole squad with you! Go and wake up the night watch, too! Now, you idiot! *Now!*"

"Got some more food for you, Mark I! Open wide!"

"*Vwoo.*"

In response to Shishi's cheerful voice, the Akaboshi Mark I threw open the refueling hatch on its back, and Shishi tossed an armful of bone coal into the roaring furnace within.

"Greedy little fella, ain't he? We've gone through half of it already."

"But look how fast he can dig now! The guards will be expecting us to try to leave through the gate, but with the robot on our side, we can tunnel straight through to the Beast Realm under their very noses!"

"Oh yeah, I guess so."

"You guess so…? Brother, are we not following your plan?"

Bisco looked at Shishi's puzzled face, then reached into his hair and pulled out a tightly rolled sheet of paper. He handed it over to Shishi, who unfurled it and saw that a fully detailed escape plan was written on it.

"What's this?"

"My partner gave it to me just before we split up. I had to wing it in a few places, but mostly that's the plan we're tryin' to follow."

"Milo wrote this? But why is it written in simple *hiragana*?"

"That's 'cause he's too dumb to write *kanji*."

"Oh, that's good. For a moment, I thought you were going to say you couldn't read!"

"You knew, didn't ya?! Then why'd you even ask? Grrr..."

Shishi and Bisco rode upon the shoulders of the Mokujin, Akaboshi Mark I, whose arms had transformed into huge drills that bored through the rocky mountain at breakneck speed. Having recalled the Kumamoto Mushroom Keepers' map to locate the bone coal warehouse, Bisco had used the Mark I's thermal cannon to open a shaft, allowing him to steal the fuel and thus recharge the robot. With the Mokujin back at full power, even the strongest tanks in the land would be no match for him.

"I never knew there were robots like this out there... I suppose there is much I do not know about the world. That must be why Father told me to seek a mentor outside the Benibishi, to broaden my horizons and deepen my noble wisdom."

"Are you serious about this king stuff, Shishi? I can't recommend bein' a leader. I've known governors, head priests. None of 'em die good deaths."

"Whether I live or die, in infamy or glory, it means nothing to me. All I want is for my people to be happy. For that...I am willing to offer everything I have. I wish to be just like my father, working his heart out for their benefit."

"Hmm... I guess that's a noble cause. The only ones I care about are my partner and my crab... Hold up, Mark I. Somethin's wrong. Stop!"

"*Vwooo!*"

"Don't get mad at *me*! I just heard somethin' weird, that's all!"

The Mark I grumpily lowered his drills, and Bisco hopped down and pressed his ear to the tunnel floor. Then he stood up, crossed his arms, and pondered.

"What is it, Brother? What did you hear?"

"Water, I think. Just under here. Sounds like a river flowing."

"A river? Could there even be a river be this far underground?"

"It'd be weird, that's for sure. But what's weirder is that the sound seems to come and go. Anyway, we can't keep diggin' here, or we'll spring a leak. Mark I, let's go around and find another way."

"AAAKAAABOOOSHIII!!"

"Uh-oh."

Just then, they all heard a man's angry voice echoing down the tunnel far behind them.

"Brother! That sounded like the guard captain! He's coming after us!"

"Didn't think they'd realize we were gone so soon. Did the heating go out or somethin'?"

Bisco cast his gaze down the tunnel and twiddled the knob on his cat-eye goggles until he could make out the scar-ridden face of the guard captain, coming down the tunnel with a squad behind him. They all wore night-vision goggles and heavy ballistic armor.

"Captain!" one shouted. "It looks like the giant's working with them!"

"Ready the salamander rockets! There's no place for them to run in these tunnels!"

"Are you sure, captain?! Readying now!"

"Fire! Fire! No mercy for jailbreakers! Blast them all to smithereens!"

Pshoo! Pshoo! The rockets streaked down the tunnel, leaving wispy white trails, but the Akaboshi Mark I instantly picked them out with his jade-green searchlights. He stood in front of Bisco and Shishi and extended his arms, which transformed into a huge, fin-shaped shield.

Boom! Boom Boom! One after the other, the rockets beat against the Mark I's shield. Each one went up in a fiery explosion, casting an orange glow across the robot's massive frame.

"How're you holding out, Mark I?! Those bastards! Don't they care if this whole tunnel caves in?!"

"Brother! The floor... It's collapsing!"

Each time a rocket landed, more and more cracks appeared in the brittle cave floor, growing wider and wider.

"Hey, you lot! Lay off the explosions! There's a river underneath, and the ground's unstable here! If you keep firing, we're *all* done for!"

"Ha-ha-ha! You'll have to try better than that, Akaboshi! At least the drain'll wash away your bodies, then!"

"The big guy's down on one knee! Keep up the assault! Fire! Fire!"

Pshoo! One last salamander rocket collided with the Mark I's shield, and then...

All of a sudden, a great rumbling came from below and the earth began to shake. The ground cracked apart, swallowing up the guards.

"Wh-what?! An earthquake?! Aaaah! I'm falling!"

"Help me! Help me, captain!"

"He wasn't lyin'... Run away, squad! Run aw—! Aaaagh!"

After dropping the guards to their fate, the cracks spread across the ground toward Bisco and Shishi. Shishi clutched Bisco's arm and squeezed her eyes shut in terror.

"It's all over! Oh, Father, please be safe...!"

"You sure give up quickly, don't ya?" Bisco grinned. "We're Japanese; if we died every time there was an earthquake, there'd be none of us left." Bisco picked up Shishi in his arms and added, "Once we start fallin', take the deepest breath you ever took. Mark I, shield us with your back!"

"...Yes, Brother!"

"Vwoo!"

Shishi held on tightly to Bisco, while Mark I wrapped its huge body around them. Then, in the next instant, the ground beneath gave way, and the three went tumbling into the darkness.

"Whoa, Doc! I can hear you! And I ain't never been able to hear out the right ear since those guards beat me up!"

"There was a scab in the inner ear that became infected with Rust. I've taken it out now, and there should be no complications."

"Outta the way, you. It's my turn. My hand's been twitchin' like mad over the past few days..."

"Get in line, dumbass! Hey, Doc? I've been getting fed up with makeup recently. You think it could be burnout? If my business doesn't make money, they'll extend my sentence..."

Patient after patient came to see Milo, and he handed down his diagnoses. Wiping the sweat from his brow, he cocked his head.

...Is this supposed to be a punishment? This is just my normal job...

After Milo finished wrapping the bandages on the last of his patients, he heaved a sigh of relief. Around thirty patients had come and gone over the course of the day, and the last one had even been one of the guards. He had come to have Milo examine some Rust warts that had been bothering him for ages, and he had really brightened up once Milo managed to remove them.

"You're a lifesaver, Doc. Now I can turn over in my bed at night without the pain waking me up!"

"Make sure you rub that ointment on it every day; otherwise they could come back."

"Got it. Thanks, Doc."

The guard replaced his black hooded robe and cleared his throat with a cough before taking out a pen and paper and scribbling something down.

"Well then, Milo Nekoyanagi. That concludes your services for today. Let's see the slips you got from your patients. One, two, three... Hmm, your business seems to be doing very well indeed."

"Erm, what exactly *are* these slips of paper that everybody's been giving me?"

"Why, they're your term slips, of course. I'll just exchange these for you; the small ones are hell to keep track of. Here you are. Looks like today you earned yourself a six-month reduction." The guard rustled through his pocket and pulled out six slips of paper, which he foisted upon the speechless Milo. "Save up forty years' worth, and you'll be a free man. There's other doctors round here, but none as good as you, so as much as I appreciate you being here, I don't imagine it'll be long before you earn your release."

...Right...I see...

The words "one-month reduction" were written on each of the slips the guard handed him. At long last, Milo figured out the workings of this so-called Human Realm.

Basically, they're bartering, using their sentences as currency. So by running a business, you can take years off your term...

The Human Realm seemed far less like a prison than the place Bisco had been taken to, and apart from Milo's weapons, nothing else had been taken from him. What's more, he was free to walk around without manacles or chains. Even the conversation that occurred when he arrived had seemed strange.

"It says here you're a doctor, is that right?"

"Oh, um, yes."

"In that case, you may use your cell as a clinic. You can purchase everything you need from the flea market in the central yard."

"Okay...what?! You mean, I don't have to stay in my cell?"

"Lockdown is at eight PM, so be careful. If you're not back in your cell by then, we'll consider you an escapee."

...And so began the latest chapter in Milo's career, the Panda Clinic, Prison Branch.

I guess that's why they call it Six Realms. Each of the sections works completely differently.

Milo found himself a little disappointed at the prison's lax attitude, but he wasn't about to look this gift horse in the mouth. Checking that there was still plenty of time until lockdown, he put on his Mushroom Keeper cloak and walked out of his cell into the vast facility beyond.

"Step right up! Fresh fruit, all the way from Kumamoto! We got redball melon, chocolate vine, whitebunch, all ripe and juicy! Three days apiece!"

"...How would you like to eat mochi handmade by Benibishi artisans, my good sir? We have red syrup and black syrup, whichever you prefer."

The central yard of the Human Realm looked to Milo like a scene straight out of his hometown of Imihama.

Is this really a prison? I've seen cities with quieter markets than this.

There were food and confectionery stalls, packed with customers. Bookshops and leisure facilities, even bars; everything exactly the same as one would expect to find on the outside. The only difference was that instead of money, all payment was settled in those so-called term slips that the guard had told Milo about.

A lasciviously dressed woman approached. "Hey, big boy, how does two weeks sound? ...Oh hey, you're actually kinda cute! Tell you what, for you, I'll make it one week." Milo brushed off her advances and slipped past her, pushing farther into the crowd.

They may be living in incarceration, but this place is just like a Benibishi city.

According to the rules of Six Realms Penitentiary, the Benibishi could never be released, even on good behavior. On the other hand, this meant they had no reason to save up their term slips and could instead spend them freely, enjoying an extravagant lifestyle here in the Human Realm. This led to the normal power imbalance between human and Benibishi being somewhat reversed, and they became more like their rich masters than anything else. Some even said it was like a care facility for them, where they could live out their lives in relative safety.

Milo pondered the situation as he stood at a market stall, finally picking out a bright-orange fruit and turning it over in his hands. Just then...

"Excuse me."

...there came a deep, commanding voice. At first, Milo thought it was aimed at the shopkeeper, and he ignored it, but soon the voice repeated itself.

"Excuse me. You there. Panda-Man."

Milo turned to see...a rather handsome man, with pure-white skin and tied-up hair. His impressive physique was outmatched only by his luxurious robe, and he stared at Milo with piercing, crimson eyes. All this indicated to Milo that this gentleman was a member of the Benibishi, but he seemed far too toned and muscular for that to be true. Despite his strange appearance, though, there was a gravitas about him that instantly captured Milo's attention.

"I hate to ask this of a newcomer," the man began, "but..."

"Er...oh? What is it?"

"Lend me a bit of cash, wouldn't you?"

"...What?!"

Here in the Human Realm, that could only mean one thing: The man was asking Milo to lend him some of the term slips that would secure his freedom. It was such a brazen question for one who looked so rich to begin with that, for a while, Milo could do nothing but stare blankly in shock.

"I fancy one of those, you see." The Benibishi pointed at the fruit in Milo's hands. "The whale orange. I simply cannot resist them myself, but they are highly seasonal, and the first batch is always the sweetest... I've just returned from death row and have nothing in my possession. That's why I need you to lend me some money."

"Listen, I think you ought to learn some manners first!"

"My Lord, how splendid it is to see you!"

Upon seeing the stranger, the Benibishi manning the stall cried out and handed over a whole bundle of the whale oranges to the muscular gentleman.

"...Please take what you desire. Your money is not needed here."

"Thanks, old chap, but it's really no trouble. This kind fellow was just about to spot me some cash."

"No, I wasn't!"

"I am simply happy to see you alive and in good spirits, My Lord. I could ask for nothing more. Please, take this fruit. Today's batch is exceedingly sweet and delectable..."

"Well, my old chum. I daresay you've put me on the spot here."

It seemed this Benibishi was well-loved, whoever he was, and even the others passing by on the street stopped and bowed their heads in reverence. Meanwhile, the fruitmonger still insisted on offering the man some fruit, and the man still steadfastly refused, such that the stalemate showed no signs of breaking.

"...Fine. *I'll* pay for that fruit."

"Oh?"

"And I'll take some fire strawberries as well. Here."

"Thank you, sir. I'll just get your change..."

"Keep it! Everyone's watching. Come on, let's go."

The crowd was swarming to the Benibishi man, and Milo wanted nothing less than to attract the attention of the guards, so he quietly ushered himself and the mysterious gentleman out of there.

"Here you go."

Once away from the crowds, Milo handed the man his bag of fruit, visibly annoyed.

"You are a generous fellow. I only wanted one."

"Forget it. You can have the whole lot. In return, stay away from me! I don't know who you are, but people seem to flock to you."

"Have you ever eaten one?"

"Huh?"

"A whale orange, I mean. Have you ever eaten one in season?"

The man swiftly peeled the orange with his fingers. Tossing the skin aside, he went on.

"You are an interesting fellow, to be sure. Come to my cell. I'll teach you how you're supposed to eat these."

"No thanks. Good-bye."

"It's just around that corner over there."

Milo watched as the man turned and briskly walked away, then headed back to his own cell...when suddenly, he realized his shoulder bag full of medical supplies was missing.

"Where did it—? Aaah!"

Milo spun around and just happened to catch the strange gentleman disappearing around the corner, Milo's bag dangling from his shoulder.

"What the...?! When did he...?!"

Feeling like he was only allowing himself to be dragged into something, Milo nonetheless had no choice but to take off after the stranger.

"Well, you sure are a contrary fellow. After all that, you decided to pay me a visit after all. You are every bit as coquettish as your features suggest."

"I don't know how you did it..."

The stranger's cell was carpeted in a sumptuous rug and furnished with a four-poster bed. It didn't look anything like a prison cell was supposed to look. Milo found himself a little taken aback by the sight but tried not to let it show as he barged in and demanded the return of his belongings with an angry voice he was not accustomed to using.

"...but you stole my bag! How dare you! Are you a nobleman or a pickpocket?!"

"A nobleman, as you seem to have surmised. And naturally, you must also be able to tell that I bear you no ill will. Take a closer look at this whale orange. Many people peel them starting from the tail, but I am here to tell you that such an amateurish approach only succeeds in making the fruit lose its fragrance. You see, you must start by digging your nails into the middle..."

What am I going to do? This man's completely nuts!

Milo had already handed off the escape plans to Bisco, and now he was working on a tight schedule. Even with unplanned eventualities taken into account, Milo's agenda was founded on an ironclad trust in Bisco's abilities, and so now he was thinking...

I'm running out of time to get everything ready!

Before Bisco managed to escape the Preta Realm, Milo would have to leave the Human Realm and pass through the Asura and Beast Realms before meeting up with him. There wasn't any time to waste, and yet Milo couldn't help but be enthralled by the mysterious stranger's wild charm.

"...And once you do that, you see, the pristine flesh of the fruit begins to show itself... Are you watching?"

"H-huh? Uh...yeah, of course."

"Very well."

The man tossed three of the orange segments into his mouth and ate them all in one go.

"Wh-whaaat?! I thought you were going to give some to me!"

"When did I say that? I said I would show you how to eat them, that is all."

The man quickly resumed peeling the orange. Milo gave a deep, incredulous sigh before sweeping up his medicine bag and turning to leave.

"I hear you landed a blow on Someyoshi Satahabaki."

The man's words stopped Milo in his tracks. He slowly turned to see the man reclining on a sofa, dropping peeled orange slices into his open mouth.

"That man is like a rampaging locomotive, while a skinny little thing like you... My goodness, it must have been like the battle between Benkei and Yoshitsune."

"It wasn't me who landed the blow, it was my partner... Wait, how did you know about that?"

"Alas, a mushroom shall never defeat a flower."

At those words, Milo instantly transformed from the good-natured doctor to a fierce Mushroom Keeper. As he scowled, the stranger simply smiled, tossed his head back theatrically, and dropped in another orange slice.

"Furthermore, the power I bestowed upon Someyoshi was that of the cherry blossom. It grants him unlimited life force, so long as he operates within the bounds of the law. Even if mushrooms cover his whole body, all they are is more food for the plants. There is no way for you to beat him."

"...You're...!"

Milo gulped. The man rose to his feet and swept his gown outward, peering down from his regal height with crimson eyes.

"I do hope you'll stay awhile longer, Mushroom Keeper. You'll never leave Six Realms without my support, I daresay."

He's the Benibishi's king! There's no doubt about it!

"I am Housen of the Benibishi. I expect there is much you wish to ask of me, but alas! The king has been wounded with thoughtless words and selfish actions, and his heart is closed off! How will the brave and intrepid Mushroom Keeper soothe his soul and earn his favor?"

King Housen chuckled and flashed a mischievous smile, while Milo simply stood there, grinding his teeth wordlessly in anger.

"A most tricky problem, is it not? Man-Eating Panda."

Just as Milo began to speak, King Housen clogged his mouth with a slice of orange, howling with laughter as Milo chewed it up, infuriated. The fruit was every bit as sweet as Housen claimed, but right now, Milo was in no mood to enjoy it.

"Ur...gh..."

Shishi groaned. The boulder atop her chest weighed a ton. It was only with great effort that she heaved it aside, and it was only once she finally stood up that she noticed the other person there in the darkness with her.

"Ah, Brother! Thank goodness you're—"

"Shishi! Get back!"

"Ah!"

Bisco's voice came not from the figure but from behind her, and Shishi leaped back just as the figure attacked from the gloom with a blade, barely grazing her violet bangs before smashing into the ground.

"Grrr. Damn, I missed..."

Shishi landed and staggered back, falling into Bisco's arms. The warm touch of his skin was the sole reassurance in this otherwise dire situation.

"Haah... haah... Not a bad little prison break, Akaboshi..."

Fwm. Fwm. One by one, a series of torches lit up the cave, illuminating its blue crystalline structures as well as their wielders, a whole squad of prison guards.

Uh-oh. Looks like these guys survived the fall, too!

"We'll have our wages cut for this, and it's all your fault. Just killin' ya ain't gonna be enough. First, we'll pull out your nails, then we'll peel your skin, then we'll electrocute ya, waterboard ya..."

"Keep talking and we'll fly the coop while you're busy countin' your chickens," Bisco shot back.

"Shaddup! ...Heh-heh. I see you made friends with the big guy. That's good..."

Here at last the scar-faced guard returned to his usual seedy grin as he held up what looked like some sort of switch with a small light flashing on and off.

"...For me, that is! If I'm gonna take a pay cut anyway, then at least I get to blow him to pieces first!"

"...!"

Bisco turned to the Mark I to see several white lights all over the robot's body, flashing in sequence with the one on the guard's device, as though something inside him were glowing with heat.

"You really think we hadn't prepared for that guy to break out? His entire body's rigged with explosives! One press of this here button and... *Boom!*"

"Say what?!"

"Vwooo!"

"Gyah-ha-ha! Look at that, a machine that knows fear! You know what, Akaboshi? You're right! I ain't gonna waste time! Take this! ...Huh? Take...this!"

"...Captain, please stop messing around and press the button...," his subordinate warned.

"I'm tryin'! My finger's...not...!"

Bisco was about to sling a stone at the guard captain when he noticed something was wrong. "Huh? What's goin' on?" he asked.

"...Brother!" came a strained whisper. *"Don't throw that. There's something else here. Back away slowly before it sees us!"*

"...Okay, got it!"

"Wh-what the hell?! Wh-what's...happening to me?!"

With substantial effort, the guard captain shone his light on himself, revealing a horrifying sight that even Bisco found hard to stomach. A whole swarm of small, hard organisms had engulfed the captain's body, from his feet all the way up to his outstretched hand, in the blink of an eye and with no sound at all.

"My legs! I can't move my legs!" cried one guard.

"Captain! What are these things?!" asked another. "Aagh, they're crawling all over me!"

"Save me, you idiots!" the captain yelled. "Get me out of here! Cut off your legs if you have to!"

"Brother, look!"

"Barnacles! Just our luck…"

Bisco, Shishi, and the Mark I all shared a glance and gently backed away, watching as the tiny creatures swarmed the guards one after the other, turning them into solid statues.

"…Aah! Brother, watch out!"

"I know! Just keep quiet. Don't let them see us, and we'll get outta—"

"No, look! It's the river! It's coming to wash us away!"

The Mark I turned its flashlight eyes where Shishi pointed, revealing a wave of muddy water surging toward them. Bisco screamed, his crimson hair on end, and all three of them ducked behind a protruding piece of rock.

"A-Akaboshi! Help! Get me outta here! I'll reduce your sentence! You won't have to work another day, I promise!"

"You guys seriously need to learn some manners. Didn't your momma ever teach you the magic word?"

"P-please! Akaboshi! M-Mr. Akaboshi, sir! Please help me!"

"That's a bit more like it! Now if only you'd said that ten seconds ago, when there was still time."

"What?! N-no… The water's coming! W-waaaaaghh!!"

The rumbling torrent of water rushed through the tunnel, and for three full minutes the three guards could only stay hidden behind the rock as the water soaked them to the skin, until finally the stream died down.

"Cough! Cough! Oh, I get it!" said Shishi. "This is the Sanzu River! It's an underground aqueduct that connects all of Six Realms, washing

away prisoners' bodies and other garbage. That's why it comes in waves!"

"...Urgh. What a way to go..."

"Brother...?"

Bisco stared, grim-faced, at the spot where the guards had stood. By now, only their feet remained, stuck to the ground by a layer of barnacles. The top halves had all torn off and washed away in the strong current, and from the leg stumps came gushes of blood. The severed feet must have numbered twenty or thirty—more than enough to traumatize young Shishi, in any case.

"W-w-waah...!"

"I don't know how they do it, but the barnacles are able to sense living things. They'll be after us once they're done with their meal."

"R-right! We need to get out of here, Brother! I'll take the lead and—"

Suddenly, Shishi was cut off as a bat, small and fuzzy, flew into her face. Before she could even react, the creature sank its tiny fangs into Shishi's neck.

"Ow! What was that?!"

"Shishi!"

Bisco grabbed the bat and tugged, spraying fresh blood from Shishi's neck wound. The animal let out a loud screech in Bisco's hand, attracting the attention of the barnacles, who advanced on the three like a wave of earth rising out of the ground.

"They've seen us! Shishi, run!"

"Okay!"

Bisco tossed the bat as a distraction, but the barnacles engulfed it in less than a second, draining it of blood and leaving only a shriveled corpse.

"Dammit. I've got nothing that can take out a swarm. I need my mushrooms!"

"Brother. Would those barnacles happen to be omnivorous?"

"How the hell would I know?! Just get outta here!"

As Shishi fled alongside Bisco, her mind was surprisingly calm. She took in the sights of the cavern: the damp smell of algae and the vine-like plants hanging from the roof, slowly putting together a solution in her mind like she was solving a puzzle.

They haven't eaten the plants, so they must be carnivores. Perhaps they use smell to detect their prey? In which case...

"Vwoo."

Running ahead of the others, the Mark I made an odd noise and stopped. The earth began to rumble, and once more the sound of rushing water could be heard from far away.

"Not this again. Already? Shishi, Mark I, this way!"

The three squeezed themselves into the shade of whatever rock they could find that was big enough to shield the Mark I, mere moments before the flash flood washed past them again. The barnacles, meanwhile, quickly shifted onto the walls and ceiling with speed unlike any other mollusk's, still bearing down on the stationary trio.

"We're screwed! I'll hold 'em off, and while they're busy eatin' me..."

"Brother, wait! I have an idea, but I don't know if it will work. Do you trust me?"

"Anythin's better than doin' nothin'! Go for it! I'll— Mmmh?!"

Just as Bisco turned around, Shishi pressed her soft lips to his, pushing the unruly Bisco's tongue aside with her own in a very unladylike manner.

"Nnnnngggghhhh!!"

"...Now! Flourish!"

In response to Shishi's efforts, there was the muffled *Boom! Boom!* of something suddenly growing inside Bisco's body. The next moment, the scattered barnacles rained down on the three from above. The bloodsucking creatures piled on top of Bisco and Shishi as they continued to kiss, completely hiding them from sight as the water rushed past...

And then, once the flow subsided...

...

...

Scuttle.

Scuttle, scuttle.

The swarm of barnacles gave up the ghost and scattered in all directions, leaving Shishi, Bisco, and the Mark I completely intact...though Bisco, for his part, was left looking a little worse for wear.

"*Cough! Cough!* Shishi... What the hell was that?"

"I am sorry, Brother, but there was no time to explain. I am relieved my plan succeeded, though."

"Succeeded?! ...Wait, you're right. The barnacles are gone, and there ain't a scratch on me. How'd you do it?"

"The barnacles track us by our breathing. I suspect they can smell the carbon dioxide we emit. Which means..."

Shishi tugged at her jaw with a finger and showed Bisco her open mouth. Inside was a mass of ivy that went all the way down the girl's throat.

"Eurgh! What the hell is that?!"

"You have the same now, too, Brother... Wait, no! Don't take it out! The barnacles are still nearby!"

"Well, then tell me what the hell you did to me and how it keeps them away!"

"The ivy goes into your lungs and causes the barnacles to mistake us for plants. Instead of carbon dioxide, we are now exhaling pure oxygen, and since the barnacles don't like plants, they go elsewhere."

"...Hmm..."

To be honest, Shishi had lost him at "carbon dioxide," but even Bisco understood that the girl's clever plan had somehow saved both of their lives, and so he cheered up quite quickly, and with a cheeky smile, he patted Shishi boisterously on the back.

"Good shit! I dunno how you pulled that plan outta your ass, but I'm sure glad you did!"

"Well, I did also think it would be a shame to die before experiencing my first kiss."

"Is that somethin' a prince should be sayin'?!"

"Now, let us get out of here before the water comes back a third time. I don't know how long those barnacles will stay fooled. We must advance to the Beast Realm before they catch on!"

Shishi ran off merrily ahead, her camellia flower in full bloom. Bisco started off after her, but at the feeling of ivy in his lungs, he stopped and coughed. Shishi turned and offered her hand, and Bisco took it before looking down into her big round eyes and enchantingly sweet smile.

"Was my power of use to you again…Brother?"

"You just asked me that. You think I'm gonna compliment you all day? Don't let it get to your head."

"You are right. I must remain humble. Now, give me a stern talking-to!"

"What the hell is wrong with you? Get moving already! C'mon, Mark I, we're going!"

With an affirmative *"Vwoo,"* the Mark I jogged after them, never realizing that, since he was a robot, the barnacles were never a threat to him at all.

"Ohhh, that's good. Right there, yes. Mmm… To think a young man like you could be so skillful… Aaagh! W-wait, not there! It hurts!"

"Stop making such weird noises! It's just a back massage! Grow up!"

Milo pushed down on Housen's hip, straightening his back with a series of loud cracks, and the Benibishi king alternated between cries of agony and delight.

"It's obvious you were fitter once, Your Majesty, but you've really let yourself go. All that slouching on sofas is bad for your spine."

"I—I know, but do you have to handle me so roughly? I am a king, remember. "

"I'm afraid so. I have to be tough just to get through all that muscle. I'll finish off with some pressure point massage, so just lie still."

"H-hold on! You mean you're still not done?! U-uurgh! Ow… Ow! Nooo! Guhhh!"

The gravelly yelps of the Benibishi monarch filled the rocky cell. It was a strange sight indeed, made stranger still by the fact that it was he who had requested the examination in the first place.

First let's see if those weedy arms of yours can help ease my aching back.

The idea had been to enjoy a relaxing massage at Milo's expense, but instead, the Benibishi king found himself at the doctor's mercy. The young boy's physical strength proved to be far beyond anything his dainty figure would suggest.

Milo, on the other hand, was as eager as always to provide medical treatment should anyone ask for it. Though this ended up being a way to get back at the king for his teasing, that had not been Milo's intent at all. In fact, he was sweating from the effort of providing the best care he could manage. Fortunately, Benibishi anatomy differed not too significantly from that of humans, so there were no troubles on that front.

"Okay! I've finished the readjustment. Now just rest awhile, and you should feel much more limber than before."

"This wasn't quite what I expected..."

"Now, as promised...," Milo began, stressing his words as he looked down at Housen on the bed. "You said you would answer my question if I did what you asked."

"Hmm, did I really? My memory's not what it used to be...," Housen replied.

"Oh, really? Well, this pressure point does wonders for recollection."

"Gyaaaagh! Ow, ow, ow! Okay, okay! You sure are an...intrepid fellow. It's been a long time since anyone treated me with such incivility."

Housen soon relented at the hands of Milo's torture...or massage, depending on how you looked at it, and he slicked back his sweat-drenched hair. Lifting a gold-trimmed tobacco pipe, he took a few puffs to settle his nerves before asking, "So? What was it you wanted to ask me again? So much for your pressure points. If anything, the shock just made me forget."

"It was how to defeat Someyoshi Satahabaki!" yelled Milo, angrily downing a glass of water and wiping his sweaty brow. "Mushrooms don't work on him, like you said. If anything, they only make him stronger. What are those strange flowers he has?"

"I'm afraid I don't know what to tell you, friend. Flowers are flowers."

"Your Majesty!"

"Settle down, my dear panda. It is not my intent to speak in riddles. As you are a doctor, I am sure you must be aware of the plant DNA that resides within the genetic code of the Benibishi."

Housen snapped his fingers, and all of a sudden a magenta balsam flower appeared out of thin air before disintegrating into petals and disappearing on the wind.

"…King Housen, what was that?!"

"I know not where it first began, but at some point, our flower genes began manifesting in strange ways. We call this phenomenon of flower-based abilities *'Florescence'* and the powers that manifest in an individual their *'Bountiful Art.'*"

"…Florescence…? A mutation in the Benibishi genetic code?"

Milo thought back to his battle with Satahabaki and how the Iron Judge seemed able to bend the cherry blossom petals to his will…

"Does that mean…Satahabaki really is a Benibishi, like he claimed?"

"Well, he could hardly be human, could he?" Housen joked, tapping his pipe to remove the ashes. "Dear Someyoshi is of the first generation, from back when we were used as manual laborers. I granted him Florescence in light of his outstanding determination and physical prowess."

"You…*gave* him his powers?"

King Housen ignored the bewildered Milo and carried on.

"Flowers, my friend, have always been vulnerable to the Rust Wind. The lightest breeze, and they wither away completely. If Someyoshi were to possess a weakness, then I could think of nothing else. Incidentally, it is also possible for flowers to draw upon an external source of life energy. For example, like this."

Poof! Poof!

With an almost comical sound, a bunch of balsam flowers appeared, growing out of Milo's head. Catching sight of himself in the mirror, he let out a startled cry.

"Ha-ha-ha. It works particularly well on Mushroom Keepers, thanks to your spores. The flowers feed on mushrooms, you see, and the more powerful the mushroom, the more life energy it contains, and the stronger the resulting flower. This is just as true for Someyoshi's flowers as it is for any others."

"…I see," said Milo, having pulled out as many of the balsam flowers as he could. "So our mushrooms only make his flowers stronger…" He crossed his arms and bit his lower lip in thought. King Housen chuckled in amusement and blew a puff of tobacco smoke.

"If I were you, I'd abandon any fanciful notions of taking him out. There is not a man alive who can best Someyoshi now. That is why I granted him Florescence and made him gatekeeper of the Benibishi's own Eden."

...I get it. Satahabaki's not just there to keep them inside. He's there to keep everybody else out. Six Realms Penitentiary is a way for them to escape human oppression.

Milo had to admit he could see the genius in the whimsical king's designs. Housen was wiser than he had given him credit for. However, Milo didn't let up on his questioning yet.

"But that's not the case anymore! Satahabaki's gone mad! He thinks you're all a threat to the peace, and he's going to execute you all in a week's time!"

"So I've heard."

"You...you knew?! Then why haven't you—?"

"Whoa, now, hold on. I only agreed to one question, and I think we've gone a fair bit beyond that by now. I'd say it's my turn. What should I have you do next...?"

"I still haven't done your shoulders."

"No more massage, I think. Let's opt for something a little less painful."

Housen snapped his fingers, and a single balsam flower grew out of Milo's chest. Ignoring the boy's shock, Housen tugged on the stem and reeled Milo in closer.

"Hmm. That's a strong look in your eyes. There are many fair faces among the Benibishi, but none with the same fiery gaze as yours. Dangerous, like a wild beast... I like it."

"...Grh."

Milo tried to avert his gaze, but Housen gripped his chin and peered into his panda-marked eye.

"There are many here who willfully offer themselves to me, and as such, I have begun to tire of my own species. The guards would make a welcome change, were they not all completely devoid of beauty and grace. I was beginning to think none here could ever satisfy me."

"So you want to try a mushroom man? I warn you, King Housen, some of us are poisonous."

"The courage you show before me! The blazing stars in your eyes! Yes, that look! I've never found anyone so amusing…"

His jaw in Housen's grip, their noses touching, Milo glared at the king with all the rebelliousness in his heart. But the Benibishi hero's smile only deepened. If anything, Milo's reluctance only delighted him even more.

Urgh. If Tirol found out I sold myself so cheaply, I'd never hear the end of it!

As a rich young doctor, Milo was no stranger to unwanted advances and had many methods at his disposal for dealing with them. However, this man, Housen, was practiced in wiles like no other, and he left not a single opening.

I don't want to resort to violence, but if I have to…I'll go for the nose…!

Milo secretly produced a scalpel from his medical bag and held it behind his back, waiting for an opportunity, when…

"K-King Housen…?"

"Hmm?"

…Housen let go of the flower and turned to the visitor with a look of sheer exasperation.

"You have the worst timing. What is it?"

Th-that was close…!

Released from Housen's grip, Milo gasped for breath as the Benibishi merchant fell to his knees at the feet of his king.

"My Lord. It is a matter of great importance," said the merchant.

"Well, so was this. What is it? Does Lady Gopis require another servant?" asked Housen.

"No!" the merchant cried. "We've just received word from the Asura Realm. They want us to send over all our children in advance of the next Byakkotai Show."

"Byakkotai…Show?" muttered Milo.

"A detestable performance put on for the rich and powerful jailers of the Asura Realm," the merchant replied, turning to answer Milo's question.

"They make the children slaughter each other and slit open their own stomachs, for their amusement. They enjoy watching our beautiful children lose their lives for no reason. It's crazy, I say! Just because we can't fight back, that doesn't give them the right to do as they please!"

"Now, now," Housen interjected. "It's not that bad. Don't cry. You're overreacting."

Housen stood up and lazily trudged over to the corner of the room, snatching up a katana that was leaning against the wall.

"Is that...a sword?! How are you allowed to have that? You're a prisoner!"

"Of course I'm allowed. I am king, after all. Someyoshi gave it to me for self-defense." Housen looked the sword over carefully for defects, then placed it neatly at his belt. "I think I'll go have a chat with these guards. You say they are coming here from the Asura Realm?"

"We have already opened the gate. They're accompanied by a great number of combat-trained helmet bears. Please put together an escort and—"

"There shall be no need. I don't intend to start a fight."

"B-but, My Lord! It is dangerous to go alone!"

"I never said I was going alone." Housen gave a playful smile and poked Milo's leg with his scabbard. "Come along now, Panda. Save my people, and I shall answer another of your questions."

Housen smiled at Milo. The boy's eyes were a pair of azure flames stoked by the frustration of what he had been forced to endure.

"Don't look at me like that. I'm offering you a chance here. Take it before I change my mind."

"Then give me a sword, too. I can't fight barehanded like Bisco can."

"Hmm. All right, then how about this *wakizashi*? You know how to use one?"

"No," replied Milo, irritated, rising to his feet and snatching the weapon out of Housen's hand. "But it has a blade; that's good enough. I'll just pretend it's a big scalpel."

The road that led from the Human Realm to the Asura Realm was only about seven or eight meters wide, enclosed on both sides by steep cliffs. Flanking the large gate stood several of the beefier Benibishi specimens, ready to serve as escorts, despite Housen's request. At his appearance, robes fluttering, they all kneeled in unison.

"What are you doing here?" Housen asked. "Stand down. You're only going to complicate matters."

"We cannot do that, my liege. We will lay down our lives to—"

"Oh, put a sock in it. I said I don't need you, so stand down."

King Housen snapped his fingers, and balsam flowers sprouted from the tongues of the brave Benibishi, preventing them from saying anything more. With a flick of his wrist, he dismissed them, and they all ran back inside the Human Realm.

Watching this, Milo interjected. "You didn't have to drive them away, King Housen. We could have just had them stand back and—"

"Heh-heh. Just like he said, it's the king himself. What a stupid old man, coming here with no security…"

Interrupting Milo was a shrill voice that came from down in the valley. Spinning around, Milo saw a pack of bears, each easily two meters tall, lumbering toward them, and riding on the shoulders of the lead bear was a chubby dwarf, wearing an eyepatch and grinning.

"These bears get mighty hungry, only ever feedin' on those Asura Realm suckers. 'Course, they know a *real* leader when they see one, so I got 'em to listen to me, but let my concentration drift and they'll eat you for supper."

"*They've trained the helmet bears?! How?!*"

"*Probably using the vice-wardens' special brainwashing methods. It's got nothing to do with that rotund fellow at all.*"

"*There's a lot of them. King Housen, be careful how you— Ahhh, wait!*"

But the Benibishi king was already striding forward, his gown billowing behind him. Soon he arrived before the lead bear and confronted its rider face-to-face.

"H-hey… Back away, old man. If you're gonna negotiate, then keep your distance!"

"Do not call me *old man*."

"Wh-what?!"

"It's an inelegant designation. It repulses me. You may call me an *Adonis*, or if that word is not in your vocabulary, then at the very least *gentleman* would suffice."

Housen ignored Milo tugging on his robe, face flicking frantically between the dauntless king and his ruddy-faced opponent.

"C-cut the bullshit!" the small man said. "Don't you understand what's goin' on here?! You know what I'm here for. We got some big shots comin' over from Kyoto, and we wanna put on a show. The kind of show you only get with people who are happy to roll over and die when their human masters ask 'em to!"

"So you want me to hand over my people, knowing full well I am sending them to their deaths? Even Gopis is not authorized to do such a thing. Someyoshi will not be pleased."

"Things ain't like what they used to be in the Asura Realm, old man! Lady Gopis practically runs the place now. That idiot Satahabaki's gone and made himself a cell at the entrance and locked himself up in it! There's no way he can monitor us from there, so we're free to do whatever the hell we want!"

The man bent over backward with shrill laughter and would have nearly fallen off his bear if Housen hadn't helped him back up. He cleared his throat, embarrassed, and continued.

"Anyway. We're askin' for all Benibishi aged thirteen and under. Else I'll sic the helmet bears on ya and take 'em by force."

"Hmm. I have to say, this doesn't sound much like a negotiation at all."

"All you Benibishi slobs are gonna die in a week anyway. At least now we'll be getting some use outta ya!"

"Indeed," Housen replied. "I suppose you are right. If we are to die anyway…"

"Right, right. Glad ya see where I'm comin'—"

"…then it matters little if I cut your filthy head off right here."

"…Huh?"

The smirk that had decorated the bear-rider's face until now suddenly vanished.

"King Housen, I thought you said you weren't going to start a fight?"

"There is a time and place for everything."

Housen cleanly drew his blade, and when the dwarf saw the flash of steel, he shrieked in fright. His bear took several steps backward in retreat, and he cried, "I-it's a revolt! Bears, attack! Attack!"

In response, a large group of bears that had been lying in wait at the far end of the valley came thundering over in a cloud of smoke.

Dammit, I knew something like this was going to happen!

Milo stood in front of Housen protectively, muttered a spell beneath his breath, and suddenly a floating, spinning cube appeared in the palm of his hand.

"King Housen, I'll hold them off while you make your escape!"

"Oh? Doubting my skill with the blade, are we?"

"Yes," Milo shot back. "I could tell from your massage that you haven't been active for a long time. You won't be as fit as you think you are."

"How rude." Housen crossed his arms, a look of displeasure on his face, then nodded and drew his blade a couple of times through the air, testing its weight. "If you are so sure of your diagnosis, Doctor, then I implore you to sit there and watch."

"…What?! Ah, King Housen! Watch out!"

The pack of helmet bears sped up, flooding into the valley and leaving no escape. As their name suggested, the helmet bears were genetically engineered to have a layer of thick skin surrounding their skulls so that they could not be killed with one blow to the head. It didn't matter how much of a master swordsman Housen was; even if he stabbed one through the heart, it would take at least two minutes to bleed out. If Milo allowed the bears to surround them, it wouldn't be long before the beasts' inexhaustible stamina won the fight.

I've never known a king so stubborn! I didn't want to have to use this mantra, but…!

"*Won/shad/keriehi/s*— (Bring target to caster—)"

But before Milo could finish his spell, the Benibishi monarch arrived before the bears, gown fluttering in the wind. With his sword outstretched, he traced a full moon circle before plunging it point-down into the ground.

Bwoom!

An enormous balsam flower immediately popped out of the earth, tossing the helmet bears aside. They crashed into the valley walls and fell to the floor, unconscious and unmoving.

"Wh-what…?!"

This is the power of Housen's Florescence?!

"Hmm. I hate to admit it, Panda, but it seems you were right. I do feel much weaker than I remember."

"Now's not the time! Your Majesty, behind you!"

"I know, I know. You're quite the tiresome fellow, aren't you?"

Housen tilted his head to one side without even looking backward, narrowly avoiding the bear's claw that sliced the air behind him. Then he spun and delivered a single magnificent slash across three of the bears, so fast he appeared to be in two places at once.

Bwoom! Bwoom!

The balsam flowers grew from the slice wound with such force that they launched the bears away, and they were unable to get back up. The normally vigorous bears seemed to have no energy, writhing around pathetically as though the flowers had sapped away their very will to live.

"From the looks of their training, I'd say these are Gopis's beasts," said Housen. "Hmm. Quite a beautiful crop, if I do say so myself."

Milo had seen many skilled fighters in his time, but Housen's techniques really took the cake.

The flowers…they're sucking away at their life force!

"Panda. Watch very carefully."

As Housen stood there covered in the bears' blood, his crimson eyes gleamed. Balsam flowers popped up in his hair, as if excited to be on the field of battle once more, forming around his head like a crown.

"In fact, let all my people bear witness…to the dance that has not been seen in five years."

The rest of the pack came after him. Housen was right. "Dance" was the only way to describe it. An awesome, beautiful, enchanting dance, with the bears offering themselves to his blade, giving themselves to the flowers that bloomed forth from their bodies. Housen whirled, eyes closed, as if the bears' sharp claws meant nothing to him. Soon a large group of Benibishi spilled forth from the gate and rejoiced, throwing themselves to the ground in reverence of their king. Milo, however, was more intrigued by something else. He gulped.

He hasn't killed a single one!

While the bodies of the bears littered the valley floor, brought low by Housen's Florescence, every last one of them was still very much alive. To strike with such care in the midst of this chaotic brawl was an impossible feat for even the most skilled sword users.

"Have I changed your mind, Panda?"

"...H-huh?"

"Having seen my dance, have you changed your mind about me?"

Housen acted as though completely ignorant of the fact that the battle was not over, giving Milo no choice but to shout back, "Yes! I have! I get it now! You're brilliant! Beyond reproach! Now get back here so I can support you!"

"Hmm. Very well."

Housen flashed a proud smile before turning and cutting down the bear behind him.

"I only wish you'd said so earlier. I was starting to think you would have me dancing all day... Now, time to end this."

With several swift hops, Housen put some distance between himself and the bears and, facing them, drew a finger along the length of his blade. As he did, the sword glowed where he touched, and buds began sprouting across it.

"Bountiful Art: Balsam Blaze."

Housen swept his sword in a semicircular arc, leaving a crimson trail in the air. This trail then became a beam of energy that launched forward, passing through all the attacking bears and disappearing into the valley beyond.

"Come, graceful flowers. Flourish!"

The very moment Housen resheathed his sword, balsam flowers of all colors exploded into being across the pack of bears. One by one, they each let out a roar of pain before collapsing to the ground where they stood.

"Our king, so mighty!"

"Our lord and savior, King Housen!"

The Benibishi were ready to kiss the earth where he stood, their heads pressed firmly to the ground. King Housen stroked his chin and gazed at the scene before him. What now filled the valley was a beautiful field of balsam flowers swaying gently in the breeze, idyllic enough to make anyone forget the bodies of the fierce predators upon which they grew.

"Hmm. Not bad, though I would have liked the color to be a little brighter. What do you think, Panda? I'd wager you've never seen anything like this these days, with the Rust Wind as it is."

"You never needed my help to begin with," Milo sulked, folding his arms. "And why didn't you start with this technique instead of putting yourself in danger like that?"

"That is because you were looking down on me," said Housen, wandering through the flower field and occasionally stopping to pick one. "Treating me like some kind of senior citizen. I had to put you in your place."

Wh-what a brat!

"Still," he went on, "I am a king, not a general. My Bountiful Art, the balsam flower, is not meant for battle. It is only able to weaken the bears by absorbing their life force."

"Speaking of Bountiful Arts... You said that Satahabaki's cherry blossoms gave him power as long as he kept to the law, right?" Milo had to run to keep up with Housen's strides, occasionally stepping aside to avoid some of the more vigorous bears whenever they snapped at his feet. "What about your balsam flowers? How do they work?"

"The balsam is the flower of kings." Housen tossed the flower in his hand to Milo, and it gently brushed his nose. "It has the power to awaken Florescence in any Benibishi who have not yet received it."

"Wh-what...?!" The king's casual remark left Milo in disarray. "You mean you can give anyone powers like yours?!"

"Didn't I already tell you? It was I who gave Someyoshi his cherry blossoms."

"But...but if you can do that, why not give it to all the Benibishi?! If all of them were as powerful as him, you'd be able to overthrow him with ease!"

"I cannot do that."

"Why not?! What is there to lose at this point?!"

"..."

Housen stopped walking, and the playful look on his face was replaced by one of solemn regality. He looked to Milo, and Milo could see the king's wisdom in his eyes as he answered.

"If I did, it is possible that the Benibishi would far outstrip humanity."

"...What? But why would that—?"

"Stay quiet and listen to me."

Milo gulped and nodded.

"You speak true. Using the power of the balsam, I could indeed awaken all the Benibishi to their Florescence. If I did so, escaping this prison would be child's play. We could conquer the whole country if we so wished."

"..."

"That is because, in gaining Florescence, Benibishi break free of their subservience to humans, and not all of us will take our forced slavery in good humor. Many will take that chance to strike back at their former oppressors, and if they did, the slaughter would be incalculable. Humanity would be purged from Japan in an instant."

"Th-that can't be...!"

"I cannot allow that to happen. I must avoid war between the humans and the Benibishi at all costs. At the same time, I wish to protect my people from human oppression."

"And so that's why you created this prison?"

"You still think it excessive? For me, it was the only choice."

Housen stroked his chin and went on. Still, he seemed to be giving careful thought to something.

"However. It is true that there is only so much I can do... A few months ago, we were graced by the most bizarre rainbow shower. I know not how it happened, but ever since then, an ivy Florescence has been manifesting in the Benibishi without my involvement. I also believe this to be somehow related to the change in Someyoshi's behavior. A king must always be in control. If there are things I do not understand, it bodes ill for the fate of my people."

Milo was stunned. The man before him now was a far cry from the irresponsible philanderer he had met in Housen's cell. Now the king spoke with the gravitas appropriate for his station, and the scale of what he was saying was far beyond anything Milo had been prepared for.

"Panda."

"Y-yes?!"

"I saw earlier that you possess a mysterious power."

"..."

"And your partner, Akaboshi. Is he strong?"

"A hundred times stronger than me."

"Hmm. Good."

Housen pointed the tip of his blade toward the valley, and a bright ball of light shot out of it. A short while later, the sound of a flower blooming was heard from far off in the distance.

"I have thrown wide the gate to the Asura Realm. Go. Your partner is waiting."

"Your Majesty!"

"You were right, my friend. If Someyoshi is not stopped, he will put us all to death. However, I am a king. I cannot lay a hand on my own people. If Someyoshi can be stopped, it will be at the hands of two Man-Eating Mushroom Keepers, and no other."

"You're telling us to kill Satahabaki? But the mushrooms don't work on him!"

"I am confident you will find a way. I can tell just by looking at you that you have weathered far worse crises than this."

With a swish of his gown, Housen turned toward the Human Realm, welcomed by the rapturous cheers of his people.

"Do not worry. With my wit and intelligence, I have always managed to turn a negotiation in my favor. I will try to speak with Someyoshi and come to a peaceable settlement. I only ask that you be ready should I fail."

"You just failed a negotiation five minutes ago!"

"Oh. That reminds me. There's something I forgot to say." It seemed Housen had no intention of addressing Milo's complaint. "I would like to ask you a favor. Look after the little one for me."

"The little one...?"

"Why Shishi, of course."

Housen's face grew serious as he spoke that name, and he looked Milo in the eye. Milo knew it was futile at this point to ask how Housen knew the two of them were acquainted.

"The camellia has taken root faster than I ever imagined possible. It is only a matter of time before the little one awakens to her Florescence."

"Isn't that a good thing? Shishi is your heir, isn't she?"

"*The king must cast himself aside. Only for the people shall his flowers bloom.*"

"...Erm, what's that?"

"The creed of kings." Housen was far off by now, but his voice carried in the dusty air. "Right now, Shishi is too young. A bud is prone to fits of passion. It can never sit atop the throne so long as anger guides its blade."

"..."

"Make sure Shishi does not succumb to the power of the Florescence. This is an order from the king."

"I'm not a Benibishi. I don't have to follow your orders."

"Then so be it. I shall leave it to your discretion. Will you save the life of a child or let it die?"

Smiling, Housen returned to the Human Realm, while Milo watched him go and bit his lip.

He saw right through me. I should have known I couldn't fool the Benibishi king...

As painful as it was to admit, he'd been strung along from the very beginning. Still, Milo couldn't let that get him down. Switching gears, he quickly set off down the valley, toward the Asura Realm.

"Come on, come on... Lookie here, it's your favorite food...!"

A prison guard hauled a handcart piled high with foul-smelling pots as countless pairs of gleaming eyes peered out at him from the undergrowth.

"Wait there, wait there. Not yet. You know what happens if you come out too soon. You get the shock!"

With practiced ease, the guardsman took a pot from the cart and scooped out its fly-ridden contents, tossing the slop into the grass. Immediately, the fierce animals lurking in the bushes began howling, rustling the trees and scattering their leaves.

"Ah-ha-ha-ha! Get along now, you animals! Can't have you tearing each other to shreds whenever it's feeding time!"

Whatever animals they were, they must have been very hungry indeed, for whenever the guard tossed the paltry amounts of feed into the grass, the sounds of fighting emerged again and again from the bushes.

"Haah...haah... Damn, feeding the animals sure is tiring. Let's just pack it in here. Nobody'll find out if I just dump the rest in the Sanzu River..."

The prison guard wiped his sweat-drenched neck with his robe and lifted open a manhole hidden in the grass. He was just about to tip the contents of the pot into it when...

"...Hmm? What's that? Something's not right with the river..."

As the rumbling shook the earth, the guard slowly approached the opening, peering into the darkness. Suddenly, his eyes widened.

"Th-the water...! It's... Aaaagh!"

A massive geyser of wastewater erupted from the hole, blasting the ground wide open. The guard didn't even have time to move out of the way; he was swept up by the current, thrown somersaulting through the air a few times, and deposited with a *Plop!* on the ground nearby. He looked up at the pillar of water, terrified.

"The river! There's something wrong with the river! Lady Gopis! Lady Gopis!"

The guard went running off, his clothes drenched. Shortly afterward, a huge red robot carrying two others in its hands flew up into the air. As all three of them bounced atop the fountain of water, Shishi took a deep breath of air.

"Phah! Th-thank goodness we're alive! I never would have dreamed of using a cave-in to block the river, forcing us up to the surface! Such a stupid, dangerous plan! That Milo is a genius, is he not, Brother?"

"Are you makin' fun of him or not? Make up your mind!"

Bisco tore the ivy out of his throat, retching as he did so. Soon the geyser subsided, and the three hopped down onto the grassy field.

"Is this still the prison? This don't look nothin' like the Preta Realm."

Bisco eyed the subtropical-looking surroundings, the thick trees and vegetation. His scarlet hair was all wet and fell limply across his face, sticking to his skin. Compared to his usual spiky hairdo, it seemed far less threatening, and somehow he now looked more like an innocent young boy than ever before.

...Now that I think about it, Brother is not that much older than me...

Shishi was captivated by the rare sight, but Bisco quickly shook his head like a dog, spraying water droplets everywhere, and in no time at all, his hair was back to normal again.

"Whoa! H-how did you do that?"

"Do what?"

"N-nothing. Ahem. You are right, Brother. This is the Beast Realm, the next section over from the Preta Realm."

As Bisco had already noted, the Beast Realm was a lot different from the Preta Realm, despite its close proximity. Where the Preta Realm had been barren and rocky, this section of the prison was full of plants and lush greenery, and the scent of the outdoors filled the air.

"The Beast Realm is home to neither human nor Benibishi. This is where the warden keeps his beastly prisoners—powerful animals that terrorize the land."

"A-animals?! He even locks up animals? Where does he draw the line?!"

"Satahabaki sees no difference between animals and people when it comes to passing judgment. Given that he could kill all these animals on the spot, though, perhaps it is out of the kindness of his heart that he grants them a place to live instead."

"I really don't understand, but I get that we don't wanna stay here for very long."

Bisco snatched Shishi's hand and pulled her up into his arms, just as a wild dog leaped out of the undergrowth, gnashing its sawblade-like teeth.

"Wh-whoa!"

"They're starvin'. Be careful."

The dog growled, chained by its neck to a post, and watched Shishi hungrily before giving up and retreating into the bushes.

"Th-that was close. Brother, I am all right now... Erm, y-you can let go of me."

"..."

"*Grrr. Vwoo.*"

"...What are you two doing?"

"Shh. Something's coming."

Shishi pricked up her ears and listened, and sure enough, beneath the sound of the wind, there was a strange chopping noise coming from far away.

"What is it? I've never heard anything like that before..."

"Looks like they sent some new shit after us. Shishi! Mark I! Look up there!"

Bisco pointed upward, and Shishi looked up to see several lizard-like creatures swooping down from the clear blue sky. Around their necks they wore some sort of propeller device that allowed them to control themselves mid-flight. This strange propeller-scarf was what produced the noise they had heard.

"Geckopters!" cried Shishi.

"So you *do* know what they are?!"

"They are animal weapons that protect the Beast Realm! There's too many of them! We can't escape!"

"Vwooo!"

All of a sudden, the Mark I gave a loud cry and stepped forward, opening its chest armor and unleashing a salvo of missiles. Each streaked toward its target in a plume of white smoke, blasting the creatures out of the sky.

"Yes! Well done, Mark I!"

Shishi watched the scorched bodies of the lizards fall from the sky like a rain of coal. Bisco, however, did not look so pleased. As the thick black smoke from the explosions washed over them, Bisco brought down his cat-eye goggles. His sensors picked up several more of the geckos, and he jumped toward his robot double and pushed him aside.

"Get outta the way, Mark I!"

"Vwoo!"

The geckos tore through the smoke, their propeller-necks cutting into the steel armor of the Mark I as easily as it sliced Bisco's flesh.

"Grh!"

"Brother!"

Shishi screamed at the sight of Bisco's blood. Bisco, however, didn't falter and stood up, scanning his smoke-filled surroundings with the goggles.

"You shouldn't have fired those missiles, Mark I. Look after Shishi. Leave the rest to me!"

"Vwoo."

"Brother! Let me fight as well!"

"Get outta the damn way! I gotta lotta stress to burn off!"

After finishing their successful swooping attack, the lizards turned around for another pass, but Bisco's goggles could pick them out through the smoke. They dived into the clouds once more, their propellers whirling, when...

Shwp!

One spinning kick from Bisco was enough to slice the poor creature in half, and its remains fell to the floor with a pathetic squeak. They continued attacking in waves, and Bisco's deft footwork dealt with the second, third, and fourth lizards as well. When the fifth came, Bisco dodged the propeller, grabbed it by the tail, and slammed it into a nearby tree.

"Seems like the tattoo doesn't care if I beat up animals," muttered Bisco. "Feel free to keep comin'. I could do this all day!"

The lizards attacked him from all angles, but Bisco's powerful body never let up for a moment. Like a god of war, he took out one after the other with his kicks, until soon the remainder fell back and hung there warily, waiting for the smoke to clear.

"...What the hell? They're weirdly organized for a bunch of geckos."

"Hee-hee-hee! You really are a witless brute, Akaboshi!"

Bisco suddenly heard a deep female voice chuckling, and a bespectacled woman wearing a white lab coat over her blue dress stepped out of the trees, surrounded by the flying lizards. As she laughed into her hand, her horseshoe earring chimed.

"You never cease to amaze, Akaboshi. I was just thinking how quiet it was at the gate. I never would have thought you'd swim through the Sanzu River to bypass it entirely! However, I'm afraid your crafty plots won't be enough to get you out of the Beast Realm."

Standing far away from Bisco, protected by the lizards at a safe distance, was one of the two villainous vice-wardens of Six Realms Penitentiary, Mepaosha.

"We meet again, four-eyes. You these things' mistress?"

"Pretty much. They're such good boys, all of them, and they're much harder to escape from than human guards."

"Makes sense to me. They do say that pets look a lot like their owners... These lizards have your teeth."

"...You damnable fungus. Don't you know how insensitive that is?"

Bisco's insult apparently struck a nerve, because Mepaosha frowned, her eye twitching, before taking a few deep breaths and calming back down.

"...Stay calm, he's not worth it," she told herself. "Just the ramblings of an idiot."

"So that the end of your little magic show? Got any white rabbits or charmed snakes? I got places to be, y'know."

"Hee-hee-hee. Oh, heaven forbid. We're only getting started. That was just a little taste of what's to come. From now on, I'll be commanding them directly. How long can you fight them off while looking after the kid and the tin can?"

"Why don't we quit chattin' and find out? I'm startin' to cool down."

"Suits me! Fly, my pretties! Chew him up and spit him out!"

At Mepaosha's order, the geckopters all descended on Bisco at once. Unlike their previous, chaotic attacks, this time they were all lined up in neat formation, jaws wide and revealing their arrays of sharp, pointed teeth.

"Hyaah!"

Bisco's kicks had reach and sharpness like a *naginata* blade, and with them, he mowed down the attacking geckos. However, having fought the man once before, Mepaosha had used her knowledge to come up with a cunning flight formation for the geckos. One that meant that no single kick could take out all of them at once.

Chomp!

"Rgh! Tch!"

"First blood!" Mepaosha chimed.

One lizard had gotten through and bitten Bisco in the thigh. As soon as he pulled it off, another formation came flying toward him.

"Ha-ha! Get it now? It's all about numbers, Akaboshi! ...Whoopsie! I'd better stay hidden. *You* might not be able to attack me through the Sakura Storm, but the Iron Giant over there's a different matter!"

"Grrr, that woman, she ain't even doing anything herself!"

"Hee-hee-hee! I do love the look on your face, Akaboshi! Fly! Fly! Don't let any of them near me! Nibble them to shreds!"

The Mark I was putting up a similarly valiant effort, but its lumbering movements were just too slow to keep up with the nimble geckopters, and their propellers kept finding opportunities in the gaps between attacks, slicing away little by little at the robot's armor. The Mark I couldn't even find a chance to transform its arms into more suitable weapons while constantly defending itself.

They're fast, and I can't just ignore them and run. She's got it all figured out!

Fending off the gecko army while also protecting the wounded Shishi was proving to be an impossible task. Slowly but surely, the enemies' attacks were finding their marks.

Dammit. If only Milo were here. He'd know what to do!

"Ah-ha-ha-ha-ha! Keep it up, Akaboshi, tin can! I don't mind using as many of my precious geckos as it takes! How many of them can you take down before you die?"

B-Brother...!

Shishi could do nothing but lie front-first on the floor, watching powerlessly as Bisco became more and more bloodied for her sake. She bit her lip hard, and the flower in her hair curled up into a bud.

I'm weak! So weak! Brother is getting hurt, and there's nothing I can—

Shishi's tearstained eyes suddenly fell upon a cage, covered in weeds. Inside that cage, some sort of feline creature watched the fight curiously.

Is that...a prisoner?

Shishi examined their surroundings. Beyond the geckos, all sorts of creatures fought against their chains, struggling for a closer look. Suddenly, she had an idea. She sprang to her feet and started running away from Mepaosha with the speed of a wild dog.

"Shishi! No! Stay close to us!"

"Aaah-ha-ha-ha! Fool, you're running the wrong way! The only thing you'll find over there is a huge cage and a dead end!"

Mepaosha grinned with glee at the sight of Bisco spurting blood and set all of the geckos on him at once.

"Hee-hee-hee! Let's say a hundred for Akaboshi, and fifty for the tin can! Time to see how many you can kill before your deaths! See if you can get a high score!"

"That bitch! We'll see who dies here!" Wiping away the blood that was dripping into his eyes from his torn brow, Bisco went back-to-back with the Mark I and faced off against the final gecko swarm. "Listen, Mark I! At this rate, we'll both be lizard food! You got any bright ideas to get us outta here'?"

"*Vwoo!*"

"What does that mean, dammit?!"

"Time to die! Go, my darlings!"

At their mistress's command, the geckopters all spun up their propeller-scarves and flew toward the pair. But just then...

Boom! The earth shook, as if from a giant's step, and the geckos all stopped short, mid-flight.

"...? What's wrong, my pretties? Huh? Wh-what's this?!"

The earthquake intensified as something gradually approached. Bisco and the Mark I both turned their heads to look.

What they saw was...

"Brother!!"

Shishi dropped out of the sky and landed between the other two. Her whole body was caked in sweat, and she had a determined look about her.

"Shishi! You're okay!"

"Mark I, take Bisco and jump! Hurry!"

"Whoa, what the hell are you—? Erkk!"

As Bisco's gaze drifted beyond Shishi, he stopped. What he saw there was a herd of giant buffalo, easily two tons each, rampaging toward them. All the animal inmates that had been eyeing the bunch until now suddenly scattered back into the long grass. The herd of buffalo trampled down trees in its way as though they weren't even there, and one unfortunate gecko who tried to escape was quickly gored on their horns and tossed off into the distance.

"That kid, she's gone and opened the Biwa Buffalo cage! How did she break the lock...?! No, there's no time! Oh, you little idiot, what have you done?!"

"Here, Shishi! Grab on!"

Bisco held on tightly to the Mark I's leg just as it fired off its rear thrusters, and he held out a hand toward Shishi. With a crack, he popped his arm out of its socket, giving it just enough reach for Shishi to grab on and for the Mark I to lift them all out of the way, narrowly escaping the buffalo stampede. One gecko that attempted to leap up and snatch Shishi's ankle was immediately caught on the buffalos' horns, and in the end, not a single one of the lizards was able to escape before being trampled by the sea of angry animals.

"...Nice going, Shishi!" said Bisco with a grin as he popped his arm back into place. "Biwa Buffalo are bred by guerillas in Shiga Prefecture to be able to cross Lake Biwa. I didn't expect to find a bunch of 'em all locked up in here."

"I am sorry...Brother...I tried... I was overwhelmed..."

"What are you sayin'? You just saved my damn life, and the robot's, too."

"Brother...!"

Behind Shishi's ear, the camellia flower shone crimson.

"*Vwoo.*"

"Don't worry, Mark I. I saw how you handled yourself out there. A word of advice, though, your movements are too big. When you're defendin' yourself against a bunch of opponents like that, you gotta be more compact..."

"*V...woo...*"

"B-Brother! The Mark I is falling!"

"What?"

"*Vwooo.*"

The Mark I tried to lower itself safely as its thrusters spluttered, until eventually they gave out completely and all three of them went crashing into the ground.

Thud!

"B-Brother! Look what we landed on!"

"*Cough.* That coulda gone a lot worse. These gecko carcasses saved our lives."

Bisco stood up and took a look around, but already the buffalo were nowhere to be seen, only the trampled corpses of the geckopters.

"Where'd that woman get to?" asked Bisco. "We need to finish things before she comes up with some new scheme. C'mon, Shishi, let's go!"

"Yes...Bro...ther..."

"Shishi? Hey, Shishi!"

Shishi collapsed to the floor, and Bisco hurried over and helped her to her feet. When Bisco's hand touched warm blood on the girl's back, however, his jade-green eyes shot wide.

"You...you're hurt!"

Turning Shishi over, Bisco saw two gaping holes, one near Shishi's shoulder blade and one in her side, spilling blood like a waterfall. The upper wound looked like something had gone right through the girl's body entirely, leaving a small opening in the front, near her collarbone.

"When you were running away from the buffalo, they got you..."

"Was I...of use to you again, Brother...?"

Shishi gave a fleeting smile, her face deathly pale. Blood dripped from the corners of her lips.

"I did all that I could...weak as I am... If this is the end for me... then so be it. Go, Brother... Save my father..."

"Cut the bullshit. I'm not lettin' you die like this."

"..."

Shishi was about to reply, but she passed out.

If only Milo were here, he began to think, but tried to suppress it. He took a deep breath and focused. He wrenched a horn from the head of a nearby water buffalo that was trampled in the stampede and, without a moment's hesitation, plunged it into his own chest.

...C'mon, your host is injured. Wake up. Wake up already!

Ignoring the pain, Bisco twisted the horn, pushing it deeper and deeper until it was touching his own heart. His blood spilled down and flecked Shishi's pale skin.

And then, tiny flecks, like molten gold, began spraying from his chest like sparks.

Yes... It's working...!

The blood dripping from the horn shone brighter and brighter until soon the two of them, and even the nearby Akaboshi Mark I, were bathed in a golden glow.

It was the glow of the Rust-Eater, the mushroom that defied human understanding. When Bisco brought himself to the brink of death, the spores lying dormant in his bloodstream awakened.

When Bisco saw his plan had worked, he pulled the horn free and slashed his own wrist with it.

"You wanted scars like mine, didn't you?" Bisco tore off Shishi's chest binding, revealing the whip marks on her back. Then he held his wrist over them, letting the Rust-Eater blood drip onto them. "Now you have battle scars, too. You can face your old man with pride."

"O-ooh... That's hot!" Shishi groaned. Bisco's brilliant blood flowed into her wounds, sealing them up in an instant.

...That's strange. She's absorbin' the spores much faster than usual...

Bisco stared closely at Shishi's incredible speed of regeneration. As soon as the Rust-Eater blood touched her wounds, some sort of thin, plantlike fiber came out of Shishi's body and sewed them shut by itself. The ivy that covered her body began changing color, too, from black to orange. It wrapped itself around Shishi, tightening around her wounds and stemming the bleeding.

Bisco knew, of course, that his Rust-Eater blood had regenerative properties, but this was quite unlike what he had expected to see. It was almost like Shishi was feeding on the Rust-Eater itself.

Is it the ivy doin' all this? Well, whatever. If it heals her, then it's all the same to me.

Bisco breathed a sigh of relief as he watched the color return to Shishi's face. Then he heard a voice.

"Ha-ha-ha! I can't believe you let Mepaosha give you such a thrashing, Akaboshi!"

A woman's loud laughter came through a megaphone. The voice was deep and had an arrogant quality quite unlike Mepaosha's. It was the other vice-warden of Six Realms, Gopis.

Bisco tied a cloth around his bleeding wrist and turned to face the voice.

"...It's the blond one! Where are you hiding?!"

"Oh, I'm not like Mepaosha, fool! I won't run or hide!"

Thud! Thud! A booming sound echoed from the forest, and Bisco turned to see an enormous creature advancing toward him, shaking the earth with each step. He watched as an incredibly large leg came crashing down, squashing cages of imprisoned beasts as though it never even noticed they were there.

"Vwooo!"

"Damn, she's crazy! What's she keepin' one of these here for?!" Bisco stood in line with the Mark I, protecting Shishi, and he looked up at the gigantic beast. "It's a Forest-Guzzler! How'd she managed to train one of those?!"

"I must thank you for making Mepaosha look like a fool, but Dahak here is nothing like that woman's puny lizards. His tongue will swallow the lot of you whole, and then I'll be the next warden!"

Before Bisco stood something more like a mountain than a living creature, casting a dark shadow across the group. The Forest-Guzzler was an evolved form of tapir, with a long tongue like an anteater's and pointed teeth, and so greedy that it could devour a village in a single bite if it so wished. It was so powerful that to get rid of one, you needed an army, and though Bisco had encountered them in the wild before, never had he seen one that had been domesticated.

The Forest-Guzzler swept up two of the water buffalos in its long tongue and cast them into its mouth while Bisco looked on in awe. The bovines let out one last cry before the creature's sharp teeth tore them to shreds. All the rest of the Biwa Buffalo had apparently become food for the beast already.

"It's big, but it's got an obvious weak point," said Bisco, huddling close to the Mark I and whispering. *"Its brains are right behind its eyes. Blow 'em out in one shot!"*

The Mark I gave an affirmative *"Vwoo,"* and Bisco lifted the unconscious Shishi onto his shoulder before running into the forest. Jumping between the trees, he worked his way up to the Forest-Guzzler's face and spun round so fast he was nothing but a blur.

"Rrraaaghh!"

He brought his heel down hard on the creature's nose in a kick that could shatter heaven and earth. The monster staggered, and in that moment the Mark I shot forward, reaching out with its thick arms.

"Go, Mark I!"

"*Vwooo!*"

From the Mark I's outstretched hands came a pair of electromagnets that landed neatly in the Forest-Guzzler's nostrils. They then began glowing with a pale light and crackling with electricity, sending a powerful current through the creature's body.

"That's it, Mark I! Keep it up! …Huh?!"

Bisco noticed the fight remaining in the Forest-Guzzler's eyes too late to warn the Mark I, and so with no other choice, he kicked the robot aside.

"*Vwoo!*"

The Mark I flew back, narrowly avoiding the monster's claws in the process. But before Bisco could even catch his breath, the Forest-Guzzler swung its huge head, smashing it sideways into Bisco.

"Grh!"

The attack was so powerful that Bisco dropped Shishi and went flying backward, where he collided with a tree and slumped to the ground.

"*Ha-ha-ha! You fool, I told you Dahak isn't like those lizards! Your feeble attempts at intimidation won't work on him! First things first…I think I'll be taking that child off your hands!*"

"Shishi! Dammit!"

The Forest-Guzzler snatched Shishi off the ground with its tongue, and in no time at all, she was pulled into the beast's mouth. Just before its jaws could close, however, Bisco displayed his superhuman might by leaping all the way into its mouth and holding its jaws open with his hands.

"*Wh-what?! You fool! How long do you think you'll last?!*"

"D-dammit…! Shishi, you've gotta wake up! Shishi!"

"…?! B-Bro…ther…"

"Shishi!"

Bisco's voice caused Shishi to open her eyes. Groaning with pain, she twisted herself, eventually managing to break free of the Forest Guzzler's tongue.

"Grab hold, quick!"

Shishi reached for Bisco's outstretched arm and was just about to touch it when…

Snap! came the crack of a whip, which wrapped itself around Bisco's wrist and pulled him out of the monster's mouth entirely.

"You think I'd let you do that, fool?!"

"Wh-whoaaa?!"

Gopis came sliding across the creature's spine and down off its nose, dragging Bisco down with her and slamming him into the floor with her whip. Looking up from the grass, he watched as the Forest Guzzler's jaws viciously snapped shut.

"Aahhh! Shishi!"

"That makes one less foolish child in the world who dared to stand against me. Heh-heh-heh. Such little meat on that scrawny body of hers; I don't suppose she'll make much more than a snack for poor Dahak here."

"You…"

Bisco stood up to protect the Mark I, who had used up all his power in the last attack and now lay exhausted on the ground. With a blood-soaked face and brilliant jade-green eyes, he glared at Gopis with an uncharacteristically righteous fury.

"Make him spit her up, right now, and I'll let you keep your front teeth. Top and bottom."

"You think I'm just gonna roll over and do what you say? You're even more of a fool than I—"

Fwsh! There was a blast of wind, and before Gopis could tell what had happened, she was flying backward. Bisco's straight punch had caught her right on the nose, launching her into the weeds.

"Ghuh! *Cough, cough.* Heh. Heh-heh. Ah-ha-ha-ha-ha-ha-ha!"

Gopis's pained grunts slowly transformed into gleeful laughter. As the blood streamed down her face, she looked at Bisco, down on one knee and growling in agony.

"Grh…Rrggh."

"Did you just hit me? You did, didn't you?"

It was the Sakura Storm, the tattoo Satahabaki had given him. In return for punching Gopis, it had grown so that it now stretched down to his stomach and across half of his face.

"You fool. It may be one thing to fight against beasts while under Lord Satahabaki's curse, but it's quite another to lay a hand on a guard! And the vice-warden at that!"

Crack!

"Gughh!"

"Your villainy knows no bounds. Death is the only cure, Akaboshi!"

Crack! Crack! Gopis's whip was like a knife across Bisco's skin, but with the Sakura Storm paralyzing him, he could do nothing but bear the pain.

"You gave me! A nosebleed! And ruined! My beautiful face! I'll kill you! I'll whip you to shreds! I'll flay your skin and turn it into a nice rug, Akaboshi!"

Gopis's leather whip tore repeatedly into Bisco's flesh. However, the jade glimmer in Bisco's eyes flared even brighter. Gopis hesitated.

"Who does he think he is?!"

Humiliated by the embarrassment of flinching from an immobile opponent, she snapped her whip once more toward Bisco's right eye. There was a heart-rending *Snap!* as her brutal attack tore up the side of his face. Seeing his eye socket dripping with blood, Gopis grinned.

"I've finally ridded you of one detestable eye, Akaboshi! Now for the other one…"

"Rooooaaaar!"

"Hold on, Dahak! I'm just getting to the good bit!"

"Rrrr. Grgh! G-grrg…"

"H-huh?! Dahak, what's wrong?!"

Gopis spun around to see the source of her pet's strange sounds, and…

Bwoom!

…something big and red erupted out of the monster's hill-like body.

"D-Dahak! What's happening?! Akaboshi, what did you do?!"

"…*Cough.* I ain't done nothin'…yet."

Bwoom! A second explosion, and a second unfurling of something large and crimson...

"*Grooooaaaar!*"

The Forest Guzzler writhed in pain and took several lumbering steps to steady itself, shaking the earth and knocking Bisco flat on the floor. Just as he was about to be crushed beneath the monster's large foot, the thick steel arm of the Mark I pulled him to safety.

"Mark I... What the hell's goin' on?!"

Bisco's eyes were glued to what he was witnessing, so much so that he forgot his pain. Enormous flowers were tearing Dahak's body apart. Giant scarlet camellias grew all along the undercarriage between the tapir's four legs, while some sort of ivy, shining like gold, sprouted forth to ensnare the colossal beast.

Bwoom! Bwoom!

The ivy reached all the way around the Forest Guzzler's tongue, while another camellia flower exploded inside its mouth. Dahak struggled for a few minutes, but before long, his life energy was sapped completely by the flowers and he fell to the earth with a crash.

"Wh-what happened?! How could this...?" asked Gopis in disbelief.

"Don't...you...dare...!"

"Wh-what?!"

From overhead, she heard a deep, oppressive voice. The body of the tapir was sliced open from within, and out crawled a young girl, drenched in blood.

"Don't you dare lay a hand on Brother, Gopis!"

"Th-the kid! How is she still alive?!"

Shishi lashed out with a whip of ivy, and Gopis retaliated with her own. Shishi's attack was deflected ever so slightly, and she hit the ground, causing crimson flowers to burst to life where the blow had landed.

"Mark I! Take Brother and get him somewhere safe!"

"*Vwoo.*"

"Shishi! How come you're suddenly so strong?!"

"There is a flower within me, too! Your blood brought it to life! But I can't control it yet, so go! I'll catch up later!"

"You fool! Think you can escape?!" roared Gopis, lashing her whip. "Flourish!"

Shishi thrust her fist, and the ivy swarmed together, forming into a blade. Using the ivy sword, Shishi cut apart the vice-warden's whip, and then as she stood there, little buds began blossoming all across its length, shining golden like Bisco's blood.

"Gopis. You have attacked not just me but Brother as well!"

Shishi's voice was no longer that of an innocent child. It was filled with hate for the woman standing before her. Gopis was sweating so hard it was ruining her mascara.

"I feel...strong. Brother has granted me the power of the sun. Now I have the power to punish you...the power to kill you!"

"*You?* Kill *me?* Ha-ha-ha! Don't get any bright ideas, you Benibishi brat!" Gopis took up a spare whip from her belt and thrust it at Shishi. "Fools, the lot of you! The Benibishi are our slaves! You can't defy humanity! It's written into your genes! You did pretty well to save Akaboshi like that, but all you've earned is the right to die in his place! The only choice you have left is whether you'll let me torture you a bit first!"

"We cannot defy humanity...?"

"That's right, so why don't you shut up and come back to being my plaything? I'll let you live if you—"

Smash! In an instant, Shishi crossed the distance between them, delivering a lightning-fast kick to Gopis's knee. The crack of her shattered shin was plain for all to hear. Before the vice-warden could even calculate what had happened, she was on her back, screaming in pain and terror.

"Gh...ghaaaaaagh?! Wh-what just...?"

"How about that? Does that not count?"

"E-eeeeeek! Ghh?!"

Shishi's eyes burned like two dark flames, kindled by the combined vengeance of her slaughtered brothers and sisters. Neither she nor Gopis could possibly know that it was her awakening that allowed her to break free of the Benibishi genetic programming. She simply knew what she had to do and did it. Within her, she felt a burning energy that turned into scorching iron, heating up her mind and spurring her body forward.

"Take this!"

Finding weakness in the girl's momentary emotional outburst, Gopis lashed with her whip. The vice-warden's aim and technique were sharp as ever, tearing at the Benibishi girl's beautiful face.

"..."

"Hah... Hah! Stay back, fool! You're nothing but a slave! A child! Know your place!"

"...You think...this is enough...?"

"...Eee...eeeek!"

"I've been such a crybaby...all this time..."

The diagonal cut across Shishi's face was dripping blood, and her eyes were devoid of mercy. She was like an executioner, ready to lay down her judgment here and now. Gopis lashed out once more with her whip, but this time Shishi caught it in her ivy, wrenched it out of Gopis's hand, and used it to strike at her broken leg.

"Gyaaagh! A...aaaahh!"

"You ugly woman...! You filthy woman...!"

Snap! Snap! Snap!

"Gwaaaah! Stoppp! Please, please let me go! I-I'll stop bullying you! I'll never do it again!"

"Where has all your pride gone, you worm?!" Shishi glowered. "Is the woman who made our lives a living hell truly so small?!"

She whipped Gopis again and again, surrendering control to the anger that drove her. The whip tore through dress and beautiful skin alike until Gopis was nothing more than a bloody mess in shredded clothes, by which time the sturdy leather whip was in tatters, and Shishi returned to her senses at last, panting.

"Haah...haah...haah...haah...!"

"Waah... *Sniff*... Waaaaah... Please stop... Please let me go..."

"..."

The woman who'd slaughtered Shishi's kin now lay at her feet, a defeated and pathetic disgrace. Any satisfaction Shishi might have felt was wrapped in a layer of meaninglessness, and instead of doing anything, she just stood there, steeped in an emotion she couldn't begin to describe.

"P-please...forgive me...," Gopis whined. "Please...just let me live..."
She wrapped her bloodied arms around Shishi's legs and nuzzled her boots.

"W-waah! What are you—? Get off me!"

"Do what you want to me," she cried, barely coherent. "Torture me, abuse me, just don't kill me! Forgive everything I've done, and let me go... Please..."

"W-wah... Stop it!"

"I'll be your slave. Please! Mistress Shishi! Master Shishi? I'll be your loyal dog. Please...please make me your slave..."

"S-slave...?"

A human...slave? To me? A Benibishi...?!

Before Shishi could even register what she was doing, she raised her foot, soaked with Gopis's blood, and brought it down hard on the fiendish vice-warden's hand. Gopis let out a squeak of pain...and then presented her body once more, as if begging to be stepped on again.

At that moment, a shiver of sweet delight swept up Shishi's spine. She didn't have the words to describe it, but it was a sadistic joy, the pleasure of breaking another and bending them to your will. For someone who had been forced to endure humiliation all her life, it was her first taste of the tantalizing nectar of revenge.

She pressed down on Gopis's hand once more. The woman emitted a feeble whimper...and crawled closer. Again, she pressed down, harder this time. Gopis didn't resist. She obeyed and whined...

"...Ha-ha. Ah-ha-ha... Ah-ha-ha-ha-ha!"

Shishi barely even noticed the laugh that escaped her lips. She went to stamp on the other hand this time, but just as she was about to bring her foot down...

"Having fun, Shishi?"

At that familiar voice, Shishi returned to her senses.

"Don't let me stop you. Make her pay for everything she put you through."

"W-w-waah!"

Her face suddenly drained, and Shishi looked down with fear at the woman curled up at her feet. Raising her ivy sword, she thrust it down as though trying to erase everything that had just happened with one fatal blow.

"Won/shad/keler/snew! (Protect target from attacks!)"

The mantra created a hemispherical shield of Rust that intercepted the attack, deflecting the ivy blade and making Shishi's wrist sting. She gritted her teeth, eyes twitching, and turned to face the direction the mantra had come from. Standing there, dressed in a jailer's robe, was a boy with sky-blue hair.

How is he here…?!

As soon as the question presented itself in Shishi's mind, she realized the answer. Escaping the Human Realm would be of little difficulty for the partner of her master, Bisco. What worried her more was his objection to what had just happened.

"Why did you stop me?" she asked. "She's pure evil, Milo. Do you have any idea how many of us she's killed? I do. I laid them all to rest. And now I shall exact my revenge!"

"Then go ahead. You've had plenty of opportunities. But I'm not going to stand by while you torture her."

"I-I'm not! Sh-she just asked me to, that's all!"

"It was beautiful." Milo's pretty face bore an expression cold as ice. "Your flower, I mean. When you were stomping her into the dirt, it looked more beautiful than ever."

"A…aaaahhh!!"

"I thought those scars made you fit to be king. I thought they were proof that you would never forget the pain of oppression. But I was wrong, wasn't I? They were nothing more than a tally; each one a grudge you sought to repay! Am I right, Shishi?!"

"SHUT UUUUP!!!"

Shishi leaped like an orca breaking the water for its prey, swinging her ivy sword at Milo, but quick as a flash, the young doctor deflected it using the sheathed *wakizashi* King Housen had loaned him. After a few indecisive exchanges, he sprang back.

"Throw down your sword!" he yelled. "I don't want to fight you!"

"Shut up! Haah…haah…! Dammit…dammit!"

"You have a darkness lurking within you, Shishi, and that's something you'll never be able to escape from. You need to accept it and learn to live with it if your life is to have any meaning."

"You're trying to say...I'm not fit for the throne!"

"Not now. Not while that darkness drives you. Lower your sword. Your power is for opening the path ahead. It's not to be used selfishly."

Shishi paused and took a deep breath, as if contemplating Milo's words, but the sword in her hand remained steady.

"That's so like you...Milo..."

"..."

"You're dazzling. You're honest, pure, and brave. You've never felt the cold steel of a chain around your ankle. You've been free to gallivant around the world...at Brother's side...!"

"Shishi. Put it down..."

"What am I supposed to do until I become as gracious as you?! Stand by while they slaughter my brothers and sisters?! Lay their cold bodies to rest in the uncaring earth without a word?! Don't talk like you know what I've had to go through!"

Shishi's crimson eyes burned with an envious heat. Her flower began scattering shining pollen that lit up Milo's face.

"...You're so beautiful, so full of life. That's because you have Brother to protect you..."

But then...

"...It's not fair. Why does he keep you around?"

...her voice grew dark, laden with malice.

"I am far stronger than you. I can protect him where you can't. All you can do is hide behind him! You don't deserve to be his partner!"

Milo had patiently listened to Shishi, letting her anger run its course. But as soon as she said those words, it was as if a bolt of lightning ran through his crystal-clear eyes.

"...I know you care a lot, Shishi. That's a good thing. And you're just a child. I know you don't mean it. But I just have to ask...

"What…was that last thing you said?"

It was like a chill wind blew from somewhere within Milo's very soul, sweeping across Shishi, turning everything to ice.

"Grh?!"

She froze, pinned to the spot by this indescribable aura. A single petal fell from the flower behind her ear. Before her stood a completely different person than the Milo she knew, an azure flame who seemed likely to burn her to a crisp with only his glare.

Wh-what just came over him?!

"You said I'm not strong enough to protect him, Shishi. Well, I invite you to put that theory to the test. I'll warn you, though. Unlike Bisco, I don't play nice."

"…Raaaaargh!"

Spurred on by the look in Milo's eyes, Shishi leaped forward and swung her sword. Milo caught it on his scabbard and drew the blade.

Ka-ching! Ching! Ching! Ka-ching!

The pair's blades, guided by their slender arms, clashed faster than the eye could follow, skimming both combatants' vitals many times, like a dance performed on the brink of life and death.

H-he knows the king's dance! But how?!

Shishi's dance of death incorporated a number of secret techniques designed for pure lethality, but Milo brushed them all aside without even breaking a sweat.

Clang!

He made it all the way to the fifteenth step! How is he still alive?!

"I saw Housen's dance, you know."

"…?! What?!"

In Shishi's moment of shock, Milo swung the *wakizashi*'s sheath, striking her hard on the wrist. Shishi suppressed her cry of pain and snarled.

"Y-you're telling me…you figured out my father's dance? After seeing it once?!"

"I couldn't even keep up with his. But yours, I can. It's written all over your face where you're going to strike next. All I have to do is pay attention and block."

"You can see what I'm planning...?!"

"Listen." Milo cracked his neck, letting his sky-blue hair fall to one side. "How are you ever going to protect Bisco like that? I'm sorry, but he's a thousand times stronger than you could ever imagine. You're free to look up to him, but don't expect him to play along with your games."

"My...games...?!"

"Come on. Don't tell me you're done already."

Shishi stood there gasping for breath, but Milo only watched her with a glacial look in his eyes, beckoning her with his finger.

"I'll play with you for as long as it takes, until you learn what my partner couldn't teach. What's the matter, lost the will to go on?"

"Don't you dare look down on me, Milo!!"

In response to her anger, the power welled up in Shishi's body once more, and the flower behind her ear blossomed into bloom, while her ivy glowed bright orange.

"Raaaagh!"

...!!

Shishi jumped into the air and swung her ivy sword with incredible force. Milo blocked it on the *wakizashi*, but there was more power behind it than anything the girl had shown thus far.

She's much stronger than before. I knew it...she's dangerous. She has too much hidden potential.

"Dance of Water! Step four! Step five! Dance of Thunder! Step six! Seven! Eight!"

Shishi's sword dance closed in on Milo without even giving him time to breathe. This time, Shishi varied the tempo of the dance, going faster and slower in an attempt to slip past Milo's defenses. Milo could still read Shishi's intent and see all the attacks coming, but now the force behind them was so much stronger that he was struggling to keep up, and the back of his neck became slick with sweat.

"How long do you think that sword will last against mine?! Give up, Milo! You saved my life, so kneel to me, and I shall let you live!"

"You sound a lot more cheerful now. That's good."

"You'll change your tune...once I land a hit, Milo!"

Shishi spun in the air and sliced the ground at Milo's feet.

Bwoom!

"Whoa?!"

"Now!"

Beneath Milo, an enormous camellia flower grew from the ground with such intensity that it made him reel backward. Shishi swung her ivy blade and...

Snap!

...Milo barely deflected her sword with his. Shishi grinned. At long last, Milo's blade had been unable to weather the constant blows and had snapped in half.

"You're in my way! If you're so eager to refuse my mercy, then die!"

She slashed at his shoulder, and Milo narrowly managed to evade. He snatched up the broken tip of his sword and gripped it tightly, drawing his own blood.

"*Won/ul/viviki...*"

"Diiiie!"

"*...snew! (Grant caster desired weapon!)*"

Clang!

Shishi's next attack, aimed directly at Milo's face, was blocked by a dagger of rust. Its blade was the piece of broken *wakizashi* that Milo had picked up, while the guard and grip were formed of green-glowing rust.

"You're amazing, Shishi," Milo said calmly as their blades locked. "Just think of how strong you'd be if you were calm."

"Still you dare to resist me! How is that shoddy improvisation going to save you?!"

"Let me ask you a question instead. Isn't that weapon a little long for someone your size?"

Milo pushed up with his blade, forcing Shishi's ivy sword overhead.

Then, in a flash, he followed up with a slice to Shishi's wrist, tearing apart the ivy itself.

"Wh-whaa?!"

Milo was like a whirlwind. It all happened so fast, Shishi didn't even feel the pain. She staggered back in surprise. The doctor's speed was on a whole new level compared to when he used the *wakizashi*. The ivy, cut free from Shishi's body, lost its orange luster and drooped down weakly before crumbling to ash.

"M-my sword! How?! That thing's no more than a toy!"

"Daggers are more my style anyway. And Bisco won't like it if you call them toys."

Shishi summoned the rest of her strength, trying to reform the ivy blade, but Milo swiftly delivered a flying kick and pinned her to the ground, holding the knife to her throat.

"R...aaargh! Dammit! Damn it all!"

"..."

"Still, you pity me, Milo! Kill me now, or else I'll make sure you regret it! I'll repay this humiliation a thousand times over! I'll kill you! Kill you!"

"I don't think you're in any position to be making demands."

Milo held her down with more strength than his slender arms seemed capable of and gazed into Shishi's eyes.

"I'm not going to kill you," he said, his azure jewels shimmering. "You can try me as many times as you like; the outcome will always be the same."

"U...urgh! Dammit! I'll kill you! I'll kill you!"

"The king must cast himself aside. Only for the people shall his flowers bloom."

"...Grhhh!!"

As soon as Shishi heard Milo's words, she stopped. The power left her arms, and soon she was just breathing in and out rapidly.

"They're a little strict for my tastes, but those are the words your father told me."

"...Fa...ther..."

The camellia behind Shishi's ear, grown rampant with anger, slowly retracted into its bud at Milo's words and at the starlight in his eyes.

...There. You've done what you must.

Milo spun his emerald dagger a couple times and stowed it away.

"Leave the rest to Bisco and me. Go wait somewhere until this is all over. Maybe by then you'll have cooled off."

"...Ah, wait, Milo! Don't you dare run away!"

"I'm perfectly happy to accept your revenge...later."

After he judged that Shishi had calmed down a little, Milo turned and took off like the wind, following the clear footprints of the Akaboshi Mark I. Shishi could do nothing but watch him go and wipe away her bitter tears.

Then, out of the corner of her eye, she spotted the defeated Gopis, attempting to crawl away on her stomach. Gripped by anger, she reached out her right hand, the ivy coming together to form her blade...

"...Ghh."

But suddenly, she stopped, took a deep breath, and clenched her fist in front of her breast. As the fires of wrath whirling within her began to flicker and fade, so, too, did the ivy sword dismantle itself, the vines retreating once more into Shishi's wrist, and Gopis escaped into the bushes.

...Milo.

Milo...

Milo was right.

My flower is the people's flower...

It is meant for far more important ends than this.

Shishi stood there, eyes closed, and shook her head to dispel her doubt. Her crimson eyes flickered open, and she set off after Milo on the trail of the Mark I, leaping across the wilderness with the grace and speed of a panther.

"So you're saying these bugs are able to reverse the effects of the Sakura Storm?"

"Hee-hee... Who knows? Maybe you need something else as well..."

"You know, there are mushrooms that attach to the brain and force their host to speak the truth."

"Eeeek! Yes, that's all you have to do, I promise! Implant the vice-warden's deluxe scarab, and it'll stop the spread of the tattoo!"

Inside one of the guards' tents in the Beast Realm lay Mepaosha, tied up in chains made for securing the animals. Milo had rescued her from her fate only to subject her to his own interrogation. Lying before him was the body of his partner, rendered unconscious by the cursed tattoo, as well as the similarly disabled Mark I, who had run out of power and was currently acting as Milo's operating table.

"Satahabaki's curse is meant to brainwash powerful criminals into becoming his prison guards, but sometimes the pollen gets out and infects others."

"I see. So that's why the guards all have these scarabs implanted in them, to counteract against infection."

"You're a smart guy, Panda. I developed this cure myself. Isn't it great? ...Hey, don't ignore me! Look, I can't fight like Gopis anyway! You don't need these chains..."

Milo ignored Mepaosha and began the procedure. Bisco's tattoo had grown to where it was even entering his body through the whip marks, and now he lay unconscious in the Mark I's arms.

…Hmm, looks like Mepaosha was telling the truth. This scarab seems to be counteracting the cherry blossoms. Once I implant it—

Milo suddenly froze as he smelled a sweet, flowery fragrance. After a short pause, he glanced at Mepaosha, then turned and walked outside.

There he found Shishi, her violet hair blowing gently in the wind.

"…"

"…"

Milo prepared to reach for his dagger at any time, but for now his hands remained still.

"So this is where you were…"

"Shishi. I already told you. If you want a rematch, it'll have to—"

"Milo. I'm sorry for what just happened. Thank you for stopping me."

"Huh?"

"…I almost strayed from the king's path. It's thanks to you that I didn't."

Milo was a little surprised. He gazed back at Shishi's face. He saw none of the fear and anger that had ruled her before.

Did she manage to rein in her emotions already? Impossible. She's still too young!

According to Housen, an irrepressible outburst of emotion followed a Benibishi's first awakening, and it took a long time for that to subside. Shishi had to deal with not only that but the unjust slaughter of her brothers and sisters, all with the perpetrator standing right before her. Never had Milo imagined she would be able to calm herself down so quickly.

However, the beautifully blooming camellia behind the girl's ear meant it was impossible for her to hide her emotions. Her gentle, determined expression was no lie.

"I'm sorry. That is all. Please take care of Brother."

"Shishi!"

As Shishi turned to leave, Milo ran up to her and embraced her. Shishi gasped in surprise before giving a sigh of relief and looking into Milo's eyes.

"I'm sorry, too," Milo said. "I said such terrible things to you. Are you really feeling better now?"

"...When I looked at Gopis, I felt my blood boil...but I'm okay now. As a prince, I must never raise my sword in anger or jealousy. I must set an example for my people, and for my father." Shishi's eyes glimmered crimson, and she looked a little embarrassed as she spoke. "It was Brother who gave me this power, so I must not use it to satisfy my own selfish desires. I must use it to defend my people, as the Benibishi's next king."

Shishi's words were quiet yet firm, confident. Shishi's peerless strength of character went straight through to Milo's heart, and he shook her by the shoulders, staring into her eyes.

"Your focus is incredible, Shishi. It's amazing! Bisco fires his arrows to satisfy his own selfish desires all the time!"

"Brother... Milo, how is he?"

"Come and see. You saved his life, so I'm sure he'll want to thank you. ...Oh, wait, he's out cold."

Shishi politely refused Milo's hand and softly shook her head.

"As long as he is safe," she said to the puzzled Milo. "With you looking after him, I am sure he will be all right. Take care of them both."

"What do you mean? Where are you going?"

"I shall go ahead to the Asura Realm. I can gather intel ahead of your arrival, and I am also worried about the other Benibishi."

"Wait, by yourself?! Just wait until Bisco is better, and we'll all go together!"

"There is no time. Now that we have attacked the vice-wardens, there's no telling when Satahabaki might resort to force to stop us. If that happens, my people will be finished. I am good at hiding; let me scout ahead."

"But, Shishi..."

"I made the Man-Eating Panda draw his blade. Do you still think I am not strong enough?"

"Urgh..."

Milo hesitated to take Shishi's words at face value, but he saw clearly the determination that sparkled in the crimson eyes, and so after a while, he nodded.

"...Okay. Just...don't do anything stupid. I have a plan. Listen to this."

Milo leaned over and whispered into Shishi's ear so that Mepaosha couldn't hear him back in the tent. Shishi listened intently, nodding from time to time. When he had finished, Milo looked a little worried, but Shishi shot him a reassuring smile.

"It was your plan that got us out of the Preta Realm," she said. "I'll trust you, and I'll get it done. Just watch!"

"Shishi, if things get dangerous, stay out of trouble. We'll be there as soon as we can!"

Shishi returned a smile and nodded before heading off to the Asura Realm. Milo watched her go, then went back into the tent, thinking.

...It's not right. Why should that one girl have to bear her family's burden? What is Housen thinking? He's her father, for crying out loud!!

"E-erm..." Mepaosha's voice broke the silence. "Since I told you about the scarabs, you think you could untie me...?"

"Shh. I'm thinking."

"Hey! I'm not joking around! Let me go! I really need to...you know...!"

"Go where you're sitting. Not my problem."

"You've gotta be kidding me! I'm gonna be thirty next year, you know! Help! Somebody save me!!"

Milo paid no attention to the struggling Mepaosha, instead turning his gaze back to Bisco. As long as his partner had the energy to run around freely, everything would be okay. With that singular thought for comfort, the genius doctor set about stitching up his wounds.

"There's a great gorge separating the Beast and Asura Realms, spanned by a bridge that goes from one gate to the other. That bridge will be heavily guarded, so there's no way we can take it. Instead, I've put up a separate bridge a little west of there."

"You...put up a bridge? By yourself?"

"Only the people I authorize can walk on it. Be careful, though, I don't know how much it can hold. Try not to take anything too heavy with you." Running low through the weeds, Shishi recalled her conversation with Milo. As she drew closer to the Animal Realm's main gate, the guards' patrols became more and more frequent. However, any rustle of the bushes was thought to be just some animal resident of the prison out for a walk, so it was a simple matter to remain undetected.

...What does he mean he put up a bridge?

Milo, and Bisco, too, for that matter, uttered such bizarre statements as a matter of course that it was difficult for Shishi to keep up. However, when she thought back over what the pair had accomplished up until now, anything they said sounded believable. So Shishi followed Milo's instructions and soon arrived at the chasm.

There's the main gate... A little west, he said.

Shishi flung off her tattered shoes and glanced at the great bridge before continuing barefoot. However, she could find neither hide nor hair of the route Milo described.

"H-huh? This *is* west, right? Where's Milo's bridge?"

Shishi slowed down in bewilderment, and suddenly she spotted something glinting out of the corner of her eye. She squinted at it and rushed over.

"...There's some sort of floating dust. Is this the bridge?"

Stretching all the way to Shishi's feet from the far bank of the gorge some seventy or eighty meters away was a mass of glittering particles. Certainly, it looked so faint that from far away it would be difficult to spot, and even up close it didn't look like anything that would take Shishi's weight. Shishi reached out over the deep abyss and gave it a tentative touch.

Crch!

"Waah!"

Shishi recoiled in surprise, but before her eyes a solid emerald floor began to form. It seemed that the girl's touch had activated the particles somehow.

"This is...Milo's bridge!"

Shishi stared at the floating platform and gulped. Now was not the time to get to the bottom of whatever strange magic was responsible for this. She steeled her resolve and stepped out onto it.

Crch. Crch. Crch.

"Oh dear, oh dear, oh dear…"

The particles crystallized, creating an emerald floating platform wherever she walked. Still, stepping out onto what was essentially dust and hoping it would hold her weight was a considerable task, made even more terrifying by the deadly drop below. Shishi couldn't keep the panic out of her voice.

I m-m-mustn't be afraid! …I have to hurry! The others are in danger!

"Hold up! What's that? Hey! We got an escapee! They're crossin' the gorge!"

"What're they walkin' on?! Hey! Bring the fanghounds!"

Uh-oh!!

Shishi heard the cries of the Beast Realm guards and turned to see a group of guards heading over, their trained fanghounds leading the way.

Shishi exhaled all the air in her lungs. Then she took a deep breath.

I can't give up here! The others are relying on my help!!

Her crimson eyes sparkled, and she began running across the floating cloud. *Crch! Crch! Crch! Crch!* With each step, another section of the bridge materialized beneath her feet.

"Follow them! Don't let them escape, or our pay will get docked!"

"Send the dogs across first! Go! Go! Bite! Bite!"

At the guard's command, the dogs rushed toward Shishi with frightening speed. Shishi was a fast runner, but even she was no match for them.

"Oh no, at this rate— Huh?!"

Crck!

Shishi's next step made a subtly different sound, and she looked down. There at her feet, she saw a huge crack in the material of the bridge. It was getting weaker.

"Th-there's too much weight! The bridge can't take it!"

"You there! Freeze! Hands up! Come back and be our slave, and we'll let you live!"

"Stop! Don't come any closer! You're in danger!"

"Gah-ha-ha! You're the one in danger here, kid. Now let's be sensible and— Wha?!"

Not even two seconds after Shishi's warning, the emerald bridge began loudly crumbling from the Beast Realm side, reverting to glittering dust and falling into the valley below.

"Waaargh! Th-the bridge! It's collapsing!"

"Help meee! Aaaaagh!"

The bridge quickly began disintegrating, dragging several of the guards down into the chasm with it. Shishi's hair straightened at the sight, and she resumed running full tilt toward the other side.

"Ruff! Ruff! Raaarr!"

Soon the crumbling bridge reached the hounds as well, and even they could not outrun its collapse. Shishi continued to run, and just as the floor was about to disappear beneath her, she made one last leap of faith and reached out her arm for the far cliff.

"Flourish!"

Vines of sunlight-colored ivy shot from her wrists like a multi-tailed whip, wrapping around a tree that grew from the earth of the far cliff.

Yes!

Shishi's brief moment of triumph was cut short by the blinding pain she suddenly felt in her ankle. She looked down to see one of the fanghounds, its jaws clamped tightly around her leg in a last-ditch effort to escape death.

"Get off!"

Swinging from her vine, Shishi and the fanghound both went crashing into the cliff face. The tree began creaking under their combined weight, and it seemed like it might give at any moment.

"Grarrr!"

The fanghound desperately clawed to stay up, slicing at Shishi's skin.

"I can't... I can't die here! I can't!"

Shishi's indomitable will caused the Florescence to well up inside her, and suddenly, from her bloodied ankle came an enormous *Bwoom!* and a huge camellia flower appeared, flinging the dog off her and into the depths of the chasm.

"Grawoo!"

After she watched it go, Shishi swung up onto the tree, springing off it just as it snapped in two and went tumbling down the cliff.

"Whew... Th-that was close...!" she said, safely ashore on the Asura Realm side of the valley. She looked down to hear the distant sound of the tree and part of the cliff as they reached the valley floor. After gazing for a while in disbelief, she patted her cheeks to refocus herself, wiped the sweat from her neck, and wrapped the ivy around her bleeding ankle.

This is just the first step. Now that I'm here at the Asura Realm, I have to save the others!

Shishi turned to face the towering onyx stadium that dominated this new area. Shouts and cheers could be heard emanating from within. Shishi hid herself from a patrolling guard, and while they were distracted by the sound of the falling tree, she extended a vine and stole a ring of keys from around their belt before slipping away like a shadow to find a way in.

Six Realms Penitentiary, Asura Realm.

This area of the prison was perhaps the most unique of all the realms, and compared to the Preta and the Human Realms, the selection criteria were a little different. To end up here, a prisoner had to be especially skilled at martial arts, but not so strong that they might escape the prison under their own power. The one who determined which prisoners met these standards was Satahabaki himself. Some of them had crawled up out of the land of hunger and despair that was the Preta Realm, while others had let their training and physical prowess slip and had fallen from the Human Realm. In the stadium, carved out of the rock itself, battles were constantly staged with no interruption, such that the Asura Realm truly seemed like a glimpse into the world of eternal strife it was meant to represent.

How was such a thing allowed to take place here, in Six Realms, famed bastion of the law? That was because of the way things worked in Kaso Prefecture, where retribution was a business. Kaso opened up the Asura Realm to visiting dignitaries from other prefectures, and the ticket fares made up a significant portion of their income. The prisoner lineup included Shimobukians, Flamebound priests, and even badgers, all highly individual and unique fighters who drew great crowds and riled them up. Even though the admission fees were high, there was no shortage of spectators, and some of the more accomplished fighters were even known to attract purchase offers by people who would free them and place them on their personal guard.

Of course, Satahabaki made sure the enterprise followed a few rules behind the scenes to safeguard the lives of the prisoners. Intentional killing in the arena was strictly prohibited, as were matches between humans and Benibishi. These rules prevented the crowd from getting *too* excited, while they also allowed the birth of a great number of rising stars.

And so it was not unusual for the Asura Realm arena to be wrapped in a maelstrom of excitement. Today, however, the atmosphere was a little different...

"...Wh-what's going on here?!"

Wearing a black robe to conceal her identity, Shishi pushed through the crowded arena seating, looking down at the fight unfolding on the sands below. Normally, battles in the arena were one-on-one, with no weapons and only the combatants' skills to lead them to victory. However, what Shishi faced was nothing of the sort.

A group of iguana riders, heavily armored, rode in circles around a band of Benibishi armed with nothing but swords and shields. Evidently, one Benibishi who attempted to fight back had been caught in a rider's whip and was currently being dragged mercilessly across the rough sand.

Th-this isn't a fight! It's a massacre!

"Yahoo! Go, go! Get 'em, tiger!"

Sitting next to Shishi was a rotund gentleman with rings on each of his fingers, laughing and clapping gleefully at the nightmare happening below.

"Hmm? Just arrived?" He asked Shishi. "Well, you're in luck! Things are just starting to heat up!"

"..."

"They were supposed to be making a bunch of Benibishi kids kill each other today, but that got put on hold, apparently, so they're showing us this instead. I have to say, my hopes weren't high, but this is even more exciting than I imagined! It's just like the fights they used to run at the Colosseum in ancient Rome!"

Shishi's face was concealed by her hood, but a thin line of blood ran down her lip, where she was biting it in anger. "What sort of fight is this supposed to be?!" she said at last. "I thought battles between human and Benibishi were forbidden!"

"Not today. Today's a special day in the Asura Realm, filled with blood and death!" The man gulped down some blue wine from the glass in his hand, spilling it down his chin and onto his clothes. "Since Lord Satahabaki isn't making the rounds, there are no rules! And anyway, the Benibishi are all going to be put to death sooner or later. They're all good fighters, so why not allow them to go out in a blaze of glory? Vice-Warden Gopis seems to think so. That's why she's put on this carnival of slaughter! Now, come on, sit down! Can I get you a drink?"

How dare you...!!

Shishi's eyes flared with anger, and her hood flew back as she jumped up onto the plump man's face, spilling his wine, and used it as a foothold to leap all the way down into the ring, slap-bang in the middle of the action.

"Something's entered the ring! What is that?!" yelled one of the iguana riders.

"An intruder!" shouted another. "Commander, what should we do?"

"It doesn't matter. It's an accident. Kill them, spectator or not!"

Shishi heard the crack of the riders' whips as they circled. The other Benibishi adopted a protective formation around her.

"It's a child! What are you doing here?!" one of them yelled.

"Protect the child at all costs! We have to get them out of here!"

"No, you do not!"

The dignified voice coming from the robed figure made all the Benibishi warriors tremble in fright. Shishi cast off her disguise, revealing a body clad in golden ivy.

"It...it's her!"

"Princess Shishi!"

"Why are you here, Your Highness?!"

"Hey, sit tight and pay attention, dead meat!"

One of the riders cracked their whip and rushed one of the panicking Benibishi. Just as he was about to tear his victim to pieces, however, Shishi extended her hand, and in it appeared a sword made of glittering ivy, which she then used to trap the rider's whip.

"H-huh?! Erm— Aaaagh!"

With the rider's whip wrapped around her sword, she swung it as hard as she could, pulling the rider off his iguana and sending him flying into the spectator seating with a crash.

"Do not think fate is the walls that surround you!" Shishi yelled to the rest of the Benibishi warriors, who all stood around, frozen in shock. "Do not think fate is the hand you were dealt! We were not born to die in the cold earth! We were born to flourish underneath the warm sun!"

"Your Highness...!"

"This is an order from your prince! You are not to die until your flower has blossomed! Follow me, and I shall lead you into the light!"

"Y-yes! Yes, Your Highness!"

"My life is yours to command, Your Highness!"

"Very good! Now take up Flower Formation: Fire No. 3!"

"Yes, Your Highness! You heard her! Flower Formation! Fire No. 3!!"

The other soldiers gave an enthusiastic yell, and their defeatist attitude from a few moments earlier completely changed. They took up their shields and entered formation.

"Wh-what's going on?" asked one of the riders. "Something's changed..."

"It's a bluff! Don't forget they can't harm humans! Press the attack!"

The riders assaulted the Benibishi formation with their whips, but the turtle-like shell of shields deflected every last blow, and with no gaps for the riders to attempt to disarm them.

"You insolent worms... Forget the whips. Draw your swords!"

At their commander's order, the riders all drew their scimitars and lunged, aiming to drive them into the cracks between the shields, when...

Schwing!

...one of the Benibishi soldiers leaped out of formation, slicing off an iguana's hind leg. The rider toppled off his mount and gave a blood-curdling cry, cut short as the beast's crushing weight fell atop him and left him little more than a stain upon the sand.

"Change to Flower Formation: Fire No. 2! Let the petals obstruct their movements!"

""Yes, Your Highness!""

"You filthy slaves, you'll pay for this!"

With the pride of the Asura Realm riders at stake, the iguana cavalry made another frenzied assault. However, Shishi's kingly strategy and techniques were second to none. Masterfully employing both defensive and offensive options, she was able to turn the tide of battle against even a superiorly equipped foe.

Benibishi may not be allowed to harm humans, but animals are a different matter. If we just target the iguanas, we can win this!

"Oh no! Your Highness, look at that!"

At her captain's remark, Shishi peered through a gap in the shields and saw that a huge tank, maybe four meters across, had entered the arena.

"Haaah-ha-ha! Ladies and gentlemen, stay in your seats. The show's just getting started!"

The enemy commander, red-faced with anger, yelled from atop the tank, made up to evoke the image of a chariot of ancient Rome. It rushed the Benibishi formation, throwing up clouds of sand in its wake, its huge treads squashing flat any iguanas too slow to move out of its way.

"Your Highness, all is lost! You must live! Please allow us to cover your escape!"

"I told you, we will not surrender!" yelled Shishi. "…Take this!"

Shishi stood before her compatriots and threw her hands to the ground. The ivy coiled around her wrists shone brighter and shot across the sand toward the tank. However, just as it reached its target, the mighty combat vehicle's caterpillar tracks tangled up the ivy and tore it off, showing no signs of slowing at all.

"G…ghah! Ghhh!"

""Your Highness!""

Any damage to the ivy was reflected on its host, and Shishi doubled over, coughing up blood. Still, grimacing, she attacked with the ivy once more, the flames of determination in her eyes ever brighter.

"...Men, offer your lives to Her Highness!"

"Your Highness, my life is yours to command."

"Mine too!"

"Your Highness, please...!"

The Benibishi soldiers crowded around her, laying their hands on her body, channeling as much of their life force into her as they could.

"Wh-what are you doing...?"

Although the soldiers had not yet awakened to their Florescence, their desperate prayers were more than enough to redouble Shishi's power, causing her to sparkle with newfound courage.

I can do this. With all their power...I can fight!

"Prepare to be run over, you worms!"

"Rrrrooooaaaaaahhh!"

Shishi and the other Benibishi stared down the approaching tank, and then they all yelled in unison:

""Flourish!""

Bwoom!

"Wha—?! Wh-whoooa!"

Bwoom! Bwoom!

Enormous camellia flowers burst downward from the ivy tangled in the tank's treads, launching the vehicle off the ground.

"W-waaaahh!"

The force lifted the tank onto its side, and it scraped across the arena floor, kicking up sand as it ground to a halt. The audience watching this strange turn of events was so confused that it didn't know whether it should cheer or boo.

"U-urgh. Dammit... How could this happen...?"

The enemy commander, barely managing to avoid injury, crawled from the top of the tank, now its side, and fell onto the stadium sand. However, just as he reached out to drag himself toward the exit...

Stab!

"Eeek!"

…one of the riders' scimitars suddenly plunged into the sand before him. He looked up to see the cold, expressionless face of Shishi glaring back.

"Wh-wh-what do you want from me…?!"

"Take it."

"…Huh?"

"Don't worry, the only ones we killed are the iguanas. Let's settle this by the rules: one-on-one, man-to-man. Any objections?"

"…Heh. Ha-ha-ha. You think I can't kill one measly child?"

The enemy commander suddenly got a nasty look on his face. He leaped to his feet, pulled the sword free of the earth and readied it, looking down at Shishi with her ivy blade by her side.

"Just because you're good at usin' your soldiers doesn't change the fact that you're just a kid. You're basically offerin' me your head on a platter…"

"Are you done?"

"Huh?"

"When do you plan to begin the fight? If I started when you picked up the sword, you'd be dead ten times over by now."

"…You won't be laughin' at me when I'm done with you, you brat!!"

The commander slashed at Shishi's head with a two-handed downward swing, but his sword sliced only thin air. It wasn't that he'd misjudged the distance; by the time his sword reached his target, the length of the blade had been snapped cleanly in two. The tip twirled through the air before embedding itself in the sand nearby.

"…Ah…ah…!"

"Never lay a hand on the Benibishi ever again. The next time I see your face, you're dead."

Shishi's ivy blade retracted into her wrist, and she turned and walked away. The commander stared in shock at his broken sword. Then, overcome with anger, he lifted it and charged toward Shishi.

"Die, you worthless brat!"

"Such a fool…"

Shishi whirled around to meet her attacker, but before she could do anything...

Splat!

...the commander's neck was impaled by a spear of green ivy. He gurgled for a second, then, with lifeless eyes, slid off the spear and collapsed into a rapidly expanding pool of his own blood.

"I will not pardon rudeness toward Her Highness. I hope you suffer in your next life, foul human..."

"You fool! What have you done?!" asked Shishi, running up to the Benibishi soldier who had intervened on her behalf. The soldier bowed reverently, dispelling his ivy spear before it could stain Shishi with human blood. "You didn't need to kill him! Such acts incur the wrath of your king! ...Wait, how were you even able to harm a human in the first place?!"

"Such is the power of these vines you have granted us, Your Highness."

Looking once more at the soldier, Shishi saw that he was covered in bright green ivy. It proved he had awoken to his Florescence, much as Shishi had not too long ago.

"Y-you have the ivy, too...?"

"Yes. We awakened when fighting together with Your Highness."

"'*We*'...? Y-you don't mean...!"

The sand clouds cleared, revealing precisely what Shishi had feared. She saw the Benibishi soldiers, weapons of ivy in their hands, standing over the human fighters, who were begging for their lives.

"P-p-please don't kill me! Please!"

"My friends asked the very same thing of you," the Benibishi replied.

"I—I—I have a family! A wife and daughter!"

"So did they. And now they lie dead."

"Ghh! Grghh...! Ghaah!"

With ruthless efficiency, the Benibishi soldiers executed their captives, every last one. Then they began to turn their hateful eyes upon the human spectators in the seats. Very soon, the Asura Realm was beginning to look more like hell as sheer pandemonium gripped the arena.

"S-stop! Don't kill! This is a capital offense!"

"My life is nothing compared to the suffering of my brothers and sisters," the Benibishi soldier replied. "Besides...it was Your Highness who granted us this power and released us from our shackles, was it not?"

"Wh-what...?!"

"That flower, the mighty camellia... It is Your Highness's flower. How fiercely it blooms, the pollen filling my lungs."

Shishi turned and looked where the soldier pointed, at the camellia that had upturned the commander's tank. Now it shone brightly like the sun, scattering golden pollen. What had awakened the soldiers' Florescence and allowed them to break free of their genetic programming was none other than Shishi's own power.

"I feel reborn. How good it feels to be free at last."

Shishi got chills listening to the soldier speak... Then, all of a sudden, she spotted up in the seating, amid the fleeing guests, a group of affluent children huddled together and a single Benibishi drawing closer and closer to them, like a vengeful spirit.

"...!! Stop... Stop!"

Shishi broke into a run, but the Benibishi was too far and seemed deaf to her screams. Drenched in human blood, he lifted his battle-ax of ivy high above the cowering children's heads...

When suddenly, a fragrant, gentle scent wafted through the arena. The Benibishi all froze where they stood, their eyes wide in shock as the vines constituting their weapons fell apart. Even the great camellia flower in the center of the ring stopped scattering its pollen and slowly retracted into itself.

"...H-huh...? What was I...?"

The Benibishi seemed to come to his senses, his ruthless demeanor suddenly gone. Shishi watched as the human children ran away, crying, and she breathed a sigh of relief.

Suddenly, there came a voice that froze the depths of her heart.

"What a sorry sight."

Before even working out what was happening, the Benibishi all turned and kneeled toward the voice, as if compelled by some primal instinct.

"Fa...ther...!"

Up on the highest seat in the stands, his gown fluttering in the wind, stood the Benibishi's king, Housen. His expression now was quite unlike the one he had shown with Milo. Solemn, dignified, majestic, regal, and stern.

He jumped from his vantage point, landing nearly twenty meters below in the center of the arena. Where he landed, tiny balsam flowers sprouted to cushion the fall. He walked, buds blossoming at his feet, across the sands toward Shishi.

Oh...oh no...

Shishi found herself unable to move, locked in place by her father's glacial stare, so several of the Benibishi laid themselves on the floor in front of her. Housen looked at their groveling forms with an unreadable expression and halted, addressing his child from a distance.

"It has been a while, Shishi."

"F-Father..."

"You have kept well, I trust? ...No, I need not ask. From up there, I hardly recognized you."

"..."

"You've found a mentor, have you?"

"I have..."

"Excellent."

"..."

Though Shishi had longed all this time to stand before her father once more, at this moment she knew not what she should say. At length, she managed to spit out a response.

"...F-Father! I...!"

"You don't have to say it. I understand."

"But!"

"Do not worry about the fate of your kinsmen. Right now, it is you who must face punishment."

The circle of Benibishi pulled back protectively around Shishi, but Housen paid them no heed.

"You killed them, Shishi," he said.

"…Ghh!"

"But, Your Majesty! It was us who murdered those humans!"

"Punish us if you will, but do not lay a hand on Her Highness!"

"SILENCE!"

Housen dismissed his subjects' objections with a mighty yell. As the sound wave swept through the arena, balsam flowers sprouted on the walls, triggered by nothing but the king's voice.

"I disagree," he went on. "The one who freed the people from their shackles, whose Florescence allowed them to kill the unarmed in cold blood… That was you, Shishi."

"…"

"I know not how this occurred. To think the prince's flower awoke such hate in the people. You have spilled blood on the king's path, Shishi. Have you anything to say in your defense?"

"No…Father…I do not."

Shishi's face streamed with tears as she walked slowly forward. The Benibishi hesitantly cleared a path, and soon she arrived before King Housen, where she fell to one knee.

"I always tried…to be your successor… I wanted to be…a great king…"

"…Shishi."

"But my Florescence…brought unrest to the people. My flowers stained the path I walk with blood. If allowed, they will surely only get in your way…"

"…"

"My flowers tainted the people! They have done nothing wrong! Please, Father, I beg of you! For their sake, for the sake of peace between the Benibishi and the humans…you must kill me!"

"Your Highness, no!"

"Oh, Your Majesty, please have mercy!"

"…"

"…"

There was a protracted silence. The Benibishi watched nervously.

"…You drove the people to slaughter innocent humans," Housen said at last. "As you say, a member of the royal family faces execution for such an act."

"...Yes."

"So then, Shishi."

"..."

"...I hereby strip you of your right of succession and condemn you to live a commoner's life."

"...?! Father! What do you—?!"

Shishi rose to her feet, furious, but Housen put a calming hand on her shoulder.

"The people only had need to unite and defend themselves because they were outside my care. That is my own failure. As a commoner yourself, there is no need for you to be executed."

"That's not true!" Shishi yelled back. "Do you mean to leave this demonic flower at large? I-if you don't... If you don't kill me here, the Benibishi will never be safe! Isn't it a king's job to do what is right to protect the happiness of his people?!"

"I have no desire to be lectured on a king's job by a commoner." Housen shrugged, dropping his stern act and reverting to his usual devil-may-care attitude. He pointed up to the ceiling. "Also, those four eyes have been glaring at me for quite a while now, and I fear what they might do if I continue bullying you any longer."

Shishi looked up to see a pair of Mushroom Keepers, red and blue, poised on the ceiling like spiders, staring daggers at Housen standing below.

"Is that any way to look at your fellow man?" Housen went on. "Your mentor sure is a fearsome one."

"Bro...ther..."

Housen turned around with a smile and beckoned his subjects to follow. The other Benibishi quickly took up defensive positions around their king and escorted him away. Several of them looked back at Shishi, worried, but soon every last one went with Housen and left.

"What a rotten old man you got. If it were me, I'd have given him a good punch."

Shishi looked up at Bisco as he landed beside her, and she smiled a little through the tears. He still had Satahabaki's tattoo on him, but thanks to Milo's handiwork, he was looking a lot healthier than before. "If you hadn't been there," he continued, "they'd all be dead! And he wants to punish you for that? Talk about ungrateful..."

"It is okay, Brother. My flowers led to death. There was no way I could ever be king after that."

Shishi tried so hard to sound cheerful, but the regret was painfully apparent in her voice. When she looked up at Bisco's pitying eyes, it all came pouring out.

"...I'm not worthy. I never was! I came so far, following in my father's footsteps, and it was all for nothing! I strayed from the path he paved..."

"Who cares about his path? You can't do this, you can't do that? You don't sound no different from the prisoners locked up here! Chuck it away; you don't need any of that! You can live life by your own rules, Shishi!"

"*Sob*... But... But... Brother!"

"No buts!"

Shishi was drawn to Bisco's glimmering jade-green eyes, flickering like emerald flames.

"Listen to me. You did the right thing. That's what you decided to do! Your path doesn't need to follow in the footsteps of anyone else. You just need to walk wherever the sun shines!"

"Brother...!"

"You'll be fine. You've got Milo and me to help. Whenever the world's rules get you down, we'll be right there to pick you back up and say, *Well done, you did the right thing.* So don't cry. Don't be scared. The only one with any right to steer your soul's growth...is yourself!"

"...W-waah... Waaaah...!"

Tears fell once more like raindrops from Shishi's eyes, wetting the arena sand.

"Brother... Broootheeer...!"

Shishi ran crying into Bisco's arms, and this time he didn't push her aside or try to break free. He just sat there as Shishi's hot tears stained his chest, clutching her sleek violet hair, wondering how so vast an emptiness could have consumed a girl so young.

"..."

"..."

"Something you wish to say, my dear Panda?"

"I was about to ask you the same question, Your Majesty."

The Benibishi king, Housen, walked back along the valley path toward the Human Realm, leading the host of evolved Benibishi, their bodies entwined with ivy. Milo Nekoyanagi strode alongside him, an iceberg of emotion.

"I do not expect a human to understand my decisions. You see, what happened back there was—"

"The king must cast himself aside. Only for the people shall his flowers bloom."

"..."

"If what you said back then was true," Milo continued, "then Shishi did the right thing." He directed his gaze to Housen, his fiery eyes liable to burn a hole right through the king's body. "She risked her life to protect her people. Knowing her flowers would only bring pain, she asked to be killed so that they could live in peace. She was willing to sacrifice herself for her subjects. If that's not the creed of kings, then I don't know what is."

"...Oh, dearie me."

"But back there, you didn't—"

"I didn't acknowledge that what Shishi did was right? Is that it?"

"..."

"You are right. If I admitted that Shishi did the right thing, then I would have needed to kill her. I needed to bend the rules for the sake of my dear, dear child."

"Even if that brings pain to the people?"

"Hmm. Rather caught up on this, aren't you?"

Housen turned back and looked at the Benibishi soldiers following a short distance behind. Not a single one of them wavered in their devotion to their one and only king.

"Yes, I admit it. I broke the rules to protect Shishi. Are you going to say that makes me unfit to be king?"

"Perhaps that's true. You do make a pretty lousy king...," Milo began. Then he smiled. "...but you're a great father. I think I can let it slide."

"...Ha-ha-ha."

Housen laughed theatrically, but his eyes were distant and unfocused. "I fear I raised her too well, that one. Shishi is far worthier a king than I, even. It is a poor lot to be chosen as king. Bound by rules, even to kill my own child, when what I wish for more than anything else is to hold her tenderly in my arms. You will find no more tragic an animal anywhere on this earth, Panda."

"So that's why you banished her from the royal family? You didn't want the throne to deprive her of her own happiness? But, Your Majesty, Shishi is—"

"I tire of this conversation. Silence, and forget everything you just heard."

"Heyyy! Come back! Wait right there, flower geezer!"

"Geezer...?"

Just as Housen was starting to look satisfied, a loud voice stopped him in his tracks. He turned to see a sour-looking red-haired young man, striding rudely toward him, hair bouncing in the wind.

"Bisco!"

"Figured you're the hotshot around here," said Bisco. "I could spot those flashy threads a mile away. Said your peace and now you're leavin', huh? That it?"

Housen's retainers stepped forward aggressively, but the king waved his hand to dismiss them. "I feel like I've said this before, but I am no 'geezer,'" he said, clearing his throat. "I am an *Adonis*. Could you at least call me that much?"

"Oh, you don't like how I talk? I can call you Mr. Fancy Flower Man if that makes ya feel better!"

"Bisco! Y-you can't talk like that! He's the king!!"

Milo sensed the Benibishi guards growing unpleasant and rushed over to cool his partner off. Bisco, on the other hand, still looked far from finished with the old monarch.

"Hmm. I believe this is the first time we've met. I don't claim to count any wild beasts among my acquaintances. Perhaps you could enlighten me as to how it is, then, that you seem so displeased with me?"

"Who wouldn't be mad after seeing what you did?!"

"And what of Shishi? Did you leave her there?"

"She passed out after usin' up all her power. To *save you*, by the way! That's all she's been tryin' to do this whole time! I'm gonna drag you back and make you say sorry for what you did, but not before I mess up that pretty little face of yours!"

"You cur!" cried a guard. "A human like you could never understand the king's feelings...!"

"It is all right. Stand down."

Housen calmed his retainer and walked over to Bisco, evidently amused by the boy's choice words. He looked the young man up and down appreciatively before settling on his sparkling green eyes, like cut jade. One of them still bore the wounds of Gopis's whip, but even the other by itself shone vigorously enough that Housen was more than satisfied.

"Hmm. I see. So you are the bud's mentor. The blackguard who made my Shishi bloom."

"All I did was give her some of my blood. The rest was her doing."

"Oh, to think my daughter has given herself to such a brutish man. Well, rules are rules. I must allow you to take her hand in marriage."

""...Whaaaaat?!""

Both Mushroom Keepers cried out in unison. Housen slipped one of the many rings from his fingers. "Long have I awaited this day," he muttered.

"Wh-what are you talking about, Your Majesty?! Bisco is already married! He has a wife! She may be a bit of a juggernaut, but she's brave and loyal, with E-cup breasts!!"

"And what is the matter with that? The Benibishi are polygamous. Shishi can be Bisco's second wife."

"Are you outta your mind, old man?! I'm human, and humans ain't—"

"I am not an old man. Call me 'Father.'"

"You've got to be joking!" Milo piped up. "Never, never, never! I won't allow it!"

Housen looked at the blue-haired boy, now panting with frenzied eyes, then shared a glance with the other Benibishi.

"What a strange fellow. Bisco I can understand, but why should *you* protest so much? …Oh, well. I'm sure you will change your mind once it's all over."

"No, I won't!"

"Well, it matters not. Now, I wish to conclude business as swiftly as possible. Was there something else? Ah, I believe you wished to 'mess up my pretty face,' is that right?"

Housen smiled at Bisco, his gown catching the wind and fluttering. The other Benibishi seemed to read his mind and stepped back, forming a circle around their king and the two Mushroom Keepers.

"Then go right ahead," Housen went on. "Punches, kicks, whatever you fancy. No need to hold back."

"What, and you ain't gonna fight back?"

"Heh. Well, I *am* interested in assessing the strength of my future son-in-law."

"Well then, suit yourself! Here I come!"

Before Milo could stop him, Bisco launched himself forward like a bullet, swinging his powerful fist right at Housen's nose…but his fist met only empty air. Bisco's momentum sent him tumbling to the ground, bouncing along the earth like a skipping stone, before he finally managed to spring to his feet.

…?! He vanished!

"Ha-ha-ha. Such spirit! Like the god Indra, or Susano'o! You remind me an awful lot of myself when I was younger!"

"…What the hell did you do?!"

Bisco wheeled back and looked at the spot where Housen had stood. Now there was only a cluster of balsam flowers floating softly to the ground.

"Oh? Did you mistake those flowers for me?" said Housen, standing calmly a short distance away. "They are truly beautiful; I'm honored."

"Quit hidin' behind your cheap tricks and stand still!!"

Bisco flew at Housen once more, his canines bared. This time, however, he suddenly stopped just short of where the king was standing.

"Hmm."

"Right there!"

After the first exchange, Bisco had already altered his approach. This time, he relied not on his sight but on his other senses, and those senses guided him, twisting his body, launching his foot sideways without even looking where he was attacking first.

Whoosh!

Another cloud of balsam petals scattered to the floor.

"What?!"

His attack failing to connect once more, Bisco found himself flat on the ground, the feeling of cold steel against his neck.

"Hmm. Very good, Bisco Akaboshi. But I'm afraid that's enough fun for now."

Bisco slowly turned to see Housen standing over him, sword drawn.

"Very admirable. Seeing through my camouflage by ignoring your sight... Just how many battles have you participated in during your few short years?"

"...You bastard. It was a double-bluff...!"

"I have no objections to allowing you to hit me if it helps you feel any better. However, I fear one solid blow from you might cause me to perish."

Housen gave a silent chuckle and sheathed his blade. The Benibishi around him all gave a sigh of relief and began murmuring in admiration.

"Akaboshi. Panda. Having seen your formidable strength, I cannot allow you to interfere any longer in the affairs of Six Realms. If you continue to meddle, be prepared to face my blade. This is a Benibi-shi matter… Furthermore, it is a matter between me and Someyoshi alone."

"So, what, we're just supposed to sit in the corner twiddlin' our thumbs? It's a Mushroom Keeper matter, too! If we don't send that big guy packin', we're never gonna get rid of our tattoos!"

"You need not worry," Housen reiterated. "I will talk to him and make him undo his Bountiful Art. There is no need for weapons in a dispute between Benibishi. I shall resolve this in a way that abides by both the law and the creed of kings."

"Dream on!" Bisco roared. "You got two conflicting ideals! This shit's gonna end in blood, mark my words!"

Housen's eyebrow twitched ever so slightly. Bisco went on, "Keep on tryin' to appease people all you like, but that ain't gonna work outside the prison! It's a dog-eat-dog world out there! You think you can just brush the dust off your musty-ass rulebook and expect the whole world to fall in line?!"

"Do you mean to find fault with the way I rule?"

"Listen to me! I'm just tryin' to—!"

"It is your right to do so, Akaboshi. If my way of rule has grown rusty, then it is only proper that it should be struck down by the force of life and a new rule rise to take its place. That is the natural way. I rule precisely because I understand that."

"…"

"The old king shall fall by the sword of the new. I have lived my whole life knowing the fate that awaits me. My only regret is for my daughter. When I am gone, and she takes up the crown, I need a strong individual who will protect her from those who seek to steal the throne. That is why I told her to seek a true man as mentor…even if all she found was this savage dog who stands before me now."

"…Wait, you've been planning this for Shishi the entire time!!"

"Since you are the one who has beflowered my daughter, it falls to you to watch over her. This is an order from the king."

"Why should I listen to you?!"

"We understand, Your Highness. Leave Shishi to us, and we shall leave Satahabaki to you."

"Hey, Milo!"

"Ha-ha-ha. Very good. It is nice to see there are some good humans after all... Perhaps the day will come when our peoples walk hand in hand."

Housen turned and, with a swish of his magnificent gown, walked calmly off down the valley path. The hundred-odd Benibishi soldiers all neatly turned in formation and followed after him.

"...Hey, Milo. You really wanna let that old geezer handle everything?"

"Of course not. I just said that to make him leave. We would've been here all day otherwise."

"You..."

"Besides, even if I did agree, I knew you were never going to listen anyway."

Bisco stared in shock at the face of his partner, who lied as easily as he breathed. Then, hearing a clanking noise, he looked up beyond Milo to see a giant figure bounding toward them.

"Ah, it's the Mark I!"

"I asked Mepaosha where to find the bone coal storehouse in the Beast Realm. He was able to get there on reserve power and eat his fill."

"That blue spiky woman? I'm amazed you managed to get the truth outta her," replied Bisco.

"Well, you know. She was barely holding it in at that point."

"Huh? Holdin' what in?"

Milo ignored him and ran over to the robot. "Mark I, I think it's hidden somewhere around here," he said. "Think you can find it for us?"

The Mark I stopped, and its head revolved in a circle, its jade-green flashlights spinning like a police siren. The two boys squinted and shielded their eyes as the light fell on a nearby wall, increasing in intensity.

"Wow, I knew it was close, but not *that* close!"

"Hey, Milo. What the hell are you lookin' for anyway?"

"A weapons store," Milo replied, knocking his fist against the wall. I sneaked into the guards' room and looked at the blueprints. Our bows and mushroom arrows should be there. We can't hope to fight anybody unless we have those."

"I'm with you on that one," said Bisco. "My fights lately have been a lot harder than they needed to be."

"*Vwoo.*"

The Mark I stomped over, picked up Milo in thumb and forefinger, and moved him gently aside before swinging his enormous log-like leg into the wall.

Crash!

The wall broke apart, revealing that it had, in fact, been a cleverly disguised mechanical door. With its destruction, a small tuft of smoke began rising off a nearby card reader disguised as a rock.

"All right. The place is going to be filled with guards. We can't hope to evade all the detectors, so we're going to have to rush through with the Mark I."

"Got it. Let's go."

"Wait, Bisco, stop! Bisco…sit!"

"I'm not your dog!"

"We don't need all three of us to do this. You should go after Housen instead."

"…Huh? What, you want me to go back him up? Isn't he just gonna go talk?"

Milo gave a small but fearless grin and scratched his ear nervously.

"I mean, I hope it goes well, too, but we're talking about a guy cursed to follow the law for a hundred years. Do you really think he's going to change his mind just because a king asks him to? I think you're right. There's no way out here that doesn't end in blood. And when that happens, your skills are definitely going to be needed."

"I see, your panda sense is tinglin' again, huh?"

"I put my trust in what you think. Now it's your turn. Who do you trust more, me or the king? I'll let you decide."

"Ha!"

Bisco slapped the Mark I on the back and took off running.

"Bisco!" Milo called after him. "I'm not asking you to start a fight! Make sure you don't make the first move!"

"I know, I know! You just focus on gettin' us our bows!"

After watching his partner disappear in the direction of the Human Realm, Milo gave a soft smile. Then, after a moment, his eyes blazed with a warrior's ferocity once more.

"You heard the man," he said. "Hey, Mark I. Wanna see who can find our bows first?"

"*...! Vwoo!*"

"Ah-ha-ha! All right, you're on! Watch closely, I'll show you how a pro does things!"

With his rocket boosters fired up, the Mark I hoisted Milo up by the shoulder and blasted off down the tunnel leading to the weapons store.

"My old friend…"

"…"

"I must beg your pardon. This burden is far too great for any one man to bear, even you."

"Whither goes your usual pride, my liege? Your heart must be as steel!"

"…"

"I have faith the king shall bring peace and harmony to our people. If I may be the cornerstone of that peace, then I shall take up the iron scales of justice without question and become the devil of Six Realms."

"…Someyoshi. Your heart speaks true. Kneel."

"Your Majesty."

"I hereby grant you the balsam's power, and with it, your Florescence. I am confident your strength of will shall make you a most splendid host."

"Yes, my liege!"

"…May your flowers be beautiful and unwavering, just as we swore together. Someyoshi, my old friend… If there is one man on earth who can make it happen, it is you…"

"Are you feeling unwell, Your Majesty?"

"Hmm?"

A guard's voice roused Housen from his deep reminiscence. By now they had long since departed the Human Realm and were nearing the Deva Realm, the grand entrance yard to Six Realms Penitentiary.

Their destination close at hand, the Benibishi were bristling with new-found vigor…all of them, it seemed, save for the king himself.

"It is nothing. Pray do not concern yourself with me."

"Apologies, Your Majesty… However, we have noticed something strange. Several of the prison guards appear to be fleeing the Deva Realm."

Just as the king's retainer said, every now and then, one of the black-robed prison guards would come running the other way past the hundred-strong procession of Benibishi warriors, emitting stammering yelps and stumbling over their own feet in terror.

"It makes me fear what is happening at the gate. Your Majesty, I advise waiting here and sending an elite squad to scout ahead."

"No need. I have a fairly confident idea of what it could be."

"Even so, we Benibishi could not allow any peril to befall you!"

"And likewise, I cannot allow any peril to befall my people. Now, remain in formation and carry on."

Housen's tone was gentle yet firm. The guard did not protest further, immediately bowing and taking a few steps back into formation.

…*Someyoshi…!*

What none of the guards noticed were the deep crimson flames that silently burned in Housen's eyes. Ignoring the fleeing jailers, the procession advanced into the main yard.

Six Realms Penitentiary, entry yard.

Before the magnificent obsidian gate stood an enormous cage of twisted wood and cherry blossoms, blocking the path. Inside that cage sat the demon warden of Six Realms, Satahabaki himself, sentenced by his own judgment to remain imprisoned until his execution. He never ate, never spoke a word, only sat cross-legged in deep meditation, a posture that seemed impossible given the thick navy-colored armor that covered him head to toe even now. Despite his incarceration, the giant man's dignity seemed as unshakable as his form. Standing just outside the cell was Satahabaki's inseparably loyal steed, Winter Cherry, nickering gently from time to time. The great stallion, custom-bred to support its master, seemed somehow lonely in its appearance and behavior, and even its striking scarlet coat had lost its sheen.

"…Khhaaah!"

From between Satahabaki's enormous pillar-like teeth came a burst of hot breath. Then, after a short pause, there came a *Bwoom!* and a grand pair of cherry blossom trees came sprouting out of his shoulders.

"…I can no longer contain the Florescence. The hour of my death is soon at hand…" Satahabaki spoke in a low, booming voice, his arms patiently crossed. "Once my life expires, and there is nothing left to hold it back, the cherry blossoms will spread throughout Six Realms, forcing the life from the Benibishi, and beyond. Soon all of Kaso will know these trees, for they will bloom all across the land, all year round without interruption."

Seeing his master stare his oncoming death in the face, Winter Cherry let out a feeble neigh.

"Do not worry, Winter Cherry. The cherry blossoms are the arm of the law. They will harm no living thing besides the Benibishi. You must live and grace the next warden with your companionship. …Hmm?"

Suddenly, Satahabaki sensed someone approaching and uncrossed his legs.

"L-Lord Satahabakiii!!"

One of the prison guards ran to the cage and threw himself before it, clutching the bars.

"The gate to the Human Realm has been opened! It's King Housen, he's leading a revolt! A hundred men, marching this way as we speak!"

"I see."

Bwoom! Another cherry blossom tree erupted from Satahabaki's back, and he plucked it off before continuing.

"The time has come. Use the key I gave you and unlock this cage."

"B-but, Warden… Even though they are Benibishi, they refuse to listen to human orders. I have reports they attacked a group of human guards and broke their swords."

"I ordered you to open this cage!!"

Satahabaki rose to his full terrifying height, such that his helmet was scraping against the bars at the top, and with a swing of his arm, he shattered the door completely.

"W-waaaah! He broke out of his own cage!" cried the guard, fleeing.

"…Hmm. Perhaps it was weak," Satahabaki muttered. "No matter. For attempted prison break, I hereby extend my sentence by twenty years!"

"As splendid as it is to see you obeying the law so faithfully, I do believe you could have handled that with a tad more grace, my old friend."

"…!"

From over in the direction of the gate leading to the Human Realm, marching in from the valley path, his sumptuous gown fluttering as he walked, was the Benibishi king himself, Housen, his soft white skin sparkling in the sunlight. Behind him stood his escort of stout Benibishi warriors, weapons of ivy in their hands, emitting an aura of confidence that kept the prison guards at bay.

"Someyoshi, my old friend! You have kept yourself well, I trust?"

The *Clunk, clunk!* of Satahabaki's armor accompanied him as he turned to face Housen's cheery voice. The broken bars cracked beneath his feet as he strode over to meet him.

"Wh-what power! He is nothing like the man he used to be!"

"Your Majesty, get behind us!"

Satahabaki stood imposingly above the guards as they scrambled to protect their king…and then, with an earthshaking *Thud!* the giant man fell to one knee in reverence.

"My liege," he said. "I beg your pardon. I have not presented myself before you in some time."

"Is that right?" Housen replied. "I had not remembered. With a man such as you, the impression of your presence lasts for quite a while."

"It is good to see you well, my liege. Your health comes above all else."

"I have your luxurious reception to thank for that, as well as to blame for these pounds I have put on as of late. But you have protected the

Benibishi well, and for that, you have my thanks. Now, listen to this. I met these two chaps, Akaboshi and Nekoyanagi. Quite an amusing duo, I must say—"

"Enough chatter!"

Satahabaki's armor rattled, and the Benibishi warriors advanced protectively, but at Housen's word, they all stepped back again.

"Leading a prison riot is a brazen act of violence. Pray explain yourself, my liege."

"I suspect you already know my reasons, Someyoshi."

"Court is now in session. I would hear it from the king's mouth."

Winter Cherry cantered over, holding the judge's giant scepter in his mouth. Satahabaki took it before continuing.

"I, Someyoshi Satahabaki, Lord High Overseer and warden of Six Realms Penitentiary, shall hear your case and decide your punishment!"

Satahabaki's booming voice gave rise to a flourishing of cherry blossoms so impressive that several of the Benibishi guards were thrown clean off their feet. Housen, on the other hand, only smiled gently, as though he had missed hearing his old friend speak so, while the shock wave ruffled his hair.

"Someyoshi," he said at last. "Have you noticed the other Benibishi yet?"

"…Hmm! The ivy!"

"Yes. They have attained Florescence not by my power but of their own wills. The time of our species' evolution is at hand. We shall be slaves to the humans no longer."

"So you wish to ask me to tear down this prison, so you might exact your revenge on them?!"

"I do not. I simply want you to open the gate."

Satahabaki's hot breath came in slow blasts, repeatedly tossing Housen's hair out of his eyes.

"Currently, the Benibishi mutation is only at its ivy stage. If the Florescence proceeds any further, the slightest spark could ignite war between us and the humans. Before that happens, I wish to travel to Kyoto, to seek the signing of a non-aggression pact between our two peoples. I believe this to be the best way of securing this nation's peace."

"Your words, though noble, are cheap! One hundred awakened Benibishi, even armed only with ivy, it is fair to call an army! It is... too...dangerous...for me...to allow..."

"Calm yourself, Someyoshi. We both seek to ensure the peace of the Benibishi race, do we not? Do not allow your Florescence to overcome you. Calm down and look into my eyes..."

"V-very...well..."

As Satahabaki's speech faltered, he dropped his scepter to the floor and began rattling uncontrollably. The guards all gazed, wonderstruck, before a couple of them noticed Housen, now surrounded by a cloud of glowing pollen. The pollen went unnoticed by Satahabaki, slipping into his helmet, filling his nostrils with a mysterious, fragrant scent.

The balsam flower's illusory technique. Thank goodness you do not have a cold, Someyoshi. As much as it pains me to use this on a friend, the only alternative would be to kill you, and I could never bring myself to do such a thing. I am sorry, Someyoshi, please forgive me...

In truth, Housen never expected to be able to talk Satahabaki down. And if it came to a fight, this juggernaut of the law would not hesitate to bring down his full might, even against his own king. It would inevitably result in the shedding of Benibishi blood.

This is the way it must be. Enjoy your sweetest of dreams, my friend.

"That...is right... We both...seek...peace...for our...people..."

"Precisely, Someyoshi. I'm glad you understand. Now, open the gate for me."

"...Yes...my...liege..."

Overcome by Housen's hypnosis, Satahabaki slowly strode over to the main gate of Six Realms, his huge frame trembling with every step. Just as Housen thought it safe to breathe a sigh of relief, however, Satahabaki's great crimson steed came galloping up to its master. It sprang off the ground, launching itself high into the air, and struck Satahabaki in the head with its mighty forelegs.

Slam!

"...!! What?!"

Housen attempted to increase the pollen density, but there was a

Bang! as right before his eyes a thick cherry blossom tree sprouted from the back of Satahabaki's head, punching straight through the helmet. The tree, lodged in the warden's brain, released him from Housen's illusion, and his faltering movements slowly came to a stop.

The next moment...

"Khaaaah..." Satahabaki exhaled deeply, and his enormous teeth began to grind and chatter. "Very close... Very close indeed!! I see now how the Florescence threatens the law of the land. I have experienced its terrifying power firsthand!"

"That horse! What loyalty! Just when we were so close...!"

"Before such power escapes these walls and leaves its mark on the land beyond...I, Someyoshi Satahabaki, must pluck those buds from their stems!"

Satahabaki steadily rose to full magnificent height, casting a dark shadow across Housen and the other Benibishi. This time, the king's guards refused to back down, and they moved to protect the king at the cost of their own lives.

"How dare you speak to the king in such a manner!"

"You are Benibishi, too, Satahabaki! Would you bar the path to your own kind? Move aside!"

"Ridiculous!!"

As Satahabaki slowly awoke from his hypnosis, his large frame creaked and shuddered, and with a *Bang! Bang!* great cherry blossom trees erupted from him, blasting apart the chains that shackled his mind.

"Your righteous rule, your noble blood, your virtuous beliefs! All of them count as specks of dust upon the scales of the law! King Housen! Do not believe for a moment that you can escape my judgment!"

Hmm... This wasn't how I imagined this going, thought Housen as a single bead of sweat dripped down his back. *I knew he had grown stronger, but I never imagined he would be able to escape my illusion.*

"I shall now hand down my VERDIIICT!!"

"Your Majesty, watch out!"

At his men's warning, Housen leaped back, not a moment too soon, as Satahabaki's enormous scepter shattered the ground where he had been standing, flinging the soldiers aside.

"For awakening the Benibishi people and subjecting the world to their limitless power, I have decided to expedite your execution date! Right here and now, you shall all become nothing more than rust upon my scepter!"

"If that is your decision..." Housen's smile vanished at last, and he placed his hand cautiously upon the blade at his waist. "Then you leave me no choice but to cut you down, Someyoshi!"

"My liege, you cannot do that. In fact, you are the only man who cannot do that!" Satahabaki's teeth gleamed like pillars of white marble. "Why is it your sword remains sheathed against one who threatens the lives of your citizens? That is because it is the law of kings to not raise a hand against their own people!"

"Your Majesty! Please stand down! He's right, you must not draw your sword!"

"We are all willing to give our lives to keep you safe!"

Satahabaki powerfully raised his scepter and swung it down toward the fallen Benibishi.

"Now crumble before the might of the law!!"

You rat!

Hosen's wild eyes flared, and just as he was about to pull his sword from his sheath...

A red meteor crashed to the ground at Satahabaki's feet and, with its momentum, stopped the descending scepter before it could reach its target.

"Gggh!"

"Mrh?!"

A spiderweb of cracks ran through the earth. Those doomed Benibishi, who had all but accepted their own fates, saw that they remained unharmed and gazed in wonder at the young man who saved them.

"I-i-i-it's you!"

"Y-you gonna lie there all day?! Hurry and get the hell up!"

The Benibishi warriors all leaped back, and so did the red-haired figure, allowing the scepter to smash into the floor.

"My! Akaboshi! You just held off Someyoshi with one hand!"

"Hey, king!" yelled Bisco, wiping sweat off his forehead. "Is the big guy right? Is that sword just for show?"

"Do not tell me how to rule. Someyoshi is a valued member of our race. I cannot raise my sword against him."

"Then you take that one instead! I'll deal with him!"

"That one...?"

Housen turned to see what Bisco was referring to and saw a giant horse, riderless, kicking, charging, and sowing general chaos amid the Benibishi ranks.

"Winter Cherry!"

Once the horse spotted Housen, it ignored the other guards and began charging directly for him.

"I see. If a horse is to be my opponent..." Housen drew his blade from its sheath, glinting cleanly in the light. "Then I need not hold back. I am sorry to have to do this to you, Someyoshi!"

"What is the meaning of this, Akaboshi?"

As the prison guards, Winter Cherry, and the Benibishi all muddled together in the background, Bisco and Satahabaki faced off across the yard.

"Whether the Benibishi live or die has no bearing on your way of life, Akaboshi. For what reason have you chosen to stand with the king?"

"I ain't standin' with him or nothin', and I don't give a shit what happens to the Benibishi neither."

"What?"

"I just can't have you dyin' on me, that's all."

Bisco's eyes burned twin holes into Satahabaki's helmet. So struck was the Iron Judge by the young man's fortitude and purehearted strength of character that he was unable to move a muscle.

"You said you're gonna kill all your buddies and then yourself. Well, I can't be havin' that. You're the only one who knows how to remove this ink me and the other Mushroom Keepers got goin' on, so I gotta beat your ass and—"

"You wish to spare me? You seek to prevent me from taking the lives of my people and falling on my sword in repentance? You mean to say *that* is why you stand against me, Bisco Akaboshi?!"

"...Did you listen to a word I said! I only need you to—!"

"Splendid!! Full Bloom!!"

Satahabaki swept his scepter overhead, accompanied by sprouting trees and a flurry of petals. His teeth chattered noisily, as though Bisco's words had pleased him greatly.

"To think I would meet so great a man in my final hours... How fortuitous!"

"..."

"Akaboshi! I go now to meet my death, covered in the blood of my own people. However! I will not forget your words, right up until my dying breath!"

"Listen to me! I'm tryin' to get you to *not* die, you great lummox!"

"Underworld Scepter! Crushing Blow!"

"Rraaaaghhh!!"

Bisco's lightning-fast kick collided with Satahabaki's mighty downward swing, deflecting the scepter backward while also sending Bisco tumbling across the floor.

"As the next warden, you must not lose to me. Get up, Akaboshi, and fight with all your strength!"

"Talkin' like a big shot, when you're nothin' but a big asshole!"

After dodging the next blow, Bisco hopped atop the giant scepter and ran along its length to meet Satahabaki, whipping out a Biwa Buffalo horn from his pocket.

"Nrh!"

The horn glinted in the light, still covered in Bisco's blood. It was the very same one that had run him through in the Beast Realm, and the awakened Rust-Eater spores living in the blood twinkled, heralding their imminent growth.

"Hrah!"

Swish! Swish!

Bisco swiped twice with the horn as deftly as if it were his own trusty dagger, slicing an X-shape into Satahabaki's breastplate. This was the dreaded Cross Slash technique, handed down to Bisco by Pawoo herself.

"Nooo! How could a mere buffalo horn manage to slice through my armor?!"

"That's because I believed I could do it, asshole!"

Bisco followed up with a powerful kick to the center of the X, pushing off and throwing himself back. The force of the kick ignited the fungal filaments, and...

Bwoom!

...with a rumbling explosion, the Rust-Eaters blasted Satahabaki's prized breastplate wide open.

"Gnrhh!"

The blood's old, so it wasn't so strong, but looks like my plan still worked!

Bisco didn't forget that Satahabaki's Florescence allowed him to feed off the mushrooms and grow more powerful, but thanks to his Mushroom Keeper instincts, Bisco knew where and when to unleash the blast so that it only touched Satahabaki's armor and nothing else.

However...

"Guess now we're on to the tough part...!"

...before Bisco's eyes, the Iron Judge stood tall, unfazed by Bisco's Rust-Eater blast.

"Nnnrrrrhhhh!!"

Bwoom! Bwoom!

Satahabaki gathered up all his strength, and two magnificent cherry blossom trees sprouted out of his shoulders, blasting off his navy pauldrons.

"How is the Sakura Storm not activating? How are you moving? Why do you not suffer?!"

"I got my own private quack, you see. It's only a makeshift solution, but it'll last long enough for me to kick your ass!"

"Then I suppose you shall have no objection if the Storm covers your entire body!"

Satahabaki swung and pointed his scepter, and a cloud of petals rushed toward his opponent.

"I shall show mercy on you no longer, Akaboshi! I shall show you a storm of petals the likes of which you have never seen!"

"Don't act like you were goin' easy on me before!" Bisco shot back.

"Bountiful Art: Revelation! Flourish! Weeping Dance!"

Satahabaki concentrated, and through the gap that Bisco had broken in his armor, the cherry blossom tattoo on his chest began to move as though alive. The pattern shifted, and out of his mighty chest came thick tree branches, growing from the skin itself.

"Whoooa?!"

The weeping cherry boughs lashed like whips, attacking Bisco from every angle. Somehow, they seemed even stronger and faster than they had the first time Bisco fought him. Bisco was able to dodge using his natural catlike reflexes, but just as he leaped to avoid one branch that tried to sweep his legs out from under him...

"GUIL-TYYY!"

"Oh shi—!"

Thuddd!

...Satahabaki's enormous scepter came at Bisco from diagonally overhead, knocking him down into the ground, smashing the earth. Bisco immediately hopped back to his feet and glared at the demon judge before him.

He still had both hands free! Now that's a stinky move!

"Come at me, Akaboshi! Or is your bravery all talk?!"

"You think you can scare me, big guy?!"

Bisco sprang aside to avoid Satahabaki's next scepter swing, leaped past one, two of the weeping cherry whips, and unleashed his signature spinning kick toward Satahabaki's head.

"Take this, you damn oaf!"

Crackkk!!

Bisco's kick connected with Satahabaki's helmet, opening a large fissure down its side. However, though Satahabaki took a few shaky steps back, the sight of his rows of massive teeth slowly opening froze the hairs on the back of Bisco's neck.

"Haaaah!"

This was his plan all along! He wanted me to kick him!

"GUIL-TYYY!"

Clench!

Grind! Grind! Grind!

"Urgh! Gruuuooohh!!"

Bisco grunted and roared in pain. One of his legs, Bisco's wings, had been caught in Satahabaki's huge mouth, and his shin bone was currently being crushed between those great white pillars that were the judge's teeth.

"I'kh oher, Akahohi! Hrehare yourhelf!"

"Shut...the fuck...up..."

"Hrhh!"

Kapow! Kapow!

"Grh! Gragh!"

Satahabaki swung his massive fists and pummeled the trapped Bisco, who was dangling from the judge's mouth as if trapped in a prison of ivory. Each blow was like being hit by a wrecking ball, and although Bisco showed incredible force of will by not passing out immediately, it would not be much longer before the darkness took him, and then everything would be over.

I have...to cut myself free...!

Even as the blood flew from his face, Bisco's jade-green eyes only shone ever fiercer.

"Hie! GUIR-TYYY!"

Satahabaki threw both arms wide, ready to finish Bisco off with both at once. With no other way out, Bisco swung the Biwa Buffalo horn up toward his own leg, when suddenly he spotted a scarlet glimmer that gave him pause.

That's...!

"Let go of him..."

Silhouetted against the sun, violet hair aflutter, golden sword of ivy gleaming in the light.

"Let go of my brother!!"

"...Nrhh?!" Satahabaki grunted, whirling around to see the bearer of that clear voice.

"Shishi!"

"Flourish! Lion's Crimson Sword!"

Shishi fell from the sky, plunging her blade deeply into Satahabaki's blind spot at the back of his neck. The sword pierced straight through the armor, and immediately there was a *Bwoom! Bwoom!* and giant camellia flowers appeared, scattering the cherry blossoms into the air.

"Grh! GAAAAAGH!"

Satahabaki opened his mouth and let out a roar of pain unlike anything he'd uttered before. Bisco, released from between his teeth, toppled out and fell to the ground with a thud.

"Incredible! Such power! This Bountiful Art can stem from none other than the blood of the king himself!"

Shishi landed by Bisco and pointed her shining sword at Satahabaki. The hot wind ruffled her violet hair.

"Let my brother...and my people...go! Lord Satahabaki of Six Realms, you have me to face now!"

"Grgh! Your Highness! A splendid swordstroke! However, I will not abide such violence!" Satahabaki coughed, and a waterfall of blood spilled from his gullet. "A member of the royal family shall not harm a subject! Such are the ironclad precepts of the Benibishi nobility. Do you mean to spurn them now before me?!"

"You fool! As of now, I am no longer bound by the royal precepts!!" Shishi yelled with all her strength in a voice that swept up clouds of dust and caused all present to tremble in awe. "I am prince no longer! Address me only as 'Shishi'! A lone wolf cub, following my heart in standing up for my brothers and sisters!"

"Nrrrhh!"

"Do not underestimate me! For I am swifter than ever with those chains unbound!!"

Shishi dashed forward, her ivy sword blazing hot and scraping the ground before sweeping upward in a strike glistening with the moon's light. The attack sliced Satahabaki in the shoulder, spraying blood and knocking him off-balance. Shishi sprang into the air after him, slicing horizontally at the warden's neck.

"Grooahh!"

"Take this!!"

Shishi's Crimson Blade sliced its target true, coating her in the torrent of blood that erupted from the wound.

"Grr...rrrhhh!"

Shishi's ivy sword was leagues sharper than any blade of steel; however, the muscles in the Iron Judge's neck were unbelievably strong, and by tensing them, he was able to stop the flow of blood before losing a fatal amount.

"Grrrrh... Grr... So weak a thing...grr...as you...grr...shall never cut me down, child!"

...How did that not kill him? What is wrong with him?!

"These wounds...are nothing but SCRATCHESSS!!"

Shishi kicked off of Satahabaki's shoulder to create some distance, but the warden swiftly clutched her in his giant fist and slammed her to the ground.

"Ghah! *Cough! Hack!* Dammit, even that did not defeat him!"

"Shishi! That's en— I mean, thanks for saving me. Guess I owe you a leg. I was about to cut mine off."

"Brother. My first attack cut right to his lung. My second sliced open his throat. Even with the cherry blossoms by his side, there is no way he should be able to weather such devastating attacks!"

"I guess, but that guy ain't normal, and you know what? Neither am I."

Shishi and Bisco both helped each other to their feet, and the two stood supporting each other. Satahabaki raised his scepter once more and swung it down toward the pair...

"Ghahh!"

But before he could finish his swing, a flood of crimson spilled from his mouth, staining both his teeth and the two standing before him bloodred. Falling onto one knee, Satahabaki steadied himself on his scepter and let out a deep hissing breath.

"It's as you said, kid. This guy's regeneration ain't normal. We leave him, and he's gonna get right back up again. Let's not give him the chance, Shishi!"

"Wait, Brother! It's too dangerous! You're almost falling apart as it is!"

"That's why we gotta kill him now! We miss our chance and we're dead!"

"Brother."

Shishi took Bisco's hand in hers and squeezed it tightly before resting her head against his shoulder and inhaling deeply.

"...You must trust me. I am going to take control of your body for a while..."

"Wait, what the hell does that—?"

Just as Bisco began to protest, a mysterious burning energy began flowing into him. A feeling quite unlike the ferocious Rust-Eater power that had guided him until then. It was a soft and gentle flow of warmth.

"I thought so. My flowers recognize your blood as their parent," Shishi whispered. "Now..."

"Hey! Tell me what you're gonna do to me before you do it!!"

"Do not worry, Brother, I will not do anything untoward like last time."

Before Bisco could respond, vines of golden ivy sprouted from between their joined hands, spiraling up Bisco's arm and around his body and legs.

"Wh-whoa!"

Deaf to Bisco's wails, the ivy first went to Bisco's crushed leg, stitching up the bone and muscle, then did the same to his arms, both all but destroyed by Satahabaki's fierce onslaught of punches.

"I have used my Bountiful Art to reinforce your strength, Brother. Please think of it as a corrective brace!"

"...The ivy fixed me up...! When the hell did you learn how to do that?!"

"I didn't...but I believed it could be done!"

Shishi's sudden beaming smile caught Bisco off guard, and he just stared in response. Then a large shadow passed over them once more, and they felt the heat of Satahabaki's breath as it rustled their hair.

"You hesitate! Strike me again if you dare! You shall not catch the Lord High Overseer unawares a second time!"

"I'll take care of those branches sticking out of his chest!" explained Shishi. "Brother, you go for his arms!"

"All right!"

Bisco leaped into action. The weeping cherries came to knock him out of the air, but they were met by a pair of slashes from Shishi's blade.

"You think a child as small as you can block all of my attacks?!" Satahabaki roared.

"My size matters not. It is my soul that acts as Brother's shield, and that, you shall find, is plenty large enough!"

Shishi's crimson eyes glimmered with a brave and noble glint.

"Flourish! Weeping Dance!"

"Dance of Water! Step four, step five! Descending Fire Dance! Step three, step two!"

Shishi's dance of twinkling steel beautifully merged both offense and evasion, allowing her to expertly handle the whipping branches. Slowly, unbelievably, the enormous Satahabaki found himself being forced back.

"Nrrrhhh! You fool…!"

"Brother!"

"Got it!"

Cornered by Shishi's dogged harassment, Satahabaki swung his iron fist, but Bisco leaped in, his jumping power strengthened by the ivy that wrapped around his legs like springs, making him so nimble now that even Bisco himself found it difficult to control.

"Akaboshi! Taste my fist!"

"How 'bout you try mine for a change?!"

The two fists collided in midair. Bisco's superhuman strength was reinforced by a gauntlet formed of Shishi's ivy, but still the majesty of Satahabaki's punch was a force far beyond reckoning.

"Gh…rhh…!!"

Bisco grimaced, and cracks began appearing in his ivy gauntlet. Satahabaki grinned, his victory all but assured, when…

Bwoom! Bwoom! Bwoom!

"Nnn…rrr…nrrhh?!"

…brilliant scarlet camellias erupted from his hand, blowing apart the navy metal of his armored glove.

"Impossible! This is Shishi's flower! You mean to say she entrusted her Florescence to you?!"

"Shishi, now!"

"Yes, Brother!"

As Satahabaki recoiled in shock, Shishi seized the initiative, switching her dance steps from defense to offense.

"Dance of Thunder! Step five, step six! Water, step seven! Fire, step eight, nine, ten, eleven, twelve, thirteen!"

As her dance ramped up in intensity, Shishi herself seemed to flash in and out of existence, stepping to and fro with incredible speed. Only the trail of her scarlet eyes marked her path through space.

"Here it comes! Dance of Kings! Step eighteen!"

Shishi's blade flashed like the full moon, tearing apart all the thick weeping cherry boughs and exposing Satahabaki's chest.

I made it all the way to step eighteen. Now's my only chance!

Shishi was on the verge of passing out, having exhausted all her strength making it this far. Nevertheless, driven only by her boundless will, she lunged her sword directly toward Satahabaki's bare skin.

"This shall end it, Satahabaki!!"

"A mere child cannot hope to harm me! You shall submit to my iron fist!"

"How 'bout my ivy foot?!"

The mountainous warden swung his rugged arm toward Shishi, but Bisco predicted the attack and met it with a swift ivy-coated kick. As soon as his foot connected, there was a *Bwoom!* as a camellia flower burst into bloom, knocking Satahabaki back. Bisco, meanwhile, did not emerge unscathed from the warden's monstrous swing, and he crashed to the ground in a cloud of dust.

"Brother!"

"Now, Shishi! Get him!"

Spurred on by Bisco's words, Shishi found her strength returning. The camellia by her ear shone bright, leaving a meteoric streak as she rushed toward her target.

"Flourish! Lion's Crimson Sword!"

Snk!

With all of her might, Shishi plunged her ivy blade into Satahabaki's exposed chest. The blade cut shallowly into the warden's flesh, then stopped.

"...Khhhh."

The peerless cutting edge of the Scarlet Sword failed to reach its target. It met its match against Satahabaki, who channeled all of his Florescence into his pectoral muscles, tensing them to keep the blade's fatal point at bay. Having expended all she had on the Dance of Kings, Shishi had no strength left to bring the blade through those vital remaining centimeters.

"Splendid, Prince Shishi... No, Benibishi Shishi. Your dance was quite the spectacle."

"No...I'm...so close...!"

"However, you erred at the crucial last stage, and therefore..."

Satahabaki raised his fists, both torn bare by the camellia flowers.

"Eight-Tenths Bloom, child!"

Ka-pow!

Satahabaki slammed his fists down on Shishi, and she felt her bones snap. Her ivy blade shattered to pieces, along with her wrist, and she hit the ground hard before rebounding into the air like a ball.

"Gh...ah!"

"Shishiii!!" yelled Bisco. Shishi clung to consciousness just long enough to hear his voice.

Bro...ther...!!

Shishi's eyes flared wide, giving Bisco a fierce look. With no power left to use her voice, she could think of only one way to get a message to him.

"...!!"

And it seemed Bisco took that message to heart, for just as he was running in to save her, he stopped suddenly in his tracks.

"Flou...rish... Ghah!"

"Turn into flowers and perish! GUIL-TYYY!!"

"Flourish! Lion Camellia!"

Bwoom!

At Shishi's voice, a camellia flower burst forth from the ivy covering Bisco's legs, propelling him into the air beneath Satahabaki's arm as it swung downward toward Shishi and pushed Bisco straight toward the blade lodged between the warden's ribs. Bisco grabbed it tightly with both hands.

Ga-bwoom!

"Ughh!!"

A huge camellia flower burst out of Satahabaki's shoulder, throwing off his aim and saving Shishi just as she was about to be squashed beneath his scepter.

Bwoom! Bwoom!

"Graaaah! Akaboshi, how many more tricks do you have up your sleeve?!"

"I see it now, big guy!" shouted Bisco. His hands were wrapped so tightly around the hilt of the blade that his golden blood spilled forth. The Rust-Eater spores within poured into Shishi's sword, which converted them into life energy and sent it straight into Satahabaki himself. "The world's full of crazy characters just like you and Shishi, just waitin' for a chance to bring us together!"

"It was not chance…that brought us together, Akaboshi!"

Bwoom! Satahabaki yelled as the camellia flower explosions rocked his body.

"It was you! Powerful ones are drawn to you! Powerful life will always find its way to you! I should have killed you when I had the chance, for you were always the one that would shatter the scales that govern Six Realms!"

Bang! Bang! Bang! Bisco watched as the scarlet flowers exploded along the length of the blade. Then he kicked off Satahabaki and launched himself into the air.

"You finally got it?! A mushroom always grows, even in captivity!"

"I shall await you in hell, Akaboshi! Let none else judge your sins but I!"

Bisco spun in the air twice, three times, like a typhoon, gradually increasing in speed, glittering like the sun and throwing off sparks.

* * *

"Case closed, big guy! All charges dropped!"

On the sixth turn, Bisco stuck out his foot and struck Shishi's blade, forcing the point deeply into Satahabaki's chest.

"...Ghhh! Ha-ha... Grah-ha-ha-ha-ha..."

Bwoom!

"Splendid, Akaboshi..."

"Shishi! Get away from there, now!"

Bwoom! Bwoom!

"Splendid! One thousand BLOOOMS!!"

Bwoom! Bwoom! Bwoom!

Satahabaki's final shout echoed in the air. The crimson camellia flowers blossomed explosively one after the other, like an uncontrollable chain reaction. Bisco fell back to the ground, rolled, grabbed Shishi, and threw the two of them clear just as one final flower blasted them away, rolling along the floor.

"*Cough. Cough.* What an explosion. What was that big guy made of?"

"Bro...ther..."

"We won, Shishi. ...Whoa, don't try to move yet. You're barely hangin' on."

"We defeated him, didn't we? Together...!"

"Yeah," replied Bisco, face smeared in blood, yet still able to crack a smile. He looked back at the garden of camellias. "But he ain't dead. I still got plans for him. We gotta get him to dispel this tattoo."

"...But you don't plan on killing him even after that, do you? After everything he did to you...don't you resent him for it?"

"Nah, I'm good. I feel a lot better after beatin' the shit out of him. Besides, I kinda had a soft spot for the guy. He's straight-talking, no nonsense. Hard to find a guy like that these days."

Bisco gave a cheery smile and tore the ivy off his arms and legs. Its duty fulfilled, it had already withered and gone limp. Shishi watched him and blinked.

"He was the judge of this place, right?" Bisco continued. "Now that his power's weakened, maybe it'll cool him down a bit, and he'll start actin' a bit like his old self from now on."

Bisco was the same innocent young kid he had always been, and already it was impossible to imagine him as the fierce engine of destruction that Shishi had just witnessed. She just stared at him wordlessly, and when Bisco looked back at her curiously, she flashed him a sweet smile.

"My, the *shishi-gashira* ferns look positively splendid, don't they?"

"Hmm?"

Bisco turned in the direction of the new voice to see King Housen standing a short ways off, admiring the garden of camellias.

"It is good to see you safe, F—," Shishi began, but she swallowed the word *Father* and stared down at her feet. Behind Housen's figure stood the great horse Winter Cherry, held in place by the Benibishi warriors and their ivy vines, its vitality sapped by the king's balsam flowers. It still snorted and groaned but was quite unable to free itself. Housen's brilliant strategies had brought it down without any collateral damage.

"Of course I am safe. Yet this wild animal showed no interest in my marvelous dance. Pearls before equine, you might say."

"If we're talkin' dances," interrupted Bisco, "then Shishi's wasn't bad, either. You shoulda seen her up against the big guy."

"Naturally, I saw her," Housen replied. Shishi perked up a little at his words, then came before her king and kneeled.

"...Why did you come here, Shishi?" he asked. "I seem to recall saying—"

"I came simply as a Benibishi, to save the others of my race," she said.

"..."

"Your Majesty's blade must never bathe in the blood of his people. I came here to protect you from that fate, and to protect my kin. That is all."

Shishi raised her head, and for a while, both father and child stared into each other's crimson eyes.

"...I see," Housen said at last. "...You did well, my subject."

"Your Majesty's words are wasted on me…"

Shishi's words were clearly spoken, yet still they seemed as though they might disappear at any moment. Housen extended his hand, and for an instant, Shishi hesitated before reaching out and…

"…Hmm! Quick, take my hand, Shishi!"

Housen's gown fluttered as he grabbed Shishi and leaped up into the air. Bisco followed as, not a second later, a huge root slammed down on the spot where he had just stood.

"Hey! If you're gonna save her, save me, too, you royal pain in the ass!"

"Mrh…What on earth is that?!"

Landing before his line of troops, Housen groaned at what he saw. The beautiful camellia flowers that littered the area were under attack from sentient branches, crawling along the ground like roots and chewing up any flowers they encountered. They fed off the plants, bulging as they sent the nutrients back up the bough's length like a pump.

And there at the center, where all the branches converged…

"NnnnrrHHH!"

"Satahabaki!! …Brother! Satahabaki's still moving!"

"Whaaat?! How is he still up after all we did to him?! He oughtta be out cold!"

"I fear Someyoshi *is* out cold, my friend. But the cherry blossoms are running rampant without him to hold them in check. They have taken control of his body!"

"What the hell?! Why didn't you tell us if you knew this was gonna happen?!"

"I have never seen it happen before. Also, I did not know. I am merely spitballing, as they say."

As they spoke, the cherry blossom branches tore into the garden of camellias, beating back the brave soldiers who charged in to stop them. They grew out of Satahabaki's back in the form of a ring that resembled the halo of the Buddha himself.

"YOu ShALL nOT PaSS. I CANNoT ALLOw IT. NoNE ShALL PaSS THrOUGH THiS GaTE!!"

Slowly, with a rumbling voice that shook the very earth itself, Satahabaki rose.

He was like a monster, a demon, a god. The cherry blossom branches enveloped him, swelling him up to nearly three times his original size. Soon the only parts of him still visible were his gleaming white pillar-like teeth.

"Protect the king!"

"Men, get in front of His Majesty!"

The Benibishi soldiers took up formation around their king, but Satahabaki's rampant Florescence was on another level. The branches that extended from his back were thick enough to be considered trees in their own right, able to reach anywhere in the yard and knock half a dozen soldiers off their feet in a single swing. Some sought refuge behind sturdy pillars or rocks, but the sweeping branches destroyed all in their path.

"*BeNIBISHI. DEStROY ThE BeNIBISHI. YOu ShALL bE ThE FOUnDATION oF mY NeW ORDeR.*"

"He does not listen to us!" Housen lamented. "Oh, Someyoshi, my old friend, just how far are you willing to go in pursuit of your mission?"

But before he'd even finished his thought, Bisco broke into a run.

"...Oh, fuck!"

"Brother?!"

Standing out in the open, raging against the thick vines that bound its legs, was the stout stallion, Winter Cherry. It was seconds away from being caught up in the carnage and crushed to death beneath the indiscriminate boughs of its unconscious and rampaging master.

"You freakin' dumbass, that's your own horse! You're gonna kill it!"

"No, Brother! You're still hurt! It's too dangerous!"

Bisco stopped before the horse and looked up to see the huge whip-like branches descending upon him.

"A little danger never killed anyone! Come on, give it to me!"

Whack!!

"Wh... Huh?"

"*Vwoo.*"

"Mark I!"

Right behind Bisco stood the gleaming crimson frame of the Aka-boshi Mark I. His thrusters at full throttle, he held Satahabaki's overwhelming power at bay by himself. Suddenly, an arrow landed in the ground between them with a *Thnk!*

"…Uh-oh."

Instantly recognizing what that arrow meant, Bisco swiftly vacated the area, leaping aside along with the Mark I.

Gaboom!!

An enormous King Trumpet erupted out of the ground, catching Satahabaki's whip and snapping it in two with its explosive growth. Satahabaki stumbled at the unexpected attack and gnashed his huge teeth.

"*StAY OUt oF mY WaY.*"

"Now that's just upsetting. He was trying to help your horse, you know!"

Before Satahabaki appeared a fluttering head of sky-blue hair, glittering softly in the sunlight.

"When you wake up, I think you owe my poor partner here an apology."

"Milo, you sonofabitch!" yelled Bisco, pinned beneath the Mark I by the force of the mushroom blast. "You're supposed to give me a warning before using the King Trumpet. You've gotten real reckless lately!"

"Hey, wasn't it you who said 'a little danger never killed anyone'?"

"I was just tryin' to stay positive! I didn't *mean* it!"

"Well, I'm afraid there's a lot more danger coming your way, so gear up."

Milo tossed Bisco his indigo shortbow and quiver, and Bisco crawled out from under the Mark I to catch them. With his trusty bow finally back in his hands, his eyes glimmered with a fierce light.

Housen, standing a short distance off, protecting his people with the dual arts of sword and balsam flowers, shot a glance toward them.

"Lest you forget, Panda! Your mushrooms cannot inflict so much as a scratch upon Someyoshi! He is immune!"

"I'm afraid I must remain skeptical, Your Majesty," replied Milo, unruffled as he leaped between Satahabaki's blows. "Is he really immune to our mushrooms? If we watch closely, and believe, and just think for a moment, there could be some way we can win, hiding right under our noses."

"That's quite the theory. But how can you be so confident?!"

"Well, I did go to school."

Milo landed beside Bisco, and the two boys stared Satahabaki down.

"You really have a way to make our mushrooms work on him?" Bisco whispered.

"Yeah. But I need to get up close. Cover me until I get there."

"You're gonna get up close to that thing?! That's suicide!"

"Only if you don't do your job, Bisco. I'm counting on you."

Milo sped off like a gale before Bisco could respond, leaving his partner red-faced, yelling as he nocked three arrows to his bow at once.

"If *I* don't do *my* job?! I taught you everything you know, you stupid Panda!"

Fwsh! Boom! Boom! Bisco's clamshell mushrooms repelled the giant tree-whip as it approached Milo, and Bisco let loose another sheaf toward Satahabaki's next attack. Milo didn't even have to dodge or block; he just kept running in a straight line toward the main trunk where Satahabaki lurked.

"Wow...! Brother's arrows are the very lightning itself! Those trees cannot touch him!"

"Yet the mushrooms only magnify Someyoshi's strength further. Panda, you had better have a plan..."

Shielded by Bisco's swift and violent arrows, Milo arrived at last within range of the main body. With a twinkle in his sapphire eyes, he began to chant.

"Won/ul/axya/viviki/snew! (Create large weapon for permissions holder!)"

The very syllables coalesced on Milo's breath, forming his emerald cube, which he held aloft while it spun rapidly, turning into the shape of a giant battle-ax.

"It worked! *President's Ax*— Whoa, that's heavy!"

The head of the ax crashed into the ground, nearly taking Milo with it.

"Milo made that?!" said Shishi in disbelief. "That's the Rust! He made a weapon out of Rust! Where did he learn to do that?!"

"Your Honor!" Milo shouted. "Did you know there is legal precedent for a man chopping down a cherry tree with an ax and getting away with it?!"

"*PRECEDENT?*"

"I cannot tell a lie, Your Honor; it shall be me who cuts the tree!"

"Stop tellin' kids' stories and get on with it!!" Bisco yelled.

"*George's Tomahawk!*"

Milo heaved the weighty ax out of the ground and leaped up into the air. He spun several times, using the ax's mass to build up speed, before swinging its emerald blade deeply into Satahabaki's shoulder.

"*?! R...G...GGHH!*"

As soon as the attack connected, Satahabaki suddenly slowed. The tree trunk whips twisting around him like great serpents all crumbled loudly under their own weight and fell to the earth in pieces.

"*WhAT hAVE YOu DONe tO mE, ChILD?!*"

"I guess you don't like my mantra as much as my mushrooms, right, Your Honor?"

Milo channeled his mantra energy through the ax, canceling out Satahabaki's Florescence. Unable to be fully controlled, the Rust began working its way up his arms, coating his delicate skin in cold metal. However, even now, with both him and his foe rapidly nearing the brink of death, Milo wore the intrepid smile of a fearless hunter.

"Flowers get one breath of the Rust Wind and they wilt," said Milo. "So I bet this much Rust is gonna cause you some serious issues!"

An emerald light began to glow right where Milo's ax bit into Satahabaki's shoulder. All of the tree trunks that stood poised to attack drooped one after the other and snapped off, crashing to the ground, while the Rust devoured the cherry blossom petals in the air and turned them into dust.

"Impossible," said Housen, uncharacteristically serious. "He caused Someyoshi to wither. I knew plants were vulnerable to the Rust, but... Panda, just how deep is the well of your strength?"

"*GNRHHH!*"

"Now! Bisco!" Milo yelled over Satahabaki's scream. "Finish him off with a Rust-Eater!"

"All right, now you're speakin' my language!"

Bisco cleanly drew a single arrow from his quiver and affixed it to the string, pulling back slowly and letting out a deep breath, focusing all of his concentration into a single moment. The Rust-Eater spores awoke and began to surround him.

"I just need four seconds. Three..."

"Bisco! Hurry!" yelled Milo, the Rust at his neck. "I can't keep it up much longer!" He groaned in pain. Satahabaki seized that moment, raising his two giant tree-arms above his head.

"KHAAAH!"

Milo threw up a mantra defense, but what Satahabaki did defied his wildest expectations. The lumbering giant ripped off one of his own wooden arms and hurled it with all his might toward Milo's partner instead.

"Oh no! He was aiming at Bisco!"

As Bisco's mind was away with the spores, he was too slow to react to Satahabaki's death-defying last-ditch attack. The arm flew at great speed, its hand open wide as if to grab him.

"...Whoa! Shit!"

"Vwoo."

"Guh!"

The Mark I tackled Bisco aside at the very last moment, but from the hand's open palm came a snakelike branch that snatched his bow and tore it from his grip.

"...! Fuck!"

Satahabaki's fist closed like a hydraulic press, shattering Bisco's bow into pieces and scattering it into the wind, just before crash-landing into the nearest wall and disappearing in a cloud of dust.

"He broke my bow! Dammit, I'll just have to deliver it myself!"

"Brother!"

Shishi grabbed on to Bisco just as he was about to start running. Bisco turned to see the tough, fearless look in her eyes and the crimson flower behind her ear in full bloom.

"I shall craft you a bow, Brother! Close your eyes and imagine the strongest bow you can!"

"…Okay!"

Bisco no longer had any doubts about Shishi's ability. He did as she asked, and glowing vines began crawling up his body, extending from hers, forming the shape of a bow in his hands with incredible speed.

…Grhh… It's no use! Brother is too powerful! My Florescence is not strong enough to keep up! If he pulls it too tightly, the whole thing will break…!

"Allowing a human the use of your Bountiful Art? You do come up with the strangest ideas, Shishi."

"…Father! I mean…Your Majesty…"

"Do not lose focus! I shall assist you. All my power is yours to command."

Housen placed his hand upon Shishi's back, and the king's power flowed into her. The ivy forming in Bisco's hand suddenly sped up, until at last what rested in his hands was a verdant plant longbow. Testing the bowstring, Bisco placed his faith in the weapon, and his eyes flared wide. The Rust-Eater spores filled the air around him, causing his hair to sparkle with golden light.

"This thing's even stronger than the Mantra Bow! Milo! Heads up, I'm firin'!"

"It's been ten seconds! Just do it already!"

Bisco's jade-green eyes glimmered, and with inhuman strength, he pulled back the bowstring. The twisted wood creaked under the force of his draw, and as the Rust-Eater spores landed on it, flowers burst into being across its length. Soon it, too, began glowing with radiant light, until Bisco appeared to be holding a curved sunbeam in his hands.

"Go, Bisco!"

"Take thiiis!!"

Bisco unleashed an arrow like cannon fire. The blast knocked Shishi and Housen off their feet, and Milo leaped out of the way moments before the sunlight arrow pierced the emerald battle-ax, sticking deep into the wound the weapon had opened.

There was a short pause, and then…

Gaboom.

Gaboom!

Gaboom!!

The Rust-Eaters fed off the Mantra Bow, each one sprouting from the giant tree faster than the last.

"GRHHHHHH."

"Direct hit! Well done, Brother!"

"…Uh-oh."

"What?"

"It's gettin' too fast! Get outta there, Milo!"

By now, the Rust-Eaters were growing at an incredible pace, blasting apart the tree's bark.

"YOu ShALL nOT PaSS. No MAn ShALL PaSS BEyOND…SiX… REaLMS…"

BAGOOM!

Satahabaki's speech faltered as one last grand Rust-Eater explosion tore the tree apart and ejected from its hot splintered bark the unconscious body of Warden Satahabaki. The chain reaction of Rust-Eater mushrooms moved down the tree's trunk and all across the ruptured soil where its roots had spread.

"Waaah!"

Unable to keep ahead of the rampant fungi, Milo was blasted into the air, and he tumbled helplessly in a spin. Bisco leaped up, caught his partner in his arms, and hit the ground in a roll.

"That was close!" the boy doctor cried. "I almost died from a mushroom schoolboy error! …Not that Mushroom Keepers go to school."

"…Fuck you. The problem was your dumbass plan." As the two lay beside one another, Bisco reached over and touched the Rust-covered half of Milo's face. He now bore a striking resemblance to Pawoo back when Bisco had first met her in Imihama.

"Oh, that's no problem. I can just cure the Rust with my shots these days."

"That ain't what I meant! If it spread to your lungs, you'd be stiff as a board right now!"

"Ah-ha-ha! It's not nice, is it? Watching your partner go off on their own."

Milo reached back and wiped the blood from Bisco's face, revealing the warrior's mark beneath his right eye.

"Now you know how I feel, Bisco."

"Khh!"

"Oh, look at the cherry blossoms! They're so pretty…"

Bisco turned to see the great tree, now hollowed out by the Rust-Eaters, bursting with life once more as the plants fed on the nutrients in the mushrooms. Where fragments of bark fell from the prior explosion, new trees immediately shot up out of the ground. Fueled by the vigorous Rust-Eaters, the brilliant cherry blossom petals now seemed to be bursting with life instead of being the instruments of death they had been only a few moments before.

"…Yeah. They are pretty… Guess that big guy had some beauty in him after all."

"And we managed to keep him alive, just like you wanted."

"Yeah, I guess so."

"So say thanks."

"…Thanks a ton, Mark I!"

"*Vwoo.*"

"To me, you idiot!! …Wait, Bisco! Your tattoo…!"

Milo shot up and wiped the blood off Bisco, examining his skin. The two of them watched as Bisco's Sakura Storm gradually dissolved into thin air without leaving a single trace.

"Whoa!"

"It appears the Sakura Storm really *can* be removed without Someyoshi's command."

The three of them turned at the sound of Housen's voice. "It is proof that the cherry blossom has depleted its power at last. I'd imagine it's not just you this is happening to but the rest of your friends as well."

Housen stopped and stood before the pair. His army of Benibishi warriors halted and, one by one, fell to one knee in a show of respect. It was honestly a little unnerving for the two Mushroom Keepers to see the hundred-strong squadron lower their heads. Housen only continued in a delighted tone. "I have lived a long life, and yet never had I dreamed a man might exist that could best Someyoshi, or rather, that embodiment of Florescence we all just bore witness to."

"Well, that's probably 'cause you spent it all cooped up in here."

"C'mon, Bisco! Don't be rude!"

"And yet... Hee-hee. To think you would go to such ridiculous lengths to keep him alive."

"Shut your royal mouth. I don't see anyone else complainin', do you?!"

Housen shifted his gaze from Bisco's peeved face to the fallen Satahabaki, lying splayed-out on the ground some distance away, and smiled.

"Quite. The truly ridiculous part is that you actually succeeded."

All of Satahabaki's armor, save for his helmet, had been utterly destroyed, yet surprisingly his skin was completely unscathed, and every now and then, he would even emit a rumbling snore.

"Someyoshi is the one man in this world I can call a friend," Housen went on. "If I had been forced to harm him, it would have taken me from the path of just rule. You have my deepest thanks. Not just from me, but on behalf of all my people."

For the first time, the two boys and one robot saw Housen bend deeply at the waist. In concert with his bow, the Benibishi warriors all lowered their heads even farther. For a king to bow his head to a pair of Mushroom Keepers was unthinkable. Milo quickly cracked under the pressure and waved his hands in embarrassment.

"It's okay, Your Majesty, you really don't have to go that far! We just did what we could, that's all!"

"What's the matter, old man, bad back? Let's see a bit more gratitude, yeah?"

"Vwoo."

"Aaargh!! Bisco!! Mark I! What are you doing?!"

The two Akaboshis crowded around Housen, eyeing his form closely, occasionally poking him into shape with their knees, like a fussy martial arts teacher. Still keen to express his gratitude, Housen raised no objection, even as his legs turned to jelly.

"That's right, keep your back at that angle, then straighten your chin and repeat after me, *Thank you, Mr. Bisco, sir.*"

"Seriously, you two! Stop it! Are you trying to start a war?!"

Milo pulled the other two back, and Housen rose back to his full regal height, his hair now disheveled from sweat. He caught his breath and cleared his throat before proceeding.

"*Ahem.* Never before have I been forced to lower my head to such an animal. I shall not soon forget this day."

"'Cause it's such a nice memory, right?" chirped Bisco.

"I shall endeavor to see it that way. After all, you shall soon be my son-in-law."

"You still goin' on about that?! I told you, it ain't happenin'!"

As it seemed Housen and his partner would be at it for quite a while, Milo turned and watched the gently falling cherry blossom petals. A short distance away, he spotted the violet-haired Benibishi girl, nobly tending to her wounded kinsfolk. Milo watched her whisper some words of encouragement to her patient, whose face lit up as she took his hand.

…Shishi. It's good to see you happy again.

Shishi noticed Milo staring at her, and their eyes met. They exchanged a glance, speaking without words for a moment, before Shishi beamed. Her smile, Milo thought, looked so much more grown-up, compared to the day they first met. For a moment, he was so taken by the beauty in her soot-covered face that he forgot to return her smile, and by the time he remembered himself, Shishi had already moved on to the next of the wounded.

…Shishi. I really don't know what to say. You've turned out so…lovely?

Her sudden transformation could only have been thanks to her short adventure with Bisco. When Milo thought about that, he felt a fiery sensation welling up in his heart that he found difficult to control. He made a face like he'd eaten a sour grape, until the sight of Shishi tending to her wounded comrades caught his eye once more. The doctor side of him smiled at her caring nature, and red-faced, he rushed over to lend her a hand.

SABIKUI
BISCO

4

Karmic Crown, Florescent Sword

Illustration by **K Akagishi**

World Concept Art by mocha (@mocha708)

Housen pressed his hand to the weighty iron doors. A bright light emerged from his palm, flowers popped into existence across his luxurious gown, and soon the great iron gate began to crack. From the cracks emerged lush green ivy, wrapping itself around the door. As the Benibishi watched on in rapt attention, Housen slowly parted his lips and spoke a single word.

"Flourish!"

Bwoom! Bwoom! The balsam chain reaction blew the door to bits, inviting a cool breeze into the yard.

"So powerful!" gasped Milo. The king's Florescence is really something else!"

"Not as powerful as our mushrooms," muttered Bisco.

"I know, I know. Can't you just agree to disagree?"

Ignoring the bickering boys, Housen spun to face his kneeling subjects, and in a solemn voice, he declared, "The time for our confinement in Six Realms is past. The world must learn of our people's evolution. But know this: Your power is a blade of unmatched sharpness. Keep it always sheathed within your heart and abide by the law of the land. Now we advance to Kyoto, where Benibishi and humanity will unite to forge a new path forward for our peoples."

The Benibishi kept their heads lowered as they received their king's words. Housen gave a nod of satisfaction and paused a little before continuing.

"…And now…I would like to end this speech on a rather more personal note."

"When's that dude ever not speakin' about himself?"

"Shh!"

"Benibishi Shishi. Rise."

Several among the crowd rose their heads to take a look before hurriedly lowering them again. A few seconds passed before there was a movement of violet hair, and Shishi stood up. The Benibishi parted like the Red Sea, and Shishi began heading down the path toward the front of the crowd.

"…"

"…"

The father and child gazed at each other before the open gate of Six Realms. After a long pause, Shishi kneeled.

"Shishi was banished from the royal family for failing to uphold the creed of kings. However, with nothing to her name, and without promise of reward or recompense, she has stood up for all of you and myself, guided by nothing but her own conviction."

Shishi didn't make a move. She silently awaited her father's next words.

"Though she struggles to control the Florescence, that is only due to her youth, and so I should like to pardon her recent jailbreak and accept her once more as my heir. What say you, my people?"

Shishi's shoulders jumped in shock, but before she could open her mouth to speak, one of the Benibishi piped up.

"We have no objections, Your Majesty," he said. "Lady Shishi is more than qualified to lead us. If she should become your heir, we are willing to devote our lives to her."

"I agree!" called out another. "Please accept Lady Shishi as your heir once more!"

"Return her to the royal family!" cried a third.

Housen nodded deeply at the sound of his people's assent and looked down again at his child.

"Shishi. My people wish for you to be my successor."

"...B-but..."

"I have seen the strength of your dance with my own eyes. That strength will be needed to guide the evolved Benibishi. There was a time I wanted nothing more than for you to seek happiness as an ordinary subject, but now I see... Shishi, become my prince once more. Soon you will unravel the mysteries of your Bountiful Art, and once it is completely under your control, you shall be ready to accept my crown."

"...No...I can't..." Shishi barely stammered out a response, her head still lowered. "I...I broke the creed. By my hand, our people committed murder. I can never be king. I can never set an example for our people."

"Shishi. You're overthinking it."

Housen bent down and whispered into Shishi's ear.

"The Benibishi are servile by nature. If you mess up a little, all you have to do is smooth things over with a little speech, see? Like I just did."

"..."

"Don't worry too much if the law says this or the creed says that. All the people need is something to worship. Once you're on the throne, it'll be a simple matter for you to sway their hearts and minds however you wish."

Just then, a soft wind blew, lifting Shishi's violet bangs and revealing the scarlet flames in her eyes.

"...I...see..."

"So what do you say, Shishi? You are brave and noble... The people shall be very pleased indeed."

"...But first...that throne..."

"Now stand, Shishi. Show them your face. These are the people who look to you for—"

"...must be repainted..."

Fwm!

Like a knife through the wind, Shishi leaped.

* * *

"...with the blood of the old."

Shng!!
Shishi moved like lightning, the ivy blade coalescing instantly in her hand, slicing off Housen's head.

SPLAAAAAAAAATTT!

The king's body remained stock-still while a fountain of blood erupted from his severed neck.

It fell like rain, bathing Shishi in sticky crimson. Her father's blood. Her father's life. Her father's death. She took it all into herself, wrapped her arms around her body, and shivered.

...
Good-bye, Father.

Shishi muttered under her breath before springing up, snatching Housen's severed head out of the air, and landing in a cloud of dust. She held it in one hand, its eyes already closed, dripping blood from its neck onto the sandy soil of the yard.

"The king is dead."

Shishi's words were punctuated by the sound of the lifeless king's body crumpling to the ground. She raised his head high and belted at the top of her tiny lungs:

"The false pretender, Housen, is dead! No more shall this *traitor* tyrannize the people!"

At that moment, she was no girl but a bloody god of war in the guise of a child. Her violet locks danced on the flames of her crimson eyes, and she exuded a petrifying aura that froze the entire yard. Housen's

hair flowed magnificently in the wind, like the closing chapter of some great myth.

As for the people…
    They were afraid.
    They howled and wailed.
    But Shishi heard not their cries. In her mind, she was already somewhere far away.
    All she felt was the warmth.
    The warm, wet sensation of blood.
    She breathed in deeply, filling her lungs with the lingering smell of balsam flowers, and as she did so, a second camellia flower appeared in her hair, just beside the first. Then a third and a fourth… Soon, a ring of them had formed around her brow, a glorious crown of flowers to mark the beginning of her reign.

"…The long winter…is over… Spring has come, and with it, new life."

The Benibishi people froze before Shishi's majesty. Their laments ceased at once, and every last one of them awaited Shishi's next words.

"You are Benibishi. No longer will you bend to the old rust-eaten laws. You are not seeds, to spend your lives trapped underground. You are flowers, to burst forth and make yourselves known!"

"Now is the time to run rampant! Fight back against your laws! Kill your oppressors! Take what is yours! I will be your guide, your prince— your king, Shishi! By our hands shall we make this land our everlasting garden!!"

Shishi's voice tore a hole through the hearts of the crowd. One by one, they began to kneel. Shishi could feel them doing so, but it no longer mattered to her. She just stared upward into the bright, sunny sky and smiled.

* * *

My path is stained with blood. But that does not mean it is the wrong path. If that is the hand fate dealt me, then let us see how far I can take it. I shall lead my people to freedom, even if my path takes us beyond Six Realms, where evil spirits roam.

So, Father…
Please…
Don't cry for me…

"…Flourish."

At Shishi's word, Housen's decapitated head became a cluster of balsam flowers, and the warm breeze carried it off high into the sky.

AFTERWORD

"Mr. Cobkubo, would you mind drawing us a map of the prison?"

"Ha-ha-ha."

"Don't gimme that!! I'm workin' my ass off here!!"

It was as a result of a conversation quite like this one that the task of creating a map of Six Realms fell to the author himself. I hope I did a good enough job.

Leaving that aside, the theme of the work this time was "Rules." Old values die out, and new ones sprout up in their place. As for our new flower, Shishi, what effect will her rules have on post-apocalyptic Japan? I can't wait to find out, can you?

I can already hear the voices saying, *"Hey, this afterword is a little rushed, ain't it?"* but unfortunately, I don't have much choice. I've only got one page, so this'll have to do!

For the next volume, I'm going to try and bring you a ramped-up action movie of a story. I'll see you then.

—*Shinji Cobkubo*

"I've been struck with a burning love, Akaboshi... Wait, have you always been so small?"

GIANT FLOWER

"There's a baby somewhere in Hokkaido."

SABIKUI BISCO VOLUME 5. ON SALE 2023!

"I permit you to kneel. I am Shishi, King of the Benibishi."

"Have you ever heard of islands eatin' each other?!"

JAPAN IN CHAINS

"Actagawa! Why aren't you retreating?! Hokkaido's going to chew you up!"

"He hates giving up, just like you!"

The Rust Wind eats away at the world. A boy with a bow matches its ferocity.